More
THAN A
Hero

MORE THAN HERO

BECOMING AN EVANS
BOOK THREE

JENNI BARA

Point Publishing

*For all of you who refused
to let me skip Nick!
Especially you Amy.*

1

MORGAN JOHANSON'S KNEES were currently touching her nose, and boy did that tick her off. At five foot ten, she was too tall to be crunched into a three-and-a-half by two-and-a-half-foot space. She would have kicked her heels off, but she worried her feet would be cold since it remained barely above freezing in the stupid under-the-counter cooler that held the bar's kegs.

Her French-manicured nails moved furiously, firing off another angry text, not allowing the fear to creep in.

> **MORGAN:** It's a 911 SOS. Seriously, guys get
> to the bar NOW!

Her damn brothers were ignoring her and, as FBI agents, this was much more their type of situation than hers. She'd already told them where she'd hidden and sent a few pictures of the situation. But they probably thought this was a "my sink's clogged" or "my car has a flat" emergency, not a "I'm hiding in a beer keg refrigerator because a bunch of guys came into the bar with guns" emergency.

She sent her big bad brothers 911 texts a lot. But this time, it was an *actual emergency*. She swallowed as fear threatened to find its way to the surface.

Morgan clenched her fists to keep her hands from shaking. She tried to convince herself it was the cold, not fear, that caused her hands to quiver. She needed to think about something other than what was going on outside of the beer cooler. *Fear makes you dumb*; her father and brothers had drilled that into her. She needed to keep it under control until the crisis passed.

And the crisis had definitely not passed. She tapped her finger on her phone, noticing, for the first time, her broken nail. It must have happened as she'd ducked under the bar's flip-up counter to hide. Most people in the bar had panicked when the two men walked in with guns and shot out the lights. She was sure most had done the smart thing and run. She had not.

Instead, she'd done everything but run as soon as the first gunshot went off. She even got a few pictures before all the lights went out, using the reflections in the mirror to get a good view of the unfolding scene. Only two of the four men were inside, and she'd gotten clear images of both. It had taken ten seconds to get under the bar, take the pictures, and crawl into the reach-in fridge where the kegs were usually stored.

She didn't think anyone had seen her open the door and climb into the small space, but if they had—

Nope.

No panicking allowed. But she couldn't stop herself from flinching every time she heard the crash of another table or chair hitting the ground. She didn't know what the men wanted with the bar. But she should never have agreed to meet her literary agent here, even if the email she'd received this morning was insistent. And this wasn't the first weird place they had met. Erica had dragged her all over Pensacola, Florida. Especially when Morgan struggled with writer's block. The crazy places she and Erica ended up always jogged her brain to start its magic.

Since it wasn't the best side of town, Morgan had brought Reed with her just to be safe, even though she knew better than to believe a boyfriend could rescue her. That had been dumb—look where it had gotten her. Alone in what amounted to an ice-cold tin can.

She shivered and wrapped her arms tighter around her legs, pulling them into her chest. She rested her head on her knees, staring at the grates below her butt.

Did bartenders ever crawl in here to clean? They must because, although it was cold and damp, it wasn't moldy or dirty or even sticky. It would be funny if someone got trapped in here—not because they were hiding, but because the door got stuck. And just like that, despite the fear, the creative juices were flowing for the best meet cute of the year. A young bartender gets stuck in the fridge and before she can find a way out she scares the crap out of the beer delivery guy. Maybe he could even drop the keg and kill the seal sending beer shooting around. But the flying beer would have nothing on the sparks that would fly as soon as the bartender met the delivery guy's eyes.

Morgan had always loved a love story. It didn't surprise her family that she wrote romances that swept people off their feet for a living.

Her leading men changed over the years. Prince Eric from *The Little Mermaid* remained her first love. Then, naturally, she moved on to Navy men. Serving their country with pride, just like her daddy and her three older brothers. But before she finished high school, she learned a Navy man wasn't all he was cracked up to be.

Now, the heroes in her books were usually accountants, or business owners. Someone stable. Someone who didn't get shot at for a living or live on adrenaline. Someone who didn't need to save the world. Who understood the term "commitment" in a relationship. And no military man would fit that bill.

Military men were good for a fun night out, but that was it. In fact, she avoided anyone with a hero complex: firefighter, police officer, or anyone who lived for the rush of saving the world. Her mantra in relationships was "No Heroes Allowed." Her current brainy chemist fit the not-a-hero bill. Morgan frowned as she thought of her boyfriend, Reed.

She still couldn't believe he'd left her tonight. A sound that might have been a siren in the distance met her ears. Maybe help was finally coming. She shivered again as a tight knot of fear found its way into her chest. If anyone opened the door—

Nope, she wasn't thinking about her current situation.

With eyes firmly closed, she went back to her idea for the meet cute. Her brain, as usual, automatically pictured a black-haired, blue-eyed delivery man. Of course, once they started talking to her, they'd develop their own personas.

Morgan smirked.

Maybe this one would be the type of man who brought home "just because I love you" flowers and did dishes to be nice after dinner. And he definitely made his girl feel like the only woman in his world.

Yeah, she was a romance writer, all about the swoon factor.

The door beside her wrenched open, and Morgan flinched into the cold metal keg behind her.

"What. The. Fuck?" That voice caused a wave of calm, and she smiled into the blazing eyes of her big brother Howard. The tight knot of fear threatening her disappeared the second his eyebrows raised up to his blond hair line. The badge on his chest bounced on the metal chain when he yanked her out of the cooler and to her feet, his eyes scanning her. "Anything bleeding? Broken?"

Her chin quivered as she shook her head.

"You didn't actually get shot, right?" Donald, her second brother, asked from behind Howard.

She tried to lock her jaw, but she couldn't stop the pool of tears in her eyes. To both her tough as nails brothers, not bleeding or broken should mean okay. Both had moved from the SEAL teams to the FBI, and handling emergencies was ingrained in them, but she wasn't used to this.

"Oh, crap, here comes the waterworks," Howard said.

She closed her eyes, not wanting to see anything inside the bar, just tucking herself into Donald's shoulder as they walked out of the building.

"Okay, Morgan," Howard said, standing by an ambulance in the parking lot, crossing his arms over his chest. "No more tears. People have questions. Take a deep breath. Let the EMT check you out."

"Yeah," Donald agreed, and gave her hair a playful yank as he stepped away from her. "You got it out of your system now, turn off the hose and do what needs to be done."

She glared at her brothers, wiping her eyes. These two had always been the least patient. The youngest of her brothers had always understood her much better. In everything from her writing to her moods. "I miss Louis," she said about her brother who'd died two years ago.

"Oh, for the love—" Donald shook his head, stepping away from her and pulling out his phone.

"We know, but he hated your tears, too." Howard gave her a halfhearted pat on the shoulder.

Louis would always joke and tease her. Make her laugh. These two just told her to stop.

"But he made me f-feel better," she said.

"Fuck's sake." Howard laughed. "Where's the tool? Can you cry on the boyfriend? I got shit to do." The mention of the man who'd left her in the bar just as all hell broke loose wound her back up.

"He's no longer my boyfriend." She sniffed twice before wiping her eyes. Morgan had this minor issue. After a crisis, she always cried a little. According to her brothers, it was more than a little, but when she was done, *she was done.*

"Since when?" Donald asked as his eyes jerked from his phone to her.

"Since he ran away and left me in the middle of whatever just happened to fend for myself."

Both men stared slack-jawed.

"Your—he—are you kidding me?" Donald finally managed. "He *left* you?"

She crossed her arms and frowned. "Yes." Both her brothers started to move away, probably to find Reed and teach him a lesson about taking care of their sister. "And to think I brought him for protection."

That stopped them both in their tracks. She almost laughed at the expression on both men's faces as they slowly turned her way. She was in trouble.

"Why, in God's name, did you think you needed protection?"

They looked identical with their eyebrows pulled together, and their heads tilted to the side, while Morgan talked about the weird email from her agent. As she went on telling them how Erica insisted they meet tonight, both jaws tightened and Donald crossed his arms, glaring at her. Finally, Howard threw his hands up in the air. Donald yanked her phone away, looking for the email. He read it at least twice before he passed it on to Howard, who finally looked up.

"You didn't realize this was a setup?"

She blew out a breath. "Well, she has me meet her all over. It's kind of our thing."

"How the hell did we help raise someone so gullible?" Howard asked, wide eyed. That was an exaggeration. Howard was almost fourteen years older than her, and Donald was twelve years older, but they hadn't raised her.

Donald shrugged and went back to her phone.

"I am not gullible!" She received two eye rolls in response. "And why should I need to be worried about my agent setting me up?"

There was only one answer for that. It had to have something to do with the two FBI agents in vice standing with her. So, she just stared at them.

It was Donald, not Howard, who finally spoke. "I would guess they were punishing me. I'm close to an arrest in the case, and Elnoz has been threatening to come after my family." He'd been working to bust the local head of a drug ring. Just last week, he'd told Morgan they were *this close* to an arrest. "I was worried. The bureau assigned someone to watch my ex and Brody."

Morgan's eyes widened, thinking of her eight-year-old nephew with his curly mop of blond hair.

"They're fine," Donald said, seeing her face. "So is Shelly. I texted her already. Plus, I'm sending someone over there now. But I didn't think about the fact that Morgan and I went to lunch last week. I bet someone saw us."

Shelly was Donald's new wife. Ten years younger than him and currently pregnant.

Howard frowned. "I would have stayed with Morgan if you'd told me. Rain's working through a tiff, anyway."

Rain would be Howard's wife number three. Younger than Morgan, and there was only one reason she would be "working through a tiff."

"*Crying all night*—you cheated on her? *Again*?" she asked, annoyed. Donald rolled his eyes at her use of the southern expression he hated, and Howard tried to look guilty, but instead he smirked.

"There are just so many fish in the sea."

"You don't get married if you want to keep fishing." She crossed her arms and glared.

"You don't like Rain," Howard reminded her, which was beside the point.

"Moey, can we do the lectures on the Holy Sacrament of Marriage later?" Donald asked, rubbing the beard he'd grown out because Shelly liked it. "Because even if no one died tonight, there are four detectives who want to get your statement. And go over your photos."

She glanced over her shoulder. All around her, red and blue lights flickered off the surrounding buildings. With that and the spotlights, no one would know it was almost ten-p.m. A crowd formed around the barriers that stopped civilians from stepping into the crime scene. Detectives stood at the edge of the barricade, waiting to talk to her. They looked at her like they were ready to pounce. If not for the two FBI agents flanking her, they would already be peppering her with questions.

"Gany!" Her boyfriend's—well, soon to be ex-boyfriend's—voice rang out into the night, and her jaw clenched. Reed didn't like Moey, the nickname her dad and brothers had always called her. He said it didn't suit her and used *Gany* instead. It didn't matter that Morgan told him it sounded like something a two-year-old called his great grandmother.

She turned toward Reed's voice. His shoulder length blond hair bounced as he tried to push his tall frame past the officers and barricade. Reed was an okay-looking chemist who spent more time in the lab than doing any kind of physical activity. There was no way he was getting through without permission.

Both of her brothers shook their heads and, just like that, they sealed Reed's fate.

"That's my girlfriend," he informed them.

"No, I'm not," she replied and walked his way. "Reed, you left me inside." His eyes enlarged in shock, and he violently shook his head before he tried to move toward her again.

"I thought you were behind me when we were rushing out. I thought you'd move—not stay inside." He tried to explain.

Morgan rolled her eyes. Not interested.

"Get him out of here," Donald demanded to one of the young beat cops.

"Gany." The change in Reed's tone had her turning to him again. Her eyes widened and she stepped back in shock at the anger on his face. It almost seemed like hatred but in one blink it was gone. "Gany, please, it's you and me." Before she could respond, another man from off to the left caught her attention.

The guy in the cuffs wasn't that tall, but he was thick, solid, and could apparently put up quite a fight because it took three officers to force him into the squad car. He was shifting and thrashing, trying to work his way out of the handcuffs or away from any of the three men around him. One officer took an elbow to the stomach before they made it in the car.

"She's dead," yelled the dark wall like man. "Kacie West might have walked out of that building sobbing on her boyfriend, but she won't live to testify. Mark my words, *gringo*. That bitch is going to have a price on her head."

Morgan's stomach bottomed out, and she couldn't take a breath. Automatically, she stepped behind Donald.

Any internet search for her picture would pull her pen name, Kacie West. She glanced at Howard and Donald. Both pairs of all-seeing ice-blue eyes tracked the car as it left the lot.

"What the fuck, boys?" said a booming voice coming through the barricades. Morgan turned toward it to see the four-star admiral headed their way. Even aged, he was still a tall, muscular man. The gray and blond hair blended together, making it hard to place him at sixty-seven years old.

"Hi Daddy," she said as his arms wrapped around her and she was flooded with the safe comfort her father provided.

"Hi princess. Not hurt, right?" He sent her a warm smile when she shook her head before he glared at her brothers.

The twin jaws were both tight, the frowns almost the same. Her brothers looked like carbon copies of her blue-eyed father. She didn't. Her red hair, freckles, and blue-green hazel eyes came from her mother. People constantly joked about her being adopted.

"I know this is my fault, but I think this just became a joint problem," Donald said to his brother, who nodded. She knew that meant her life was about to turn upside down.

2

NICK EVANS LOOKED up from the crap cards in his hand. He had nothing, but that didn't matter. Most of these idiots sucked at poker. The only one that might call his bluff sat across from him, but Nick didn't glance at Seabass. Watching his right-hand guy—rookie move, and he wasn't a poker rookie. Nick loved poker because it was a game of reading people without giving his own hand away. As long as the room thought his cards were good, he had the upper hand.

He picked up his beer and took a sip.

Seabass and Nick had been together since their days with the SEAL teams. A little over two years ago, Seabass came with him to Jersey to start life in the private sector. Neither was sure how that shit would go. But with help, Nick got his feet under him, starting NAE Securities.

Although it wasn't an easy transition, his company filled the void that leaving the SEALs had left in his life. A specialty firm, they dabbled in investigation, protection, and surveillance, even taking on a few government contracts. His guys, all former military, were the best. And Seabass had stepped up to help run things with him.

"Hey you ever going to stop being a speed bump, new guy?" Seabass asked one of their first hires, the former Marine, Wyatt Cross. Wyatt wasn't paying attention. Instead, he was talking too damn much. Although good at many things, *eyes open, mouth closed* wasn't one of them.

"Shaking the entire table again, asshole," Nick's brother-in-law Marc Demoda said to him, pointing out Nick's inability to sit fucking still.

"Don't be whiny, pretty boy." Nick smirked, watching Marc roll his eyes. Not that Nick would say this aloud, but he loved the guy. And he was all kinds of good to Nick's sister, Beth. Still, Nick loved to give him a hard time when he could, because Marc was so easy to pick on.

"I'm out," Wyatt finally said and tossed his cards on the table.

Nick's longtime friend Chuck folded next.

Seabass said nothing, just pushing a few chips into the center. His dark hair fell back as he tipped his chin to Nick before sending him a rare smirk.

Fucker.

"We all know you're folding, Marc. Don't make us wait. Your crap poker face is yelling 'I got nothing,'" Nick teased.

"Why do I come to poker night?" Marc groaned.

"Because you want to get away from the missus since she's got that crazy pregnancy mood going on?" Donovan, another NAE guy, asked.

Marc frowned.

"He's not picking," Wyatt assured, defending his coworker, before Marc could say anything. "We all love Beth, but she cried for ten minutes the other day because I said her hair looked pretty."

Marc chuckled. "Yeah, our house is full of roller-coaster moods lately. But she's working double the hormones since she's growing two little people."

He had that "my sperm is so awesome I knocked her up with two" face going on. Nick threw a chip at his head.

"That's my baby sister, douchebag. I don't want to think about that shit."

Marc laughed again. "I call," he added, tossing in his chips.

"Too rich for me." Donovan dropped his cards on the table, leaving just Marc, Seabass, and Nick.

Nick flicked a few chips to the center.

"You know, you really need to put something besides a poker table and a pool table in here." Chuck glanced around.

"I got a couch and a TV." Nick took another swig of beer.

"Dude, we're in your kitchen and the only table is the poker one," Wyatt pointed out.

"There's that shit too." Donovan tipped his beer bottle at the large island.

Nick had bought his sister's house when she'd moved in with Marc a few years ago. And he'd settled in nicely. Pool table, poker table, sofa, TV, food. It checked all "the shit you need" boxes.

His basement door opened and Wyatt, Seabass, and Donovan all turned in sync to watch Bex Carmicheal head into the kitchen from Nick's home gym. Bex hated the weirdos at the gym, so she always came to exercise at his place.

"How's the game going, boys?" she asked.

The woman was beautiful—Nick would give her that. And her spandex workout outfit showed off all her curves. Nick noticed—he wasn't blind—but he couldn't force himself to be interested.

His brothers assumed that when Bex got divorced, Nick would move right in on her. Nick honestly would have thought that too, but Bex's marriage and divorce had left her one hot mess. Nick liked her too much to become another fuck-her-and-leave-her guy. She'd had enough of those with her ex—James—plus some douche bag she dated for a couple of months last spring. They had a whole friendship thing going and it worked. He didn't want to mess that up.

He didn't have too many friends, apart from his family and his brothers in arms. Nick avoided getting too close to people. He didn't need more people to read his "if you're reading this" letter that every SEAL had. Because every goodbye a guy said before he got on that airplane to go do his job could be his final one. Many a person told him every soldier must have a death wish. That wasn't the case—he didn't know a single guy who went on a mission hoping to die. They just went to do their job. And do them perfectly because any less wasn't good enough. Then they'd blow off steam after the fact. Work hard, play hard.

"How was the workout, Belle?" He used the nickname he'd called her for years. Ever since her coming out party when she was eighteen and a dead ringer for the princess in Beauty and the Beast. They'd first met when he was her formal escort for the stupid party her parents insisted on having.

"You know I love your gym, gimpy," she answered, chuckling at his frown. Few people could get away with calling him gimpy, but Bex Carmichael had never been just anyone.

"Leg's been good for over a year," Nick reminded as she moved closer to the table.

"So has the nickname," she chuckled, along with the rest of the guys. They loved when Bex gave him the crap they couldn't.

"Where are the kids?" Chuck, Bex's brother, asked, referring to Bex's two.

"Their dad is showing them the new house and taking them to dinner," she said.

"Did they close on the house already?" Marc asked.

"Yeah, last week, but they aren't moving in yet. Haley wants to do some work or something," Bex said. Her ex had just remarried, and they were moving to Ambra. Since Bex was a better person than Nick, she was supportive. Nick wanted to toss the asshole off a cliff.

Donovan glanced at the center of the table as the chips clattered.

"Mr. Wiggles can't sit still," Marc said, and Nick stopped his leg from bouncing.

"Put your cards down, fucker." Nick dropped his nothing-but-a-Jack on the table. Seabass's top card was ten.

"Pair a queens." Marc reached for the chips.

"Holy poker face," Wyatt said.

"Aw, our little guy is finally learning to play poker." Nick chuckled.

"May you be blessed to fall for someone with brothers," Marc said to Nick as the guys laughed.

"I can't wait to meet the girl who knocks him off his feet." Bex smirked. "But I'm gonna head out. I want to beat the kids home."

"I'm going too." Marc stood up. "Go out on a high note. Plus, I want to get home and check on Beth."

"You just know you can't win again." Nick laughed.

Marc rolled his eyes and said his goodbyes.

"I'm out." Chuck looked up from his phone. "GPS says it's only fifty minutes to my place. I'm going before an accident closes the tunnel. Either of you two assholes want a ride or are you Ubering?"

Both Wyatt and Donovan, who lived in New York like Chuck, jumped on the offer and suddenly the house was almost empty.

"You ready to head out tomorrow?" Seabass asked as he tossed his beer bottle into the recycling bin. He turned, his ever-present scowl on his face.

"I'm picking Wyatt up at o'five hundred and then we'll go."

"Need anything?"

"Nah, you know me. I love chasing drug dealers." Nick smirked but Seabass's dark eyes didn't look amused.

"Don't assume it's going to be easy. That's when shit always goes south." Seabass frowned. Nick wasn't the happiest guy in the world, but sometimes even he thought Seabass needed to lighten up the doom and gloom.

"Seriously, what could possibly go wrong?"

3

HALEY COLLEN PUSHED a white peppermint mocha across the table as Morgan sat down in one of the many Starbucks that dotted the New York City streets.

"Crying all night. It's cold as sin out there." Morgan pulled off her gloves before grabbing onto the lifeline of warmth and caffeine with both hands.

"I'm as *sweet home Alabama* as you, but I've never understood that expression. Not really sure about *lord love a duck* either." A soft chuckle pushed through the back of Haley's throat as the deep southern twang she couldn't shake, even after years in the big apple came through with every syllable.

"What do New Yorkers say—Holy shit? Either way, I'm lucky I have fingers. I hate New York." This wasn't the first time in the last month and half she expressed that sentiment to her BFF. Since about Halloween, Morgan had complained about the ever-dropping mercury. It was a big change from the warmth of the Florida panhandle. She had grown up and lived in Pensacola, Florida, for most of her life. Yes, Florida wasn't normally considered "the south," but Pensacola was practically Alabama, and no one called *that* the north. Nor did it ever get cold enough that it hurt to breathe.

"But I'm here." Haley smiled at her. She'd come to New York after college to get a taste of the big city. Falling in love, first with the city, then with multiple crappy men, had kept Haley here for the last eight years.

"Yes, which is why, when I was forced into exile, I came to this freezer." Morgan sighed.

It had been late spring when the fiasco at the bar in Pensacola had taken place. Since Donald had confirmed that they'd been trying to get to him through her and she was a witness that could place one of the big guns in jail, Florida wasn't safe for her until after the trial. The cartel down there didn't have enough resources to track her all over the United States, so she just needed a place to stay for a few months.

New York had seemed like a good idea. Easy to blend in with the sheer amount of people. And, of course, Haley was here. She had thought it would be fun to spend some time with her bestie.

Haley, however, had other ideas. Not two days after Morgan moved in, Haley met a man. Haley always met a man. She was the pretty, perky blonde who attracted males like ants at a picnic. Within a few months, Haley had moved in with James Collen, vice president of a pharmaceutical company. That had been August. By September, they were engaged and had a small, almost nothing, wedding during the first weekend of December. A whirlwind romance if Morgan ever saw one.

It left Morgan lonely for her friend. She was happy for her, but now that Haley was married, her priority was her husband. As it should be, but for a single best friend, that kind of sucked.

"You don't hate it here that much." Haley chuckled. "You're awfully cranky. Is Reed bothering you again?"

Morgan frowned. Reed hadn't bothered her in months. Not since she'd blocked him on all her social media.

"No, he's not. I just never see you anymore, and you're moving," Morgan said. It was the first weekend of January and she'd only seen Haley once since the wedding at a party on New Year's Eve.

"It's only to Jersey." Haley smiled. "We want a yard, not an apartment for the kids."

James had two kids from his last marriage. The guy had married at twenty because of an unplanned pregnancy. According to James, he had been too young and too dumb to put any effort into being a husband or father. He became a serial cheater, and that ended his marriage. Morgan called that par for the course. She'd heard that story too many times and didn't quite believe James was as reformed as he claimed to be.

But Haley kept assuring her that James had changed. All of her brothers' wives believed the same thing until the truth knocked them in the teeth. A part of her wanted to believe the happily ever after her friend kept trying to sell her.

To be fair, James was everything Morgan and Haley had decided they were looking for. Averagely good looking, but nothing that would cause women to flock to him. A businessman, with a well-paying job who worked in an office with numbers and computers. Nothing exciting. Nothing brave or heroic. He had money, but not an exorbitant amount.

Most importantly, Morgan noticed when the three of them were together, James had to work to pull his eyes off his wife. He noticed things like when her drink was low or she looked tired. There was also a tenderness in James's glances, and that was something Morgan hadn't seen before. All of that gave her enough to feel hopeful, and yet, the ex-wife and kids left a crap taste in Morgan's mouth.

Which was exactly why she was here today.

"She's going to be here in like ten minutes." Haley chewed nervously on her pink thumb nail.

The ex-wife, Rebecca, was meeting them for coffee. Haley was supposed to be getting to know the ex so the kids could have a more active role in James and Haley's life. They wanted a more shared parenting time schedule, but Rebecca had full custody and held all the cards. Poor Haley was terrified. Morgan was moral support. At least for the first twenty minutes, then Morgan had to head out for her own date.

Supposedly, this ex-wife was the picture of perfection. She was beautiful, smart, classy, and old-money rich. In fact, she came from money so old that it was probably brought over on the Mayflower. And to make it worse, she was nice and supportive of getting to know Haley.

Morgan couldn't believe this chick could be everything that Haley had made her out to be.

Morgan watched Haley panic and glance out onto the street repeatedly as they chatted about work and Morgan's new guy, Stew, who Haley hadn't found time to meet.

Finally, Haley said, "That's her."

Morgan's eyes ran over the woman as she walked their way. This woman's hair was the chestnut color of a Clydesdale and thick, falling long past her shoulders. She had a nice figure under her pea coat and jeans, but Morgan towered over her, even though this woman's expensive boots had heels. Rebecca sported the features of an aristocratic European royal blood line and had deep honey-colored eyes.

Haley cleared her throat. "This is Rebecca Carmichael."

Morgan stood and reached her hand out to the woman.

"Nice to meet you," Rebecca said and flashed Morgan a perfect white smile.

"You too," Morgan agreed hesitantly.

"Your hair," Rebecca said. "It's beautiful. It's the most amazing shade of red."

"I always tell her that," Haley agreed.

"Thanks." People loved her not quite red, not quite auburn hair, but Morgan always found it boring. It was pin straight and a bit too thick to be pretty.

Haley and Rebecca spent the next ten minutes chatting, and Morgan sat back and watched. Her poor friend was so nervous, it was almost awkward. In fact, it would have been if Rebecca hadn't been working hard to continue the conversation and put Haley at ease.

Morgan had wanted to dislike this woman on principle, but it was almost impossible. Rebecca seemed genuinely happy for Haley to be married to her ex-husband, and she made it a point to say how much happier James was since meeting her. She even mentioned the kids seeming to settle in nicely and praising Haley. The woman sure knew how to work a conversation.

Morgan watched her more carefully, trying to find something to grasp onto, anything to give Haley a reason to be worried, but this woman was just *nice*.

After a half hour, Morgan tapped Haley's arm and eyed her watch.

"Oh gosh, I'm sorry," Haley said. "Morgan has a date we're keeping her from."

Rebecca's eyes widened just enough to reveal surprise and apology. Her mouth flashed another perfect smile. "I'm sorry we're keeping you."

Morgan figured they wouldn't miss her all that much. She'd said almost nothing, and as nervous as Haley was, the women seemed to be getting along. Morgan had to admit that was nice for her friend, although it brought another wave of loneliness.

"You got this," she whispered as she gave Haley a quick hug.

She walked the ten blocks to her apartment in the cold. Wishing it wasn't winter, wishing she could be home in Florida. Even in January, in Florida, cold was like fifty. Today, with the wind chill in New York, it was two degrees. She hated the cold, which was why she and Stew were ordering in and watching a movie.

Before she'd made it halfway back, she felt a chill creep up her spine. Spinning quickly to see who was behind her, Morgan crashed into a woman who mumbled something about paying attention before she hurried off. Although no one seemed to be watching Morgan, she couldn't shake the feeling that she was being followed. It was probably dumb—and dramatic, but since New Year's Eve she couldn't shake the idea that someone was watching her. A few more people walked by but she still saw no one she recognized.

She jumped as Sweet Southern Comfort blasted into the air from her phone. She pulled off her glove, cursing herself for not having the touch screen kind.

"Hello?"

"Morgan, is that you?" The sound of the old woman's voice in her usual greeting had Morgan chuckling despite the cold. Morgan didn't know who Ms. Fishman thought would answer her phone, but she always asked the same question.

"Yes, Ms. Fishman," she replied to her eighty-two-year-old neighbor. When she'd moved into her fourth-floor walkup, it had shocked Morgan to see a little old lady on the same floor.

Even more so when she learned Ms. Fishman lived alone. Well, besides the four stray cats she'd brought into her apartment.

"I'm out of milk and tuna," she informed her. Morgan rolled her eyes—she was always out of milk and tuna fish. Being a good neighbor, Morgan had given Ms. Fishman her cell phone number and told her to call if she needed anything. But Ms. Fishman took that to mean Morgan would be her personal grocery shopper.

"Okay, I'll stop on my way home. I should be there in twenty minutes."

"Normal good old-fashioned milk. None of that weird stuff." By weird stuff, she didn't mean almond milk or soy milk. She meant two percent or, God forbid, skim. After six months, Morgan knew better.

"Do you need anything else?"

"Just milk and tuna today." And every day. But hopefully a quick pop into the store would let Morgan get over the creepy feeling she got walking home alone.

Dropping the groceries off had given her less time, but she was never one to be late. Morgan was dressed and ready before Stew arrived. They'd been dating for about two months, nothing serious or exclusive. At least not yet. Stew checked the right boxes: boring, steady, average. An accountant who knew how to dress to impress. He brought flowers to every date. Ordered take out because Morgan could not cook to save her life. But Stew didn't mind, which won him some major brownie points. Tonight, it was Thai food, one of her favorites. Things had been going well. Until it was time to watch the movie.

In hindsight, it was dumb to let *him* pick the movie. But it had been over a month. She'd invited him over to her place—he should've known he was setting a mood. Morgan realized too late that it had been a test she hadn't intentionally meant to give. And yet, Stew failed it all the same.

The mood he picked—a shoot 'em up, beat the crap out of them, action movie—was not romantic. *At all*. Going into the night, she thought it would be *the* night they took their relationship to the next level. She'd pulled out all the stops. Extra time in the bathroom, even new underwear. But that kind of night would have called for a love story, or even a romantic comedy.

Morgan rubbed her arm as she noticed the goosebumps. She'd changed into a deep purple lace dress after coffee. But it had clearly been for naught. Unwilling to suffer being cold for no reason, she wanted a sweatshirt.

She glanced at the time again. Just over an hour into the movie, and about the time the hero slept with whichever girl he happened to be saving. The relationship was an afterthought—just to throw some sex in for the male audience. She rolled her eyes as the beautiful actress threw herself at Mr. Tall, Dark, and Handsome on the screen.

"I'm going to get another," Morgan said, shaking her empty White Claw at Stew. "Need a beer?" She had bought a six-pack of what he liked, which was apparently a waste of money.

Stew barely looked away from the movie to nod. It was a good thing she had good self-esteem because he didn't even glance at her butt or her long legs as she stood up—and she knew she looked damn good in the dress.

Morgan flicked her bedroom light on and grabbed a sweatshirt from the back of the closet. It was Donald's big, bulky black FBI shirt. She missed him and Howard. It was strange being far away from her dad and her brothers. Weird not having someone to call when the bathroom tub was clogged with her endless amount of hair or she needed something hung on the wall. She could do all those things herself, but she missed having someone to do them for her. Mostly because of the joy she got annoying them by asking them to do it.

Both Donald and Howard, along with Louis and her father, had been SEALs; they traveled even though they spent most of their careers stationed in Pensacola. As a group they were rarely all there at the same time, but one of them was always around. And she never moved far. Even in college, at the University of Alabama she'd never been more than a few hours' drive from any one of them. Anytime she called, they would eventually show up. Now, in New York, it was just her. She missed them.

Tomorrow morning, Donald and the district attorney were flying up to meet with her for pretrial prep and to get her ready to testify. She'd be glad to see him. She'd saved two paintings especially for him to hang on the wall and she'd have him rearrange the furniture in her bedroom. He'd be annoyed, especially because she was only supposed to be in New York for another few weeks. But what was the fun in having brothers if you couldn't drive them crazy?

She grabbed the drinks before tucking herself into the sofa. The movie had moved to gunfights and buildings being blown up while she was gone. She reached over and grabbed her manuscript off the end table. She'd rather work than watch this drivel. Stew didn't seem to notice.

She had read about twenty pages when she heard the whine of what sounded like a firework being set off. The sound should have been coming from the movie but, instead, came from behind her.

Outside her window.

Everything from there happened in slow motion. First the realization that it wasn't the right time of year for fireworks, then the only other thing that made that sound. She rolled to the floor before she considered what she was doing, dragging a confused Stew with her.

"Fuck, if you're in the mood—" He didn't have time to get the thought out of his mouth before the building shook with the force of bricks being shattered.

Morgan had forced their heads to the floor, so the sofa blocked most of the heat waves that blasted out of her bedroom. But, the blast raised the temperature of the room at least forty degrees instantly. She knew the window to get out before the fire engulfed the entire apartment would be a short one.

"Oh shit, oh fuck fuck fuck. We're going to die," Stew chanted as he rocked against the base of the sofa while Morgan took stock of how quickly the fire was spreading. "I'm not ready to die." His voice broke in a sob.

Morgan looked over, disgusted at the tears flowing down his face while he gave up. They weren't going to die—all they had to do was *leave*. Whatever had hit the building hadn't hit the family room. They could get out if they moved. The initial explosion had engulfed her bedroom, but the long hallway gave them a few seconds before the fire made escape impossible.

Luckily, the basket of her throw blankets wasn't far, and she grabbed one for Stew while pulling her brother's sweater shirt around her like a tarp.

"Run to the door," she demanded, but she stopped for her keys and her go bag. He didn't need to be told twice. She also learned the idiot didn't understand how fire worked. He left the blanket on the floor giving himself no protection, then opened the door in a burst. The second the fresh air hit, the fire exploded again, throwing them both to the ground. It was hot as Hades, but they were at least in the hallway.

Stew stood up, thanking God that they were okay. But Morgan knew she couldn't leave Ms. Fishman. So, although Stew looked at her like he was questioning her sanity, she turned toward the fire.

Alone, of course, because Stew was a wimp. If she hadn't already decided to dump the guy, that would have been the nail in his coffin.

How did she always manage to find the idiots?

Luckily, Ms. Fishman had given her a key about a month after she'd started delivering the tuna and milk. The second Morgan was through the door, she saw that the fire had easily spread into the living room. So she pulled the sweat shirt over her face, and dropping to her hands and knees, crawled through the smoke filled hallway to the bedroom. She was sweating, her eyes stung from the smoke that had already filled the place, and every breath burned her lungs. But she had to get her neighbor out.

Ms. Fishman was sound asleep in bed. All four cats were yowling their heads off in an attempt to wake her but without her hearing aids, they weren't having any more luck than the blaring alarm. Morgan shook her. Ms. Fishman's brown eyes opened wide in terror.

"Fire—no time—we gotta go," Morgan demanded. She ran to the window and slowly cracked it open letting all four cats free into the night. She carefully opened it wide before moving to the bed. The woman was still sitting where Morgan left her. The only difference was the wheezing hack coming from her. "Come on," Morgan called desperately. She knew they didn't have long.

When she realized Ms. Fishman couldn't hear her, she ran back and yanked her to her feet, all but dragging her out the window onto the fire escape. Ms. Fishman's brain had finally checked into the current situation, and she hurried down the steps. Morgan followed as fast as possible without pushing the old woman.

She could hear the sirens now that she was outside. The ringing alarms, along with the wail of the fire trucks, filled the city street. She could see the flashing blue and red lights. They had to make it down two more stories and then she would have to drop the ladder. All too slowly, she helped Ms. Fishman along. The combination of what Morgan assumed was fear and the biting cold of the night had the poor lady shaking. Morgan felt neither. She wrapped her sweatshirt around Ms. Fishman before pushing the ladder down as the right side of the fire escape started to wobble.

"Hurry," Morgan said, letting Ms. Fishman go first. A bright burst of light and heat shot out from the window above them. It rocked the fire escape as more windows shattered in both Morgan's and Ms. Fishman's apartments. Morgan looked up to see the bolts holding the fire escape loosening from the wall around the window above her. Her heart beat frantically in her chest. They were losing time.

The fire escape teetered to the left, then swung to the right, as Ms. Fishman moved slowly down the ladder. With the ladder swaying as it was, she knew she had to wait until Ms. Fishman was on solid ground before she moved. She shivered as the cold air bit at her skin. Her legs felt like Jell-O, so she locked her knees to keep herself upright. Another window blew out, causing a burst of sparks and smoke to choke her lungs. It was the longest minute of her life.

Morgan was five rungs down when the fire escape let go and she and the ladder dropped. The last thing she thought as she fell to the concrete was *no good deed goes unpunished.*

4

NICK EVANS'S PHONE buzzed in his pocket. Not a good sign, since there were only a few people who could reach him when his phone's do not disturb feature was on.

Habit had him tracking back into the woods the quarter mile to his cave before he pulled out his phone. At the clipped run it had probably been three minutes, but his training taught him not to risk something like a phone call during an op. He might just be at James and Haley's resort doing some initial surveillance, but some things were ingrained in him.

Once safely in the darkness of the hole in the side of a hill where he'd been staying, he pulled out his phone, shocked at the name on his missed call list. An ocean of things he didn't want to think about or feel crashed through him before he could blink.

"Admiral?" he asked when the return phone call was answered on the first ring.

"Nick."

Admiral Richard Johanson's voice was both a balm to his soul and a pin prick to a scab that couldn't heal. Nick winced. He respected this man a hell of a lot. He'd been his example through most of his years on the SEAL teams, and he was a hero to the country.

Didn't mean Nick *liked* talking to him.

He could never be sure if it was survivor's guilt, because Nick was still walking around while the admiral's son had died, or if it was the fact that the admiral had sent them on the mission that had killed half of Nick's team. But something made talking to this man hard.

"How the hell are you?" the admiral asked when Nick hadn't spoken.

"Hanging in." Nick couldn't say he was happy. That was too strong a word—he was—settled. He leaned against the stone next to him. The space was small but it kept him out of the wind and snow in the open air. January was brutal in northern Pennsylvania. He'd spent the last few days placing hidden cameras in the trees and buildings around the resort.

"I've heard the business is doing well." The statement sounded like a question.

"Getting off the ground," Nick answered.

"We miss you," he said.

Nick grunted at his former boss.

Admiral Johanson was the liaison between the President and SEAL team six, DEVGRU, but Nick doubted they missed him. New—younger, stronger—guys always filled in the voids the old has-beens left behind. And he didn't have time for this bullshit at the moment.

"Admiral, I hate to cut this short but I'm in the middle of nowhere on business. If this is just a how the hell are you, then I'll call when I hit home base," Nick said.

"It's not."

Nick froze as his entire body clenched. His heart skipped a beat. While the night air was frigid, that wasn't what caused his blood to turn to ice.

"Hewie and Dewie?" He forced the words out quickly, checking on the two surviving sons. Not wanting to hear bad news.

"Are fine," the admiral confirmed. Nick's fist unclenched and he took a breath. "But Morgan—well." He cleared his throat. "She's in trouble."

The admiral had four kids. Morgan, the baby of the family, was also the one every single one of the Johanson men had a soft spot for. If she was in trouble Nick was sure the admiral wasn't the only one worried. Hewie and Dewie—Howard and Donald—were probably upset as well.

"What kind of trouble?" he asked. Neither of the brothers had reached out yet. But it wasn't shocking. Since Lewie died, he hadn't talked to the family very often.

The admiral began to explain and Nick listened to the story.

"I would like someone to sit on her until trial. Just another week. Lewie always said if we needed someone, go to you," the admiral said.

Nick swallowed thickly at the mention of his best friend. "Call my brother Danny. He's an arson investigator with the bureau out of NY. If he's not already, see if he can get on her case—you have enough pull. I'll take it from there," he promised, knowing there wasn't another answer he could give. Yet a huge part of him knew he wasn't ready to deal with Lewie's family. This was the last job he wanted to do.

He listened to the details before hanging up and calling his right-hand guy.

"Got a job," Nick forced out as soon as Seabass answered.

"I need you to go meet Danny and Johanson's daughter at the hospital and bring them out to me."

MORGAN WOKE UP briefly in the ambulance, remembering bits and pieces after her fall. She could vaguely remember the smell of disinfectant, and the bright light from the ride to the ER. When Morgan opened her eyes for the second time, she was in a hospital room. There were people talking to her, but she felt like she might have a migraine coming on. Her eyelids were heavy, so she gave in, closing them again.

She didn't know what she had said to the tall man watching her, but she remembered he'd laughed. A lot. The same unknown blond man had been there the next time she opened her eyes too. Along with another man who was definitely Navy. She recognized the vacant empty look in his eyes that all three of her brothers came home from tours of duty sporting when the trauma they experienced overseas forever changed them. Closing her eyes was easier than trying to discover who these two men were, so she slept.

She didn't know how much time had passed, but she finally felt coherent the third time she woke up. Memories of the weirdest dreams of talking fish and dancing around as Snow White with the seven dwarfs flooded her mind. One of the dwarfs even had bright blue sapphires instead of eyes. Her imagination amazed her sometimes.

Sun light shone in the window as she glanced around. Although currently alone in the standard hospital room, she could tell others had been there. The drapes stood open, and three chairs were pulled up around her bed with coats discarded on them. The tray table that was meant for her held empty coffee cups and two cells. The television was on ESPN, and no matter how out of it she was that wouldn't have been her doing.

Her head hurt. Not too bad—just a dull throb. Her left hand reached to the back of her skull and she winced in pain when her fingers skimmed the bump. She moved her right hand and her feet; everything else seemed to be in working order.

The clock on the wall said eight but the not even mid-day sun told her it was morning. The toilet in the bathroom flushed, and after a moment, the door opened. The military man froze when he saw she was awake. His entire outfit from his T-shirt down to the toe of his boots matched the black of his hair. The gun on his hip said he was some sort of law enforcement, and the black hair long enough to touch his eyebrows said he wasn't Navy anymore.

"You know where you are?" His dark eyes were flat, but she watched them take in even her smallest movement. It was the same way her father and brothers had taught her to take in a room.

She nodded, and then winced at the pain that came with the motion of her head. He asked the typical follow up questions. What's your name, what year is it, who is the president.

"Am I fit?" she asked, and got a twitch of an almost smile from the serious man.

"You have a concussion, Ms. Johanson. Do you remember what happened?"

She almost nodded before she thought better of it and blew out a breath. "The fire escape fell on me because Ms. Fishman wasn't fast enough."

His lips twitched again, but he appeared too grumpy to smile.

"Do you remember what happened prior to the fire escape?" Grumpy asked.

It took her a second. Waking Ms. Fishman, Stew running away, the heat of the fire, the grenade. Then she crossed her arms and winced as the motion hurt. She probably had some bruises.

"Does that mean no?" he probed, and realization hit her.

"What's with the interrogation?" She scanned the room again. Grumpy's arms crossed over his chest as his jaw clenched. Her eyes landed on Howard's bomber jacket. "Where's my brother?" she asked before he could say anything else.

His gaze narrowed. "They both just stepped outside."

"I'll answer questions when they get back." She swallowed the lump in her throat.

Grumpy shook his head. "Listen, there is no reason to be afraid of me. I'm private security. The company I work for was hired by your father, and I've known Hewie and Dewie for years."

Hewie and Dewie—the stupid nicknames her brothers picked up in the Navy.

"I never said I was afraid." But she was. She wanted to feel safe, and that only happened in one of her big brothers' arms. "What about—"

"Ms. Fishman's fine. She was admitted for smoke inhalation, and her son is on his way from Florida," he said. "And before you ask for the fourth time, *the dress* is also fine. No one dared to cut it." The man rolled his eyes as he said it.

She exhaled a breath. Although that wasn't her top concern, the dress was too perfect to cut. It fit her in all the right places, and the color worked on her. And as a redhead, not everything did.

The door cracked open like someone was about to come in, and she heard the voice. The wonderful voice of her big brother. Howard stepped in through the door first and doubled his footsteps when he saw she was awake.

"Moey, you okay?"

She nodded as she felt the first fat tear stream from the corner of her eyes. As soon as he was close enough Morgan threw herself into Howard's arms, wincing as her bruised body banged against him. Her head hurt and she was tired. The tears were flowing before she could stop them.

"You get the water works. It must be my lucky day," Donald said as he came in behind Howard.

Howard awkwardly rubbed her back as she soaked his shirt. "She didn't do this any other time she woke up." Morgan could hear the confusion in his voice.

"Guess she was waiting for you," Grumpy answered.

"Moey, could we do the abridged version of the sprinkles?" Howard asked.

"Aw, be nice you can't rush a good cry." Donald's smirk was just visible above his beard.

"*Can't rush a good cry?* Jeez, first the constant calls with the wife, now this. Did you get your period today, Don?" her brother asked over her head.

"Pregnancy hormones, more likely." Morgan looked up to the new voice, and saw the giant blond man with happy eyes. Almost like he was the polar opposite of the grump. The man's happy eyes stayed focused on Morgan as he smirked at her brother's scoff. "Wife's pregnant, right?"

Donald nodded.

"My sister's pregnant as well. But her husband—" The blond laughed out loud. "—He's become a moody bitch lately."

Morgan forgot about the tears when the blond laughed again as Howard asked if he was talking about his very famous brother-in-law, the former all-star baseball pitcher, Marc Demoda.

"One and the same," the man said and finally addressed Morgan. "Do you remember who I am?"

She looked around the room at the four men. She almost shook her head before she remembered that it would hurt like a son of a gun. Instead, she cleared her throat and said, "Other than you're not Navy, like the rest of the guys in the room, I've got nothing."

"It's because of my happy, happy, glitter eyes, right?" He smiled.

She almost laughed. "I'm not sure those would have been my words but—" She shrugged.

"Ooh—those were your exact words, doll." He laughed again. "Then you told me you'd be Snow White because two of the seven dwarfs were already in the room. Happy." He pointed to himself, then turned to the dark haired grumpy former Navy man. "And Grumpy."

Now she did laugh; her dreams were starting to make sense. "Well, when I'm right, I'm right."

"And when you're concussed, you're funny as hell," Happy Eyes informed her.

"Or drunk," she added.

Her brothers both frowned at her. They didn't enjoy her drunken shenanigans at all. Probably because she and Haley had called them a few too many times to bail them out of a drunken mess.

"So." She sat back on the bed and looked at the big blond man. "Do you have a name or should I stick with Happy Happy Glitter eyes?"

"I'm Danny Evans," he said as the grumpy guy with dark hair finally cracked.

Morgan feigned shock with a gasp. "Wow, I have to change your name to something other than Grumpy now."

He cleared his throat and apparently remembered he was supposed to be pissed off. "It's Seb Ashton."

"Sebastian?" she asked.

He shook his head. "No. First name: Seb. Last name: Ashton. And yes, my mother was high—just call me Seabass. Yes, like the fish, and yes, I know SEALs give shit-ass nicknames." He crossed his arms over his chest. Morgan wasn't sure if he meant any of it or not. She turned to Danny, shooting him a look full of questions.

"I was there for that conversation too, and my name wasn't as fun," Danny said.

"Why are you here Mr. Evans, and why do you have Mr.—" She paused again looking at the serious face of the Navy man and decided he didn't know how to joke. "—Ashton giving me the third degree?"

"Seabass. No need to call me Mr. Ashton," he corrected.

Danny reached into his pocket and flipped out a badge. Morgan frowned as she took in the FBI logo. "If you say you're changing my name to Agent Whatta Waste, I'm going to start to believe I've been transported into Groundhog Day," he said.

"What?" Howard demanded.

"Last time I flashed my badge, I was told my name should be Agent Whatta Waste because no one as good looking as me should be law enforcement." Danny turned to Morgan. "Another exact quote from you, doll." Morgan shrugged. Again, it was too true to argue with.

"Were you doing drugs last night?" Donald asked her, and she rolled her eyes.

"Drug test came back negative," Howard answered.

Morgan glared. She had never in her life done drugs. She'd never even smoked pot like others had in college. She was way too chicken to try it. It would either be laced with something and kill her, or she'd be caught and arrested, and her brothers and father would kill her.

"With the way you were going on we had to check," Danny assured her.

She sighed. "What department are you with?"

"Arson."

Morgan blinked. "Arson," she repeated.

"I'm asking questions to find out why someone set your building on fire, well set *your apartment* on fire to be accurate." Then Danny turned and frowned at Seabass. "He's asking questions because he's a nosey fuck."

A growl slipped through Grumpy's gritted teeth. "I'm asking questions because I'm being paid to keep her alive. If I know what happened it will make my boss less pissed when I talk to him."

"Oh, yes, he's not a patient asshole, that's for sure," Danny agreed. Morgan snorted. When were assholes ever patient?

It took a second for the comment to sink in.

"Wait a second." She glanced around the room, her eyes falling accusingly on both siblings. "You told me I was safe in New York, but the FBI is here asking me why my apartment was set on fire and you're hiring people to watch me?" They'd gotten her into this, and now they were going to dump her on someone she didn't know and thought she'd be okay with it.

"Donald—you told me that if I went to New York, it would be fine. No one would come after me. Now you're saying they did?" Her voice was screechy.

"Moey, calm down. Let's talk about this," Donald started.

"Nope," Howard interrupted. "This is not a discussion. Neither of us can follow you around for the next week and a half before you need to be in Tallahassee. We'll stay for a couple days until you're released from the hospital, but then we need to head back to Florida. And by the charred remains of the place you call home, someone clearly has—"

A knock on the door interrupted him.

"Good morning. Looks like Ms. Johanson is finally awake." An elderly man with kind eyes and a white coat walked in. He smiled at her. "I'm Dr. Larson." She returned his smile before the kind old man turned into a hungry bear and snarled at the men around the room. Although the doctor seemed to have a good bedside manner, his don't-fuck-with-me attitude proved he was a New Yorker. "Anyone not in a hospital gown—out, now." There were protests all around. The kind doctor turned to her. "Is there anyone you want to stay?"

She looked at both her brothers and then the grumpy man they were apparently paying to babysit her.

"Nope," she smoothly answered. There was not a damn person she wanted to see right now.

5

NICK WALKED DOWN the dirt road that led to his brother Grant's barn. He had been out in the woods for forty-eight hours straight, and the chill seeped into his bones. It was cold as balls this winter and not a thing in the breath-taking panoramic view that was his brother's property looked alive. Still, Nick knew there was work to be done on the farm. Without a doubt his brother would give him some menial task to complete. And it would definitely involve shit.

Boots, not cowboy, but black Durashocks, the same brand that had been protecting his feet for almost twenty years, silently tread through the grass next to the dirt road leaving no evidence. He automatically covered tracks that on his brother's farm, didn't matter. His blue eyes scanned the horizon, looking for a threat that would never come. But the habit was part of him. Knowing his surroundings had kept him alive. If he was driving, he watched for an ambush or braced for a land mine. If he was walking, he watched not only his six, but his three sixty. If he opened a door, he saw who knocked, but he looked for who else might be there. And he always found the threat.

That sixth sense, as people referred to it, had saved not only his life, but others.

At eighteen, Nick Evans had left the small New Jersey town he grew up in to head to the Naval Academy, then BUD/S, and from there he served his country as a Special Ops Navy SEAL until he was forced to retire two years ago. His leg was fine, but the fact that he had more metal than bone made him unfit to serve his country. It was crap. He could do anything he'd done before the incident he didn't like to think about.

His tread became hard for a moment before he stopped in his tracks. He smelled metal, hot metal, and the rust of blood. He wasn't on the farm anymore. Instead, he was half a world away. He sucked a breath through his teeth, trying like hell to block out the flashes that just thinking about his leg caused. He focused on breathing in and out steadily, and automatically put his hand into his pocket to find the flat engraved silver rectangle. He let his fingers trace the rounded edge until his nail caught on the hole. He knew what was engraved on the thin piece of stainless steel. Just like he knew where he was.

"I'm on Grant's fucking farm. I'm in the grass and I'm about to shovel a ton of shit," he said aloud. He was talking to himself. He knew that made him sound crazy, but talking to himself helped keep him sane. Fucking flash backs. He opened his eyes and found himself in the grass in Pennsylvania.

Months of therapy—he was man enough to know when he needed some—had taught him how to keep the demons away. But truthfully, it wasn't the leg that made him unfit, hells to the no, it was the flashbacks.

Fucking flashbacks.

Before he realized it, he had taken in his surroundings again and was moving. He heard Grant and someone else in the barn. Nick glanced around to the open window and chuckled as he scaled his way up the side of the barn, through the window, and onto the loft ten feet above the floor below. Stealthily, he moved to the edge, seeing his brother leaning on the stall, holding Bullet, Nate's horse. Nate was in the stall brushing the horse with his father's direction. Nick eyed the lower rafters until he found his path. His DuraShocks silently moved along as he walked the tightrope. Halfway to them, he saw Nate glance up. Nick's finger moved to his lips and Nate glanced away.

Not a minute later, Nick pounced down, yelling as he flew through the air. Grant's entire body shook, and he spun around.

"Motherfucker son of a bitch. What the fucking hell is wrong with you, asshole?" Grant snapped. He grabbed his chest, huffing as he bent in half. Two breaths before Grant spun to his son. "Do *not* tell your mother."

Nick chuckled at what his sister-in-law, Trish, would say about the string of curse words his brother had just let loose in front of their ten-year-old.

Nate just smirked. "Yeah, we already have a curse cup he puts messages in because he can't help himself."

Grant glared. "You all love the IOUs I drop in those cups."

Nate nodded. "The best is an extra hour of riding."

Then Grant frowned. "How did Nick not scare you?"

Nate smirked again.

"Because your son pays fucking attention to his surroundings. Unlike his old-ass dad." Nick pointed out the obvious.

"Language," Grant snapped.

Nick just raised his eyebrows.

"You scared the piss out of me, that doesn't count," Grant replied and Nate laughed.

"You should have seen yourself." Nate fist bumped Nick's hanging hand. "Mom says you shouldn't keep doing that to him, though. You're going to give him a heart attack one day."

"We gotta keep this old guy young."

"I'm younger than you. You're my older brother," Grant snapped.

"Only because I was born eleven months before you. We both know in mind and body, you've got me by ten years." Nick chuckled.

"That doesn't make sense." Grant shook his head and passed Nick a pitchfork. Nick knew what was coming. "If you're going to be here and act like a—" He paused, and his brown eyes cut to his son. His brother wouldn't call Nick an asshole in front of Nate again, but Grant's eyes said the words. "Like a douche. You muck the horse poop out of the stalls."

"His favorite punishment," Nate frowned. "Better you than me." Then Nate paused, his chocolate brown eyes looked from the tip of Nick's black boot to the top of his black beanie. "Why do you look like you've been mucking stalls for two days?"

Nick shook his head. That kid. Not only was Nate ten going on twenty, but nothing got by him. Nick ruffled Nate's straight, jet-black hair that looked nothing like his father's mop of curls. They wouldn't look alike; Grant had adopted Nate from a deadbeat fucker who was currently serving multiple life sentences. Still, love trumped blood every time and this father son duo proved that.

"Doing a surveillance for fuck-face's family's company for the last two days," Nick answered.

Grant sighed. "Your girlfriend's ex needs a new, more appropriate name."

"Bex is not my girlfriend, but the name fits James to a *T*," Nick corrected.

Grant's teeth gritted. "More appropriate for the audience, not the man."

Nate smirked again when Nick looked at him. "There is a reason they coined the term 'cuss like a sailor,' Dad." This kid. What ten-year-old says "coined the term."

Nick laughed. "Don't tell the others, but you're my favorite." He gave him a noogie.

"Gah." Nate pushed him away. "You say that to all of us. I've heard you tell Steve that same thing, Uncle Nick."

That was true. He loved them all.

"Why are you here?" Grant rolled his eyes.

"Am I not welcome?"

Grant sighed.

Nick gave in. He'd be serious for a few minutes. But the truth of it was he rarely got to just be the fun guy in life and with his brothers, all six of them, and his sister and sister-in-law, it was nice to relax. His big-ass family was the breath of fresh air that always kept him sane no matter what shit happened during active duty. He was the oldest now that his older brother Bob had passed away. Next came Grant. Followed up by five more. His sister Beth had married Marc. And Grant, of course, had Trish, who Nick protected as fiercely as if she were his own sister and happily let the woman feed him at any chance he got. Which, besides the location, was the reason he'd come to the farm today.

"I was supposed to be doing surveillance on James and Haley's resort, which is forty clicks from here, but I got a call from Lewie's father." Nick's hand reflexively went to his pocket, and he swallowed.

Grant froze. His eyes went from annoyed to sympathetic instantly. "Nick." His whole family knew his best friend, Lewie.

Nick put his hand up. The flashback ten minutes ago was too close, and he couldn't. It would swamp him. The *L*-words killed him. Things like leg, long road, and Lewie were off limits. He swallowed and then sucked air through his teeth.

"Anyway, after he called Hewie and Dewie called. They all need a favor," Nick said flatly.

"Wait." It was Nate that spoke. "Your friend Lewie has brothers named Hewie and Dewie? Like the Disney ducks?"

That actually made Nick crack a smile. Somehow, Lewie's name coming out of the kid's mouth didn't send him down a rabbit hole.

"The second thing about sailors, son, is they give crap nicknames. They aren't actually named Hewie and Dewie," Grant explained.

"Oh." Nate agreed, like it suddenly made sense.

"What's the favor?" Grant asked cautiously.

Nick cracked his neck left, then right. "Babysitting. Their little sister got into some shit and needs protection for a week. They're meeting me here."

"Let me guess, Daisy?" Nate asked and giggled, finally showing his age.

Nick shook his head, and Nate frowned. "Moey—Morgan." He corrected, not using the nickname her family called her. He'd heard Lewie refer to her as Moey often enough that it seemed strange that her name was Morgan. But he doubted she'd want some guy she didn't know using Lewie's nickname.

Grant crossed his arms. "What kind of trouble and why, in the name of all things holy, are you bringing trouble to my house?"

Nick smirked. "Actually, Danny is bringing the trouble," he explained, referring to their little brother.

Grant's eyes scanned Nick before they got wide, "Danny. His new arson case?"

"Yeah." Nick shrugged. Not that Nick would ever tell Danny to his face, but his little brother was the best arson investigator the FBI, or anyone for that matter, had ever had. Not only was Danny fascinated with fire, but he was like a dog with a bone once he was interested in something. And any fire interested the fuck out of Danny.

"So, you two decided to bring this here? To my house? To my family? Without asking," he snapped.

If Nick had even a tiny inkling that any of this would put his brother's family in danger, the woman wouldn't get within a hundred miles of this farm. Nick protected what was his—fiercely. However, his dumbass brother should know that, so instead of pointing that out, he went a different way.

"Well, Danny called Trish and asked her if we could all stop by and if she'd make meatloaf. Your beautiful wife said, of course," Nick replied, sweet as pie.

"Fucking Danny." Grant shook his head.

"Should I not tell Mom about that one either?" Nate smirked.

Grant simply pointed to the second pitchfork leaning against the wall, and Nate sighed. Nick patted his shoulder.

"Sucks when your dad's a hard-ass, huh?" he whispered.

"Especially when you have to learn to divide fractions," Nate agreed, and the two spent the next couple of hours mucking out the horseshit before Nick walked to the house with his brother and nephew.

The porch door slammed shut and Nick turned. His guy, Wyatt, stood on the porch in the standard all black uniform of NAE Securities, shit-eating grin and a bag of what looked like Trish's homemade dinner. Wyatt had been out on the job with Nick and came out to Grant's before heading to Jersey.

"Meatloaf?" Nick asked, and Wyatt nodded.

"Your brother is one lucky fuck. I swear I miss the days when Trish made me three meals a day." Wyatt pushed his hand through his white-blond hair. Unlike Nick, who'd spent the last two hours cleaning horse shit, Wyatt had gotten to visit with Trish.

"Go home, punk," Grant called and closed the door behind him. Wyatt laughed. Nick had met Wyatt when he was part of the Marshal team protecting Trish from her crazy ex-husband. But as much as his brother pretended to hate Wyatt, it didn't escape Nick that Wyatt had been invited out for long weekends multiple times over the last year.

"So, you still okay to juggle both these jobs?" Wyatt asked.

Nick nodded. "Yeah, the admiral's daughter is just going to hang out while I figure this other shit out."

"If you need me—"

Nick cut him off. "It's fine. Didn't you ask for the next two days off for your dad's procedure?"

Wyatt's father's diagnosis of early onset Alzheimer's was the reason he'd left the marines for the Marshals. He wanted to be closer to home. It was also probably the reason Nick was able to steal him away from service with the idea of a permanent New York home base. It was damn lucky for NAE Securities because Wyatt was sharp as a tack and had all his legendary father's computer and coding skills.

"Yeah, Dad's thing is tomorrow," Wyatt mumbled.

"Don't feel guilty about being there for your family. Family first, jarhead," Nick ordered.

Wyatt smirked. "I know the rule, but shit, this is Admiral Johanson we're talking about."

"His family doesn't trump yours," Nick said. "Plus, I got to do this myself."

Wyatt nodded. After a long beat of silence, he added. "Well, the cameras all over the grounds and offices are live. We have every angle we need, and hopefully it doesn't take more than a day or two to figure out who's selling the drugs."

Nick nodded. Having two people call in favors from him at the same time sucked. But he couldn't deny the Johansons anymore than he could Bex. Even if it was for her idiot ex.

"I just hope we catch whoever is doing this before we have another OD on James's resort. Four is enough. Plus, my contact with the DEA said we have a week before they move in unless someone else dies. Because then they will shut everything down," Wyatt reminded him.

"Go home, Wyatt, we'll be fine," Nick assured. Wyatt nodded one more time and headed off Grant's porch to his car just as another car pulled in.

"Bro," his brother Danny called as he stepped out of his black Range Rover onto Grant's gravel driveway. Danny's eyes did the typical government skim-around before landing on Nick with a smirk. "Figures you'd be covered in horse shit."

"Just finished. About to hit the head." The shit portion of the day was done. But the shower hadn't happened yet—beer was needed first. Nick didn't care if Trish said he couldn't stay inside because he reeked. He'd gladly stand outside in the cold for a minute. He probably wouldn't have another opportunity for a drink for over a week. He glanced toward the empty car. Danny was supposed to have the Johanson siblings with him as well as Seabass. "How far did your heavy foot get you ahead of my—ward?"

"Ward?" Danny asked, his smirk turned full smile.

"Lew—" Nick crossed his arms and frowned. His friend's name died on his tongue. He cleared his throat. "Hewie and Dewie's sister," he said instead.

Danny showed no sympathy for the struggles Nick had just speaking Lewie's name. Danny, being government trained, knew PTSD and he wanted Nick to admit he had an issue. The problem was Nick knew he did. He just didn't talk about it with his family.

"When was the last time you saw Lewie's sister?" Danny asked.

Nick shrugged. The right answer should have been at the funeral. But fuck if life had screwed him and Nick had been in a hospital in Germany for the funeral, unable to attend. Couldn't be a pallbearer at his best friend's funeral. The guy that was another brother to him. The guy that he still wished he could trade places with. . .

January was usually cold but suddenly he was sweating. It was miserably hot. The Humvee didn't have air conditioning— the windows were down, but it was too hot outside for it to be comfortable.

"Why are you turning?" Nick asked from the back seat. It was weird for Nick to not be in control. He was always in charge, but today, Lewie had taken over.

"Order says no more trips through towns," his second-in-command answered from behind the wheel.

Nick gritted his teeth. Keeping the fight out of the towns wasn't bad, but keeping his guys on the back roads tripled the chances of hitting an IED. If he'd been behind the wheel, he would have said fuck off and stayed off the road riddled with hidden explosives. But Lewie rarely bucked the chain of command. It was one of the reasons Nick should be in charge.

"Can we close the windows? This is ridiculous," said the woman beside him, pushing her hair behind her ear.

"You're in a war zone." Lewie's blue eyes cut to Nick as his custom smile appeared on his face. Lewie loved to give people shit. Nick rolled his eyes. They were on a mission. It was time to focus, not tease, even on an easy op. His head needed to be in the game. Lewie was always the light to his dark. The smile to his glare, the laughter to his serious scowl. "Your hair doesn't matter, T-cup."

Nick bit his finger. He couldn't laugh because he sat next to the woman they'd dubbed T-cup.

He, Lewie, and Seabass were stuck with the girl on this deployment. In actuality, the entire team was stuck with her, but they were Alpha One, Two and Three and they were charged with keeping the reporter alive on what was basically a supply run. Added to the stress was the rock on the girl's finger, given to her by Alpha Four, their brother in arms. Not only did they have to deal with her, but none of them were going to tell Jeremy that they hadn't done everything in their power to make sure his girl was safe.

Nick couldn't wrap his head around the fact that his team-mate's fiancée was with them. Nick didn't have a girl. He didn't let himself; he knew he wasn't ready for the commitment. There were women he cared about. His sister and Bex were at the top of the list. And even though it was different from what Jeremy felt about T-cup, he knew there was no way in hell he would ever let Beth or Bex be involved in the danger that even something as run-of-the-mill as a supply run would require. So, if T-cup was Nick's girl, shit, she'd be at home in the good ol' USA. Loved ones stayed home, stayed safe.

Jeremy had wanted T-cup with him in the second car. But Nick, the commanding officer, knew well enough how minds worked. Nick would rather have Jeremy focus on the car in front of him, than on the woman in the seat behind him. At least if his girl was in the front car, Jeremy'd be looking ahead. He'd also decided that if Jeremy was on an op, more complex than a simple supply run, T-cup couldn't come.

"I don't care about my hair but the sand kills my eyes." T-cup sighed.

Yeah, something about the desert. It not only burned his eyes, but the dryness bit at his skin, sucking the life out of it.

"Just shut 'em," Seabass said from the front seat.

"Shut my eyes and miss the story I'm supposed to write? You know me better than that Seb. Life goal: famous journalist." T-cup reached forward and pulled Seabass's hat over his eyes. Seabass cracked a smile.

Lewies fingers tapped on the wheel, and he began to hum "Stand by me," his favorite, and Seabass groaned at the song they'd heard too many times.

The last thought Nick remembered having before life turned to crap was that there wasn't a news story here.

"Dumbass."

Nick didn't hear the words but felt the bitter sting from the slap to the face.

"He's good," Grant said, nodding.

Nick took in his surroundings. The bottle that had been in his hands was lying by his boot on Grant's porch. Grant's farm, where he was currently standing. He was safe. His finger moved to his pocket to finger the silver dog tag. Nick was half a world away from the flashback. This had been a long one, not a few seconds. Grant had already showered, but he looked relaxed. As opposed to Danny. Everything in Danny's stance said he didn't believe for a second that Nick was okay.

Nick glared. The front of his shirt was soaked with sweat and horse shit. The horseshit had been there for a while, since Nate wasn't the best at not sending it flying in the air. The sweat, though, was new.

He didn't know how long he'd been out. He went to run his hands through his hair, but he had a beanie pulled low on his head. He tried to speak, but he couldn't find his voice. The flashbacks had been under control. One call from Lewie's father, and they'd come back with a vengeance.

"I'm going to voice this aloud again; this is a shit idea. You're not ready for this, and you're not going to be able to keep Morgan safe." Danny shook his head.

Nick's hand ran along the three days of black beard before grasping at the back of his neck, unwilling to admit that Danny might be right. "I'm doing this," he said instead, using his "don't mess with me" look.

Danny frowned, but before he opened his mouth, Nick spoke.

"If it was your partner at the bureau and you made him a dying promise, tell me you wouldn't do it. No matter what shitty shape your head was in, no matter what shit you had going on."

Danny's eyes flitted shut for a moment.

"But as your brothers," Grant stated when Danny was at a loss, "it's our job to worry more about you than some random chick."

"She's his kid sister, not a random chick," Nick stated.

"When was the last time you saw this *woman*?" Danny asked again.

Nick shrugged. "I don't know. She's probably twenty by now, but in my head, I see a gawky teenager with frizzy hair, braces, acne, glasses, with her nose in a book."

Nick's eyes tracked the car heading down the road. A black Escalade that belonged to his security firm. That had to be Seabass with the Johanson siblings.

"You said you had to remind yourself she was a job?" Grant asked Danny.

Nick's head shot to Danny. "Off limits," he snapped, and Danny smirked. It was a team rule. Every SEAL knew it; sisters were off limits. Danny was younger than Nick, but still, twenty was young, even for Danny.

"I don't mix sex and cases. No worries about me," Danny, his playboy brother, assured him. "And Grant's already shackled to Trish. I wasn't worried about him either."

"Shackled?" Grant shook his head. "My wife is the best thing that ever happened to me. I'd give everything I own to keep *her* shackled to *me*."

"Whipped." Danny coughed.

Grant smiled. "And proud of it. Don't hate on my girl."

"We all know Trish is the best," Nick assured Grant, rolling his eyes at his baby brother. Danny needed to stop heckling Grant about being happy, especially if Danny wanted meatloaf tonight. And Nick wanted meatloaf; it was melt-in-his-mouth, beg-for-more, good.

"Do you still have a thing for redheads Nick?" Danny's random question had Nick glancing away from the incoming car again.

Hell yeah, was the right answer. Nick had always had a soft spot for the ginger girls. Something about a natural redhead just called to him. But lately he just didn't have time for any woman. Instead of agreeing, he just shrugged and turned to watch Seabass approach.

Their conversation ended as the SUV pulled to a stop ten feet from the brothers. All three of them turned their attention to the opening door.

Nick watched the black stiletto heel appear on the gravel driveway, followed by a long, pale leg that just kept going and going and going. The fact that the skirt the woman was wearing didn't even show three quarters of her long shapely leg almost had Nick swallowing his tongue. Especially as the rest of her appeared.

In one quick glance, Nick saw the entire woman in front of him. His eyes moved from the black shoes up her legs, to the perfect curve of her hip in her tight black pencil skirt. From there, he tried not to gawk at the cut of her belted waist pinching in. The swell of full breasts under her white blouse and just a sprinkle of freckles dusted the flawless skin of her chest before leading up to the beautiful line of her neck. All topped off by a soft jaw, full pink lips, aqua green eyes, long lashes, and pornstar thick red hair.

"Who is she?" Nick mumbled to Danny, assuming one of his partners from the FBI had ridden along. Nick might need to make some time for dating.

"Your ward." Danny chuckled.

Nick's head snapped around to him.

This was Lewie's little kid sister? Where the fuck had time gone? She was sixteen in his mind. But that didn't make a lick of sense because she had been sixteen during his and Lewie's first tour together. Damn, that would have been—probably—fourteen years ago. And clearly, Lewie's sister had grown up. Had he really not seen her in fourteen years?

Nick shook his head.

"Off limits," Danny whispered in a sing song voice

Nick glared. *Of course* she was.

"God, I hate you both," the beauty snapped and slammed the car door. Her big eyes lit up with a sparkle as soon as she saw Danny. "Agent Whatta Waste, next time I ride with you, Grumpy and my jerky brothers are poor company."

Nick eyed Danny. Who was Agent Whatta Waste, and what the hell did that mean?

"Personally, I prefer Happy Happy Glitter Eyes," Danny teased.

This sounded like flirting. Nick's glare heated.

Seabass got out next and his face told Nick without words that the car ride had been hell. But Nick's eyes in return said one thing to Seabass, *Lewie.* Seabass glanced down at his own leg. Both Nick and Seabass were discharged from the teams at the same time. Both for similar reasons and both had legs with more metal than bone. Seabass had lost his leg, whereas a rod and some screws had fixed Nick's. Neither man, however, could seem to get their heads on straight. Seabass raised his eyes to Nick before nodding at Grant.

"Trish made meatloaf," Grant said to the man.

"Hooyah." That got a rare smile and a fist pump out of Seabass.

"That's two!" The beauty declared with a five-alarm smile full of lush lips, white teeth, and sparkling eyes. Nick forgot how to breathe for a moment. He needed to pull it together and remember that this was his best friend's sister.

"Morgan, stop being annoying," Donald said as he climbed out behind the woman, opening the door she'd slammed in his face. His eyes scanned the area before landing on Nick.

"Hawk," he said with a smile. Howard was out of the car right behind him, and Nick greeted both men with a shake and a back slap while Danny introduced Morgan to Grant.

Morgan's cute little nose scrunched up, causing the freckles to disappear as she came closer to Nick. She spoke in a soft southern voice that echoed in his bones. "What's that smell?"

Nick knew it was him. "Shower," he said and left the porch. It was going to be a cold one.

THE DOOR SLAMMED behind the stranger before Morgan had received an introduction. But at least the putrid odor of what she could only assume was sewage went with him.

"Well, that ray of sunshine was my oldest brother, Nick," Danny said, chuckling. "And for the record, he was what smelled like shit."

Morgan wasn't sure how to reply. Truthfully, she didn't understand why she was here. The car ride was a waste of time. Her asking questions, no one answering them. They'd all just told her they were meeting Danny and Seabass's boss here.

"Put him to work while he was here?" Seabass asked.

Grant didn't reply, he just opened the door and motioned for them to enter the storybook house.

When they had pulled up, Morgan immediately jumped into story mode. The quaint white farmhouse with the huge wrap-around porch looked like it had jumped out of a winter romance novel. The enormous windows, the slam screen doors, the porch swing—she could just imagine love growing here. Walking inside the house didn't disappoint either. All wood—walls, floors, ceilings. Big open space, lots of windows.

It was gorgeous. And had that homey feel that made a person want to stay. Old sofas, cozy drapes, throw pillows, bouquets of flowers, and family photos.

This place screamed *home.*

"Your house is beautiful," she said to Grant.

"My wife," he replied gruffly and nodded to the brunette standing at the stove. Morgan could just see her through a large opening in the wall.

Danny sighed. "He means his wife, Trish, is what makes this place great. It was a dump before she moved in."

Grant crossed his arms and glared at Danny.

"I do like how you opened the wall in the kitchen though." Danny ignored his brother's angry eyes like he was used to it.

"Everyone here?" The brunette, Trish, said, wiping her hand on her flannel shirt. Leggings and Ugg boots completed her look.

But Morgan's eyes cut to Grant. The second Trish had spoken, Grant's focus shifted, and his entire being softened. Brown eyes warmed with a look that said *my world is heading my way.* His arms uncrossed automatically once she was near and found their way to the small of his wife's back. His face lit up in a smile as he introduced Trish. In that small second, she saw a lasting love, and because of that, Morgan couldn't help but like Grant.

"Dinner still at six?" Grant asked.

Trish nodded, then paused. "That okay?"

Grant smiled. "Anytime you want to feed me is perfect in my mind." His brows gave a waggle, Trish flushed.

Morgan covered her smile as she realized Grant was probably talking about more than one type of "eating."

A sharp cry came from the kitchen area, and Grant reacted instantly. "I got her." He let go of his wife and moved to scoop up a tiny little girl from a swing. His big hands tucked the small little bundle of pink onto his shoulder before another small voice came barreling up the basement steps.

"Heidi needs me! I am here to help." The girl looked around four years old and had her mommy's dark hair and big brown eyes.

Grant squatted down, scooped up the second little girl, and took both of his daughters to a well-worn easy chair, settling in as his older daughter pulled out a book about princesses to have him read. To Morgan, there was nothing sexier than the sight in front of her.

"How old is the baby?" Morgan asked.

"Heidi's four weeks," Trish said, eyes on her husband and kids.

"Wow, you look amazing," she said to the woman. She didn't look like she'd had a baby in the last year, let alone a few weeks ago.

"Grant's shirts hide it well," Trish assured.

"I think you look great," Morgan corrected, and her eyes flicked to the chair with Grant reading to his girls. "And that is the picture of perfection right there, isn't it?"

Trish's eyebrows raised.

"A man who loves his family is the sexyist thing ever," Morgan explained. And then she added, to make sure Trish knew Morgan realized Grant was very much taken, "I write romance, and I swear I'm going to use the way that man looks at you to describe the hero in my next book. I'll even thank you both in the acknowledgements."

"He's not a big attention fan, so he'll hate that," Trish finally said, but she smiled at Morgan. "I have to finish up dinner— you're welcome to join me."

"I'm useless in the kitchen, but I'll be happy to keep you company," Morgan confessed as she followed Trish.

"Oh, it's just mashed potatoes and gravy. It's easy," Trish explained. "Nothing fancy."

That might be true, but Morgan could ruin any meal. She'd burned soup a few years ago when she'd gotten lost in her novel and forgot it was on the stovetop. So she let Trish work, mixing things in some kind of pan while she took a seat on the stool nearby.

"I wish I had your ability to cook," Morgan said as she watched the easy efficiency with which Trish prepared their meal.

"Most people think cooking is a dying art," Trish said. "You said you're an author?"

Morgan nodded.

"I write romcoms. I was supposed to have a book come out in a few weeks, but life's been complicated lately." She was going to miss her deadlines for the first time.

"Danny told me you got yourself into some trouble." Trish let that hang.

Morgan frowned. Of course, the story would be that it's her fault, not that her brother's case put her in danger. "I'm not supposed to talk about it."

It wasn't anything new. Growing up in her family, she learned what classified meant at a young age. She was twelve when she signed her first nondisclosure agreement. And even before that, her brothers and dad had constantly told her she could never repeat anything she heard.

Trish's eyes were kind, as if she understood.

"My sister-in-law's father is the Vice president. I get it," she agreed.

"So, there are what? Four Evans siblings?" Morgan asked. Trish's eyes flicked over to Morgan before looking away.

"Eight," Trish corrected. "Nick, the oldest, is upstairs. Then my husband Grant. There are twins, Luke and Will, next. Beth. Then Danny." Trish nodded her head toward the other room. "Then Joey. And Clayton is the baby of the family."

"Was Nick the guy on the porch?" Morgan asked. Her thoughts flicked to the tall man in all black. His beard was thick, his skin a dark tan. Sunglasses covered his eyes, and his frown was pronounced.

"I told him he best clean up for dinner if he wants meatloaf, and I happen to know he does, so he'll come down clean and fresh," Trish agreed. "I hope he gets that scruff off his face. It doesn't suit him, makes him look mean as a snake."

Yeah, that was the impression she got from him in the thirty seconds she was in his presence.

"When I first met him, he had long hair and a thick beard. I was terrified of him," Trish continued. "It took me a while to realize he's as much of a softy as all the Evans men. They're a good family."

It took Trish another ten minutes to get the food on the table before calling everyone. The first one to sit was another child. He looked about ten and was ready to eat. Morgan moved to join him when she heard the soft tread of boots on the stairs. She glanced over her shoulder and did a double take.

Her heart skipped two beats and her stomach did a backflip.

The man walking down the stairs looked nothing like he had on the front porch. The beard was gone, showing off a smooth, hard jawline. His lips were tight in an almost frown as his slate-blue eyes scanned the room. His hand came up to run through his dark wet hair.

She swallowed, letting her eyes track over the fitted T-shirt that showed off his broad shoulders. Holy biceps. This guy was built. But more than that, he was a dead ringer for the man she used to start off every single book she ever wrote.

Prince Eric had just walked into the room.

NICK TREKKED DOWN the steps, seeing the guys in the room waiting for him. Howard, Donald, Seabass, and Danny were all braced before he came into view. Their stances relaxed a bit once they saw him. Grant never looked up from the girls in his lap—he was too fucking trusting. Although it also could be that Grant realized he was in a room full of people who would take care of any issue before he even knew it happened.

Special ops never left you.

"Ah, pretty boy's back," Howard said after viewing Nick's cleaned up appearance.

"Fuck you, never gonna be that," Nick snapped before Trish suck in a breath across the great room. He winced, feeling his neck heat. He really hadn't meant to upset his sister-in-law. "Sorry."

"Cuss again in front of my children, Nicolas Evans, and you're not eating with us." Trish frowned. Nate smirked from the table but his eyes said he hadn't told his mother that Nick had been cursing in front of him all afternoon.

"I'll definitely make it through dinner." Nick crossed his heart and sent Trish his most charming smile, causing her to shake her head.

"At least I was right. He cleaned himself up and doesn't smell like a toilet. Now we'll work on the potty mouth," Trish said to the woman Nick's eyes had been avoiding.

A cold shower had taken care of any kind of inappropriate thoughts he might be having. However, another look at the beautiful woman in the kitchen made his gut tighten. He moved toward her and held out his hand.

"Nick Evans," he said, and she let him take her hand. Hers was soft, smooth, but her grip was firm enough that she didn't come across as weak. He respected that. Crap handshakes set his teeth on edge.

"Morgan Johanson," she said quietly, the thick southern accent still clear in every syllable. He released her hand after a quick moment and simply watched her. This was his best friend's sister. Lewie's letter home. The one he sent twice a week, telling her as much or little as he could. The person he loved more than anyone else in the world. And the idea that she'd spent the last two nights in the hospital made Nick's fist clench.

Lewie's mom had died during childbirth with Morgan. Nick knew Lewie and his brothers had helped raise this girl. She was practically their daughter rather than their sister. He talked about her often enough; it was still hard for Nick to wrap his head around the fact that he hadn't seen her since she was a sophomore in high school. He'd probably never officially met her.

Still, she was the one person Lewie wanted taken care of if anything happened to him. Nick had said he would be the person to do that. Yet Nick hadn't even checked in on her in the last two years. He scratched the back of his head in guilt before looking at her again.

Her blue-green eyes stared at him in amazement, and he narrowed his own. He had expected fear to radiate off the woman he was supposed to protect, but that wasn't what he saw. He'd been around women who looked him up and down, inspected him like a prize steed, blatantly objectified him. However no one had ever looked at him like he was a superstar they'd always wanted to meet.

"Sorry," she apologized, but didn't stop staring. "It's just . . . you look a lot like someone."

He cocked an eyebrow. He'd never heard that before. No one ever said things like, "wow you're a clone of Chris Hemsworth." He definitely didn't resemble those Hollywood pretty boys.

"Who?" he demanded.

She shut her eyes, but a whisper came out of her sweet, full lips. "Eric."

Was he supposed to know who that was? He glanced over to Howard and Donald. They were both silently laughing. What the fuck?

"Is that the moron who cried when your apartment blew up?" Nick demanded, and his hands slammed to his hips. "Because I sure as—" He stopped himself as he saw his sister-in-law's warning gaze. "I guarantee I won't be crying."

Morgan finally opened her eyes and looked at him again. She shook her head. "Eric. From the Disney movie."

Who?

He heard both Trish and Danny laughing, too. *What the hell?*

"He's a cartoon, but I have to say, I see it," Grant said through a chuckle. "Katie has his doll."

He nodded his head and moved toward his daughter's bin of plastic dolls across the room. Nick stomped over behind him and plucked the little thing out of Grant's hand.

Morgan thought he looked like this tool? He had plastic black hair that looked like a poof on the dude's head and a weird-ass nose. He scowled as he saw what looked like eyeliner around the eyes.

"You've got to be kidding me," he snapped as he dropped the doll back into the pink basket. "I don't resemble that tool. Katie needs some GI Joes or something," he added to Trish and watched Morgan's eyes narrow.

"Wait—" Her hand came up in front of her before her eyes cut from him to her brother's and back again. "How exactly do you know my brothers? Trish said you own a business, but exactly what kind of business?" she asked warily.

That seemed like an odd question for her to ask. What did she think he was doing here? He glanced at her brothers and then paused as they both vehemently shook their heads. He saw Morgan's eyes follow his own.

"Mr. Evans?" she asked.

"Lieutenant Commander Evans," he corrected automatically, and heard her groan.

"Of course. What an *idiot*," she mumbled.

His eyes widened. "Excuse me?" he snapped.

"Not you," she assured him. She moved closer. Her soft hand patted his arm, and he was knocked back by the sweet scent of lilac. He was transported to the calm spring of his childhood yard—to everything safe and good in the world. Lilac was the smell of home. She smelled like home. Which was impossible. He'd just met this woman. He had to get these thoughts under control.

"Me. I'm an idiot," she assured him, drawing him back to the moment.

Nick had no idea what was going on. This woman was throwing him off. Nothing threw him off. He'd gone through massive amounts of training to teach him how to be on top of his game in any situation. But at this moment, he was utterly lost.

"You're Seabass's boss. Who we're meeting. I assume you're my babysitter until the trial next week?" she asked.

He gave her a clipped nod.

"DEVGRU, right? Part of my dad's black ops team?" she asked. Her tone was way too innocent for such a statement. The team she flippantly mentioned wasn't even supposed to exist, let alone be spoken about.

Nick had run it for years before he left the teams. But—he frowned—he'd never confirmed that to anyone. His family didn't even know. It was *classified*. His eyes shot to Seabass first, who shook his head, then her brothers.

"She's got an NDA," Howard confirmed. Nondisclosure agreements were given to families of a lot of SEALs, and DEVGRU, just to allow them to talk about the basics.

Still.

"No one else does." Nick glared first at the brothers, then at the chatty woman.

"DEVGRU, black ops?" Danny asked, rubbing his chin.

Nick grunted. Danny's eyes ran over his face before moving on to all four former SEALs in the room. They'd all been DEVGRU. And it probably meant more to Danny than anyone else because of his work in the FBI. He might know what DEVGRU did.

"All four of us are retired. None of us will confirm or deny anything about our time serving our country," Nick answered automatically and then sent a glare that could have put little miss chatty pants six feet under.

"Sorry." She mouthed. But the flush of her cheeks was almost unbearably attractive. When his eyes raised to both the Johanson brothers, he saw the apology in theirs too, but apparently, the black ops team wasn't a secret in their family.

"What's DEVGRU black ops?" Nate asked from the table when no one else had spoken.

Nick's eyes flitted closed. Nate saw everything. Including a lie when it left your mouth. He wasn't going to lie to the kid.

"Well, basically what it is—" Morgan's voice moved away from Nick as she spoke, "is a group of super-secret, awesome, best-of-the-best soldiers who do all the stuff no one else can," she explained and Nate was enthralled. He didn't blame the kid. "And although everyone who was ever a part of it is a huge hero to our country, it's also like the ultimate secret. They can get in big trouble for even confirming it's an actual thing."

"It's really a secret?" Nate asked.

Morgan met each of the four former DEVGRU members straight in the eyes, her apology clear. Then she nodded to Nate. "No one can ever tell anyone, even their family or their best friend, if they are part of it. And it was mean of me to ask your uncle. So I owe him a big time apology. He's a former SEAL and a hero, and to put him on the spot was disrespectful of me."

Nate's eyes moved to Nick's. "I could believe you were the best of the best, and if you weren't, the country's dumb for not picking you." Then Nate hugged him. Nick's eyes flitted to Morgan.

"Thank you," he said silently. And he saw something in her eyes. More than just an apology. Something that said she understood this kid shouldn't be let down because kids needed to stay innocent as long as they could. It was crystal clear this woman had lost her innocence too soon, and Nick wanted to know what happened. And lucky for him, he had a full week to find out.

7

"YOUR SISTER'S GOT a big mouth," Seabass said as soon as Grant and Trish shut their bedroom door behind them. Morgan had gone up about an hour earlier, claiming she had a lot of writing to do. Nick had done a quick scan of her room before leaving her. His instructions were simple: do not leave the room for any reason. The halfhearted shrug of agreement meant she wouldn't listen to him.

"No one else wants any?" Donald held up two glasses of scotch for Howard and himself.

"Don't drink on the job," Seabass, Nick, and Danny answered in stereo.

Nick bent down and opened his bag pulling out his computer and his reading glasses. "Can we talk about the case?"

"It's classified." Danny smirked. "I guess I need to know your clearances."

None of the four former SEALs even smiled. Nick focused on the laptop as it slowly booted up.

Danny took a sip of his Diet Coke and watched all four over the rim of the cup. "I'm kidding, but DEVGRU, black ops, really? All of you?"

He might have a general idea of the code word clearance level missions Nick's special ops SEAL team had run, but Grant's living room wasn't going to be where they'd hash it out.

Nick eyed Seabass who stood and moved to the black bag he'd brought. Files landed on the coffee table. Nick put on his glasses before he reached for one. He flipped through the still photos from every camera within two blocks of Morgan's apartment the night of the fire. He pushed the only one that mattered onto the table in seconds.

"Hawk at his finest." Howard shook his head.

"Did you tell him?" Donald asked Danny.

"Tell him what?" Danny's eyebrows pull together.

"Where the grenade was launched from? Trajectory possibilities?" Donald pushed.

Danny shook his head and reached for the photo. "Is this the building north by northwest of Morgan's bedroom? Fourth floor three windows over? How do you know?"

Nick ignored him. Besides showing him the exact spot the suspect stood to launch the grenade, and a small glimpse of the swirl on the unknown subject's shirt, the photo didn't tell much. He reached for the next file. All the stills around the building in question for thirty minutes around the attack. He flicked the photo of the fucker who blew up Morgan's apartment onto the table.

"Damn, dude. Lewie was right; you're a beast," Donald said. "We spent hours looking through these while Morgan was sleeping before we found the unsub's photo."

Nick raised his eyebrows at Seabass. He wasn't sure how his right-hand guy had missed the bag the unsub was carrying or the same white swirl on the black hoodie that reflected off the glass from the first photo he'd pulled.

"Why weren't you at the hospital?" Howard asked.

"Busy on another case." Nick dismissed the comment, unwilling to admit he couldn't force himself inside a hospital. "Did you run it through our facial rec?" he asked Seabass.

"*You* have facial rec software?" Danny asked. "Who the fuck are you guys?"

"NAE Securities," Nick answered and then turned his eyes to Seabass.

"I didn't, but I had Wyatt run it for me when he got to Jersey an hour ago. Nothing. He says it's too grainy, and not even a great profile."

"There a better angle?" he asked, looking at the other files. Seabass shook his head. "It's New York City, for shit's sake. You're telling me that no other cameras got a picture of this fucker? What if we hack the traffic or NYPD cameras?"

"I'm sorry, what?" This time it was Howard asking. But Nick and Seabass ignored him.

"Wyatt's trying all the traffic cams, ATMs, the four building security cameras, and even two cameras from cop cars, but he's not having much luck. I told him to call it a day. We can worry about it after his dad's thing," Seabass said. "This son of a bitch either knows what he's doing or he's a lucky fuck."

Nick scratched his head. There had to be another shot of this guy. He stared at the lanky man in the ball cap and hoodie. He couldn't even tell this shithead's race.

"Are you still covert special ops?" Donald asked.

Danny shook his head. "No. They aren't employed by the government." Nick glanced up at Danny whose eyes said what his mouth didn't. *Neither of you two could pass any sort of psych eval.*

Nick looked each man in the eye, "I'm private sector, and above board. However I employ some of the best. Be it hackers, coders, snipers, or security. We get every job done every time, and we don't fuck up. Do you want to ask more questions about my company, or do we want to figure out who bombed your sister's apartment?"

No one asked anything else as Nick stood up. Unable to just sit anymore, he needed to burn some of the useless energy pulsing through his body. He paced the room as Danny's hand came up and rubbed his forehead.

"Look, I know you've got Morgan in New York to keep her away from the drug ring you're breaking up in Florida. But I don't think they did this," Danny sighed. "I didn't see this because none of you bothered to show me this shit at the hospital." He flicked the shot of the apartment window to the table. "Or this dude." He pointed to the grainy photo. "But I can tell you the firebomb was homemade. I'm not calling it amateur because that's not accurate. It wasn't. Whoever built it knew what they were doing, and yet it wasn't military, ours or anyone else's. Or the kind you can buy on the black market."

Nick's eyes narrowed. "Why?"

He wasn't an arson specialist, but that didn't mean he would just accept *A* plus *B* equals four. That's how mistakes were made.

Danny's hands moved in front of his face like he was praying. "The chemicals were sophisticated. Everything about them you would find in any grenade or missile our government launches." His eyes flicked to the photo of the unsub. "The casing though—the delivery method. It was amateur. Almost unstable. Like I want to call the unsub a lucky son of a bitch for not blowing up the building he launched from."

"Tell me why that's not the Florida guys," Nick said.

Donald sighed this time. "Because most of the time, they would buy the shit from the black market, and it would be real."

Howard added a second thought. "And they don't work alone. They work in a group. You would see three to five guys around. Not a lone unsub."

"We have ears on the ground, but we have no buzz about anyone going after her again, or moving north," Donald finished.

Nick flopped onto the sofa as the other four men sat back, letting that sink in.

"You're telling me you want the working theory to be that Morgan is in hiding from one set of people while someone *else* is trying to blow her up?" The accusation in Seabass's voice played into the ridiculousness of the theory.

"Is she using her real name in New York?" Nick asked.

"No," Seabass answered. "New alias is Morgan Potter. And before you ask, she was offended at the idea that she would mess up her name for any reason."

"Did this Potter person just jump up when Morgan moved to New York?" Nick asked.

"No," Seabass answered. "Someone, I'd bet vice, made a nice little backlog. None of this can be traced to Morgan Johanson. From everything we can tell, she's been careful."

Seabass handed him a folder, and Nick skimmed it quickly.

Nick chucked his reading glasses on the table and rubbed his eyes. He was going to let Danny in on his secret. There was no other way to open this case up.

"We need a minute of honesty. The drug ring has to be working theory number one, because that seems most like-ly. However, we can't discount the idea that they don't use homemade shit. But we all know there are many people who do." He eyed the brothers. "I can't do my job unless we realistically admit that you two have some enemies. If someone I cared about was almost blown up, I'd have an idea."

Both men glanced away. Howard's jaw clenched and Donald rubbed his legs.

"Give me some names, boys," Nick ordered.

"What is your security clearance?" Donald asked Danny, pulling at his beard and shifting uncomfortably in his seat. It was one thing to joke, or hedge, it was another to give details.

Danny shook his head. "Nowhere near DEVGRU, but I'm not dumb. I know the reality we are dealing with." Danny frowned and glanced away before meeting Nick's eyes. "Look, I need your list, too. I'm going to assume you and Lewie were on the teams together."

Nick blinked.

"Nick was Lewie's commanding officer," Donald said.

"Holy shit. You ran DEVGRU, black ops?" Danny snapped.

Nick's teeth ground together. "This can never leave this room. No one in our family can ever know this." Danny met his eyes. Nick saw a million questions but instead of asking them Danny only nodded. This wasn't fodder. This wasn't gossip. It wasn't a joke; it was code word clearance.

Seabass cleared his throat. "I ran ours already, Danny. After the conversation with Hewie and Dewie at the hospital," he said. Danny raised his eyebrows. "We were all teammates. As soon as I realized it was a possibility, I pulled my list. I also pulled Nick's from our drive; former teams guys hold one on file. I'm going to assume between the two of us we covered Lewie."

"Is it safe to assume the fire had nothing to do with Lewie?" Danny asked.

Nick rubbed the smooth metal in his pocket, trying to stay in the moment. He reminded himself of where he was, and what was going on around him. But he started to smell the dessert, and he knew he was going under. He sucked in one final breath before he was transported to hell.

Nick glanced at the small dark-haired woman next to him to see how she'd react. He'd only just met her this morning, but she was a firecracker. Nick's sister had gotten married yesterday, or maybe two days ago. The time changes and the international dateline were messing with his mind. He wasn't sure what day of the week it was at this point. But he'd arrived at camp this morning. Just in time for the supply run, which Lewie graciously offered to drive. Between the wedding fun and the long-ass flight around the world, he was happy to let his second take the lead.

"Shut my eyes and miss the story I'm supposed to write? You know me better than that, Seabass. Life goals: famous journalist" T-cup *said as she reached forward, pulling Seabass's hat over his eyes. Seabass cracked a smile.*

This was a supply run. There was no major story here.

The Humvee pitched forward before a wave he didn't see coming struck Nick. It racked his body as a roar louder than a train running directly over him pierced his eardrums like sharp needles being plunged over and over again. His body was moving head over feet or possibly in a circle, but the migraine-like throb in his head made it hard to focus.

The vehicle hadn't even come to a full stop before Nick was aware of what happened.

Roadside bomb.

He couldn't see. He wasn't sure if his eyes were injured or if the gray blackness surrounding him was smoke from the blast. Still, he knew it wasn't a direct hit. It didn't come from below, but behind.

Vehicle two set off the bomb.

The roar in his ears turned into a ringing as the Humvee finally stopped. Pitched forward, his harness locked him in place. The first thing he noticed was the hand clawing at his leg. And he reached to cover it.

The diamond bit into his palm as he squeezed, letting T-cup know he was alive. She probably couldn't hear any more than he could. He ran his hand up her arm to find her face. He turned her in his direction, which was awkward as he hung like the car had landed on its hood facing the ground.

Her face started to appear in the gray haze as he pulled her closer, assuring him that his eyes worked. But although her mouth moved, forming rapid-fire words, he couldn't hear any of them. He pressed his finger to her lips, then banged his ears and shook his head. She nodded like she understood. He pointed a finger at her and then made the okay sign. From what he could see, she had glass in her hair and cuts on her skin. Her one eye was swollen, but it could have been worse. Her good eye widened, almost like she was going to panic, before she swallowed. Tears pooled, but she just nodded.

Her mouth formed two words. Nothing broken.

That was what he needed to hear. As the smoke cleared, he glanced forward. He could make out the outline of Seabass and Lewie in the front. Seabass was moving almost manically. Nick tried like hell to focus, and finally he saw it. The metal in the man's leg.

Without thinking, he reached for the belt at his waist and tossed it forward, smacking Seabass in the face. With every moment, visibility got easier and he could clearly see Seabass now. His head spun toward Nick before he took the belt with shaking hands, and used it as the tourniquet Nick intended.

Finally, he turned his attention to Lewie. It was like a second explosion rocked Nick. His stomach dropped, the air leaving his lungs in a swooping blow.

Vacant, blue eyes stared lifelessly back at him.

"Is he okay?" The voice cut through the pounding of his head and suddenly, instead of soot, the scent of lilac filled his nose. The moments coming out of a flashback were always marked by confusion and instinct.

"He's doing his thinking thing," Seabass said.

"Thinking thing?" Morgan asked.

His whole body relaxed at the sound of her voice, and he could see he was in Grant's living room. In *this* moment, he was safe, and the desert was half a world away. He turned to the smell, and there stood Morgan, all long legs and too much skin.

Once again, his thoughts abruptly changed directions. He was here and now and couldn't take his eyes off her.

"You okay? Because I want to know why everyone's talking about Louis?"

Nick sucked in another breath through his nose as he patted the seat next to him. She looked like she had just showered, and the floral scent flowed off her thickly. For that, Nick was grateful. He was not as happy about the barely there tank top and skimpy shorts. Short enough that ninety-nine percent of her legs were on full display. Long shapely legs that had him picturing them wrapped around his waist, or thrown over his shoulders. Great fucking legs.

He glared. He had to *stop* this.

This was his best friend's baby sister. The guy who died behind the wheel of the Humvee that Nick should have been driving. He was a bastard for thinking of her that way.

She tucked her long legs under her as she moved next to him. Nick listened while her brothers explained what Lewie had to do with anything, but he noticed they left out the fact that he and Nick were on the same SEAL team and anything to do with their friendship. Almost like they knew that would make Morgan less likely to stay with him and, of course, it would.

Saying Lewie's name aloud was hard enough. Hearing them talk about him almost sucked him under again. But having to admit what happened would be impossible. To tell Lewie's siblings that Nick was responsible for putting Lewie behind the wheel of the car that killed him—he couldn't. He lived with enough guilt. He couldn't watch the blame flicker in their eyes.

Instead, he sat staring at the freckles that dusted the pale skin of Morgan's chest. He'd love to taste every one of those freckles—just run his tongue along her skin. Her hair was still wet and as she tucked it over her shoulder, the water soaked into the material of her shirt. His eyes dropped lower, and his mouth went dry at the almost see-through material. What the fuck was the matter with him?

Lewie's little sister. Remember that asshole.

Nick tossed a throw blanket at her because he couldn't think while she sat there with her high beams flashing at all of them. And it bugged the crap out of him that both Danny and Seabass were looking. She needed to cover the fuck up. It was winter, for shit's sake. Why didn't she have winter clothes to sleep in?

"Goosebumps," he said. Her eyebrow raised and Danny sent him a "you're full of shit" smirk.

"Thanks?" she replied, but it seemed like a question. Her eyes looked brighter green with the dark forest hues of the plaid fleece wrapping her shoulders. When they met his, he forgot what they were talking about. Her face was shower-fresh, not a speck of makeup. In fact her lashes still held the beads of water on them. Still, she took his breath from his lungs.

"Morgan," Danny said, pulling her attention from Nick. "Can you think of anyone who would want to hurt you? Not them." He pointed to her brothers. "Not Lewie, but you."

She shook her head.

"What about your boyfriend?" Danny asked, and Nick's body jerked, almost as if someone shocked him.

Boyfriend?

"I'm assuming you mean the idiot, Stew," Morgan said. "Even if he hadn't *cried* and *run away* instead of helping my nice old neighbor out of the *burning building,* I would have ended it with him. And we weren't serious enough to use a label. But no, he's boring. No one would hurt him. My dad though—"

"He's a special advisor to the president," Danny interrupted. Morgan nodded, but Nick hadn't thought it was a question.

Nick pulled at the back of his neck. If it was someone trying to hurt her father, that had the potential to be a cluster fuck.

Nick cleared his throat. "He's the DEVGRU point of contact—liaison—between the teams and POTUS."

Danny huffed. "Of course he is, because this couldn't be easy."

"Sorry." Morgan shrugged.

"You're the only innocent person in this room, doll," Danny assured, and Nick glared at him, causing Danny to chuckle.

"We all gotta leave in the morning," Seabass said.

Nick nodded.

"Yeah, Grant's going to have my head if he realizes what I brought to his house," Danny said.

"Grant can't ever know." Nick sighed. "But—if we killed the trail leaving the hospital, keep low and off the grid, I doubt anyone will find us."

"We killed the trail," Seabass assured, and Nick turned his attention to Morgan's brothers.

"You two—look into anyone with a connection to the drug ring in Florida who might have come after her. I don't want any surprises when she and I get down there. And keep Danny in the loop." Nick waited for them to nod.

"Thanks for taking over my investigation," Danny complained.

Nick rolled his eyes before turning away from him. "Seabass, have Donovan check everything again—twice. Wyatt has two days, and then he's meeting Morgan and me to do the drive to Florida."

"Why not Seabass?" Morgan said and for the first time Nick saw the nerves that he had expected her to feel about the situation. His hand moved before he thought it through and he reached out to take her hand in his. Her soft trembling hand clung instantly to his, causing a surge of protectiveness to run through him.

"One of my other guys, Wyatt, is a former marshal. He's trained for witness protection. He's brought many witnesses to testify in the past. He knows what he's doing." He gave her hand a reassuring squeeze and her eyes more green than blue at the moment flicked up to meet his. Fear she hid well swam in the depth of those beautiful crystal waters. He watched her swallow. Come hell or high water, nothing would happen to this woman on his watch. "And until then, we keep you off the grid and safe."

"Where are we going?" Morgan asked.

"To a resort nearby. You're going to pretend to be Nick's wife for the next few days," Seabass said and Morgan's mouth dropped.

8

"CAN YOU EXPLAIN now?" Morgan asked once they had pulled out of the long driveway. It was seven in the morning. Nick had rushed her through a quick breakfast before demanding she get into the car. He'd been a bossy shadow since last night. He'd even slept on the floor outside her room. She'd tripped on him at about three am when she got up for a glass of water.

"We've been in the car ten seconds and it took you thirty minutes too long to get the hell out of the house." Nick frowned at the road straight ahead of him. He was as stubborn and unwilling to share as any of her brothers. It wasn't at all shocking that he was Navy. He had every one of the traits. She wasn't sure if he was on the teams with Donald or Howard, but even if none of them confirmed that they'd served together she knew it had to be true.

She just wished he wasn't so damn good-looking. Every time those intense slate-blue eyes swung her way, her stomach flipped. And this morning he already had the brush of a five o'clock shadow darkening his jaw that enhanced the sex appeal that wafted off him.

"I've waited seven hours," she huffed. It blew her away that she was supposed to pretend to be married to the man who looked exactly like her first crush.

Since he was busy driving, she took the opportunity to study him again. The Ray-Bans covered his blue eyes and jet-black eyebrows, but not his straight nose, the hard jawline, or the thin, reddish-pink lips. She swallowed. Just watching him caused a current to zap through her body.

"Stop staring at me. I don't resemble a fucking cartoon prince," Nick said, and she glanced away. He was watching the road—how did he even know?

"I'm waiting for you to tell me what's going on. You said you couldn't tell me in front of everyone else. I've been patient, but why the hell do we have to pretend to be married?"

Nick's lips vibrated as the air blew out between them.

"Obviously, that's not my ideal situation either," Nick said. "But I'm in the middle of another job, and my wife and I were scheduled to check in to a resort I'm looking into for a friend."

"You're *married*?" Morgan wasn't sure why this shocked her. She hadn't even been with the man for twelve hours, but somehow, he gave off a single vibe. And last night, when he'd held her hand, it had felt like more than just comfort. A frown immediately covered her face. She glanced at his left—ringless—hand on the steering wheel. *Navy.* No-good cheaters, incapable of commitment.

"Freckles." He turned his head and shot her a glare. She pulled at the neck of her shirt, covering up the hated freckles that spread across most of her chest. "If I was married, there is no way in *hell* I'd be going to this resort with you."

"You just said *wife*," she reminded him.

"This isn't the type of place where you get a room alone, but I need to be onsite for a few days. The resort belongs to a friend, and they've had some issues with drugs."

Morgan froze. Her problems had all started with her brother busting up a drug ring. Apparently, they'd even followed her to New York.

"It's nothing to stress you out." Nick's hand came over and rested on top of hers. The rough skin of his hand caused a zap of heat up her arm, and she tightened her shoulders to stop the shiver from rushing down her spine. "It has nothing to do with what happened in Florida." Morgan breathed out a sigh of relief at his words. "A string of overdoses. My friend asked me to look into it because the DEA threatened to shut them down. I need to be onsite—a wife gives me a cover reason to be there. A friend, in need of a bit of R&R, was going to help me out. Then your father called; plans changed." Nick frowned again.

"Sorry I ruined your plans," she mumbled. It was stupid to be jealous of his girlfriend. She hardly knew Nick, and he definitely wasn't the type of guy she wanted to date. So what if he had a girlfriend? But her jaw still clenched at the idea.

"Didn't ruin, just adjusted. Doesn't matter to me who I'm staying with." His scowl seemed to make that statement a lie. "And Bex is coming with Seabass. She'll still get her R&R."

"You're letting your girlfriend stay with someone else?" Morgan asked, shocked. Even her brothers, who couldn't stay committed to one woman if their lives depended on it, never let their girls do something like that.

He shot a look of disgust. "Again, she's a *friend*. And if I wasn't fucking single, I wouldn't be going to this resort with you."

"You have a new text message from Danny." The car chirped

at Nick before she could respond, and he hit a button. The car spilled out a slew of messages as he banged buttons on the dash.

DANNY SAID: Okay, we have to talk about how unbelievably hot Legs is

JOEY SAID: On a scale of one to ten how hot are we talking?

BETH SAID: This conversation is degrading. You guys are idiots

DANNY SAID: I'd definitely call Legs a nine

LUKE SAID: No shit I need an introduction

CLAYTON SAID: Me too, I'm with Nick about the gingers

BETH SAID: Neither of you are even on the east coast

DANNY SAID: Nick's big on her being off limits. I doubt any of you assholes will get to meet her

GRANT SAID: Yet he can't seem to keep his eyes off her

"Fuck." Nick pounded on more buttons, finally ripping the cord connecting his iPhone from the car. But apparently that didn't stop Bluetooth. Morgan's eyes widened as she realized they were talking about her, but Nick couldn't seem to get the car to stop reading.

TRISH SAID: It was cute he was flustered

MARC SAID: Nick was fucking flustered?

BETH SAID: Language hotshot

WILL SAID: Why are the girls on this chat

GRANT SAID: Don't hate on my wife Will

MARC SAID: Or mine

WILL SAID: This just seems more boys only - its why we have that fucking chat

DANNY SAID: My bad. I meant to use the other one but I was too excited to fuck with Nick

LUKE SAID: Is it, he wants to fuck her flustered, or he knows he cant fuck her so he's flustered?

"Jesus." Nick finally opened the phone, and the voice stopped. "And those, ladies and gentlemen, are my siblings." He sighed, tossed his sunglasses onto the console, and ran his hand over his face.

Could any of that be right? Did *she* fluster Nick?

No, she didn't think so. But her eyes glanced over the dusting of pink on his cheeks.

"Are you blushing?" She couldn't stop the chuckle that slipped past her lips.

"I don't do that." Like the idea that he could blush offended him. And of course, it did. Blushing was probably too girlie for the big bad SEAL. His phone buzzed about twelve more times, and he sighed heavily.

She liked the idea that she flustered him. It made her feel like they were on more even ground. If they were going to spend the week together, they couldn't both be awkward all the time. She relaxed and rolled with it rather than ignoring the conversation.

"I guess it's only fair I get a nickname too."

"Huh?" he asked.

"I'm guessing Agent Whatta Waste named me Legs?" She glanced down at her long legs. The reason heels made her taller than most men.

"If at any point you wore something that covered them, maybe he wouldn't call you that. It's winter. You could wear pants." Nick glared at her legs quickly before looking back to the road.

"And it's freezing too," Morgan agreed. She would love

pants; this white skirt was short enough it was almost impossible to wear. "I wish I owned more pants."

He shot her a look that said "what the hell?"

"My apartment blew up, remember?" She raised an eyebrow.

He nodded like he understood. "Why didn't your brothers buy you pants when they went shopping for your clothes?"

She scoffed. "My brothers didn't get my clothes. They stayed with Seabass at the hospital with me."

He raised his eyebrows.

"Danny showed up with clothes before we left to meet you. And I have some leggings that were in the bag but since I didn't know where we were *going*, I wasn't sure if leggings and a long sleeve T-shirt were appropriate."

"*Danny?*" Nick's voice raised two octaves. But she wasn't sure what had upset him.

"I didn't ask him to," she assured. "I would have rather gotten my own clothes, but I wasn't allowed to go anywhere. Everything he got is short, tight, and lace." Not to mention Danny apparently had a thing for thongs, because that was all she owned at the moment. Nick seemed to be choking, and she turned to him. "Are you okay?" she asked.

He didn't respond. His eyes flicked between the road and his phone as his fingers seemed to fire off a massive amount of texts.

"You shouldn't text and drive," she said as he glared at the phone. "You could get distracted."

His gaze wandered up from the phone to hers again and this time a smirk played at his lips. "Trust me, freckles, I'm trained to multitask."

It wasn't a statement that should have been sexual. But somehow, the rough sound of his voice vibrated over her skin and caused her to shiver.

His phone buzzed a few more times, and he turned to it, firing off a couple more texts before dropping it in the cup holder again.

"Are you going to tell me exactly where we're going?" Morgan prompted.

"Grab the black portfolio back there," Nick said, nodding to the back seat. "Seabass put all the info in there. Along with our new IDs."

"IDs?" She reached for it.

"We're hiding you. That means new identities again. Copy that?" Nick said.

Morgan sighed. She should have realized that. Someone was trying to kill her, and no one was sure why. Surprisingly, she wasn't more off balance by the whole thing, but truthfully, she trusted Nick's statement about staying off the grid, and being untraceable in the middle of nowhere Pennsylvania.

She unzipped the black leather case and inside was a red folder, a manila envelope, and a white felt string bag.

Nick yanked the envelope off the pile and flicked it open with the hand not currently steering. He dumped the contents onto her lap. Two driver's licenses and two Visa cards fell on top of the red folder.

"Can you read them out to me? Name, address, birthday," Nick demanded.

"Morgan Stewart," she read, then followed it with an address in Delaware and a birthday in August one year before hers.

"Learn your deets. Mine should say Nicolas Stewart, 203 Berdane Ave, Miltport Delaware. DOB December 12, 1986," he said, and she agreed. "We need to see if those fit. I had to guess your ring size."

Nick reached over, swiping the white bag off her lap. He opened it and dumped three rings onto the console between them. He flung the bag on her lap and picked up what looked like an engagement ring.

"Give it a go."

The white gold band was toothpick narrow and in the center was an enormous square diamond sparkling up at her. It was simple, elegant and exactly what she would have chosen. Weird to say it was her dream ring. Even more odd was how the real-life version of Eric sitting next to her just handed her this ring. She slipped it on without a problem and then frowned at it.

God must have a serious sense of humor to provide her with her childhood dream but in such a twisted way.

"Hate it?" Nick asked.

"Huh?" she asked.

"You're glaring at it like it offended you. What would you have picked?" he asked.

She glanced at her hand again. "This. This is my dream ring."

"You dream about an engagement ring?" He chuckled.

She glanced out the window, feeling silly. "I mean, I write romance. Most stories end with a proposal, and I have to describe a ring. I've done the research and know what I like. And it goes with the happily ever after I sell to my readers. My brother, Louis—" But before she could go on, he sucked in loudly through his teeth. Nick's jaw was tight when she turned to look, and he was breathing hard through his nose. "Are you okay?"

"Right as rain. What about your brother?" Nick's jaw seemed too tight for him to be good. She wondered if he thought she was reading too much into these rings.

"He used to call me his girl who loved a love story," Morgan said.

Nick made no comment. He just stared straight ahead, breathing hard through his nose. Morgan thought maybe she was annoying him, so she glanced at the rings and picked up the single white gold wedding band and slipped it on too. As she glanced down at her finger, she felt the car pull over to the side of the road.

"What are you doing?" she asked.

"Talk. Anything. Just keep your voice going," he asked softly, breathing hard in and out of his nose before he rested his head on the steering wheel.

Morgan cocked her head to the side watching his white-knuckled grip on the wheel. It almost seemed like he was hanging on for dear life. She knew what trauma looked like. She couldn't believe she hadn't made the connection last night. Sympathy rushed through her, relaxing her back into the seat. Flashbacks were something many soldiers dealt with, so she did what he asked.

"I grew up with all boys and around a bunch of military men, so I gravitated toward girlie things. Dresses, nail polish, princess movies. Love stories. And romance books were just perfect for that. By the time I was thirteen, I was chewing through them. My dad let me get away with it because he didn't know what the books were about. I loved a love story so much I majored in English in college because I wanted to write my own. And it has to be happily ever after, even though real life isn't like that. It's nice to have a fun escape." She continued talking about her work for another few minutes while Nick simply sat, resting his head on the wheel.

"Thank you," he finally said. And she turned to see his

haunted gray-blue eyes watching her carefully. She nodded. He picked up the silver ring on the console and slipped it onto his finger before putting the car back in gear.

"How long have you been having flashbacks?" she asked hesitantly, wondering if he was about to deny what had just happened.

His jaw tightened as he stared straight out the windshield. She continued to wait for so long she assumed he wasn't going to answer.

"Almost two years," he whispered and put the car back in park. "But don't worry, I won't run around naked screaming or shoot you or anything. From what I've heard, I just stand there staring into space."

"I wasn't worried. With my dad and brothers—do you think I'm scared of flashbacks?" she asked.

"My job is to keep you safe. I don't want you doubting my ability to do that. But it also means you need to know the truth," Nick said.

"I don't doubt it. All of my brothers had flashbacks, at one time or another, so did my dad, and yet they're the people I trust most in the world," she said honestly. She watched him shut his eyes and lean against the headrest. "I'm assuming, since you own a business and seem like a highly functioning person, you see someone?"

Another clipped nod and a tweak of a jaw.

"Do you have triggers?" she asked.

Another clipped nod, and then he sighed.

"Hospitals. Certain smells. *L*-words." He opened his eyes and cleared his throat. "Leg, love, long road, life." He listed a few, but still stared straight ahead.

The entire conversation since they'd left his brother's house had been riddled with triggers for him.

"I've been good for over a year." He paused again. His left hand reached into his pocket as he sat staring straight ahead. "I actually hadn't had one in over a year," he said, finally turning to look at her. He looked apologetic. "It's just these last two days have been bad."

"An anniversary of the trauma or something?"

"Or something," he agreed.

"If you ever want to talk about it, I've probably heard it before," Morgan suggested.

Nick's eyes narrowed, but he didn't turn away from her. "You shouldn't have a general idea of what happens in war, let alone details."

"My brother—" She stopped, realizing her brother's name was an *L*-word and she would try to help him. "The one who died. He used to write me—notes. He'd talk about his friends a lot, especially his best friend. Boots, he called him, although I never really knew why. He'd tell me about places he went or people he met. I'd send him the meet cute for my books, and sometimes dialogue for scenes with guys because he'd always say I messed them up. I sounded too lov—sweet." Wow, this *L* thing was going to be hard. "But he also told me stuff that happened. Getting it off his chest helped him. . . get through the bad times."

Nick said nothing. It shouldn't surprise her since they hardly knew each other. He had no reason to tell her anything.

"You know al-Tarf?" he asked hoarsely.

"Syria," she agreed. That was where Louis had died, but she never knew the details. Her eyes scanned his face—had he been with her brother? He'd yet to say he knew Louis.

"Fucking Syria. I go back there every time. I never realized how clearly I knew the smell of sand. Dingy basement dust with a hint of herbs. No one ever thinks sand smells like spices." Nick slowly shook his head. "And we give people shit for complaining that it burns their eyes, but *fuck*—it does. Even in the cold desert like Afghanistan in the winter; the dry cold burns. I still don't leave home without eye drops and sunglasses."

Morgan reached out, carefully placing her hand over his on the console between them. His eyes focused on her hand for a moment before he flipped his over to let their fingers tangle together. Her breath caught as his warm palm pressed into hers, enveloping her hand in the heat of his. Her heart skipped a beat when his thumb rubbed circles on the inside of her wrist.

He simply glanced out the window, unaffected, and she swallowed.

"It wasn't cold that morning. It was hot. Hot as Hades. The windows in the Humvee were open, and we were all still sweating through our skivvies." Nick didn't say anything for a few minutes and they sat holding hands. His thumb continued its distracting movement. "We were land force," Nick said. "Supply run. Long fucking road. Our convoy took a hit. Bad one. I shattered my leg trying to get everyone out. Lost a lot of lives."

She heard the *L*-words. Land, long, leg, lives. She got the trigger. Morgan waited. She was patient, but after over five minutes of silence, it became clear he was done talking.

"I learned that each of my brothers, and even my dad, had things that helped pull them back from a flashback. Do you have something?"

He sighed and pulled his hand from hers. He glared out the window before finally running his hands through his hair, but he didn't speak. It was strange because she knew, *knew* Nick was the type of big bad Navy SEAL hero she always avoided because they were larger than life. He had this air of capability that surrounded him. But at the moment, he seemed vulnerable. The exact opposite of everything she didn't want. The type of sensitive guy she might want. Almost like he was letting her see past the hero shield to the true man underneath.

And that flipped her stomach.

"If I can pull you out of them, it would help me to know how."

"You do," he assured her. And before she could ask what he meant he went on. "You smell like flowers from my childhood backyard. When I start to fall, and I smell those flowers I'm pulled back here to reality."

"L—" She started to say lilacs, but she stopped herself.

"I know it's lilac. Not every *L*-word sets me off." Nick sighed. "And there is something about your voice. I can hear it when I'm under. It pulls me back from the edge."

His haunted eyes finally looked up to her own. Every part of her wanted to lean into him, wrap her arms around him, and pull him against her. But he had already pulled away.

"Okay." She nodded instead. "So, I use a lot of lotion and I never shut up. That'll be easy. I've always heard I talk too much."

Nick's chuckle warmed her belly. "Don't worry freckles, I might be a head case, but I'll keep you safe."

"I trust you," she said. And what was more surprising was that she meant it. Because outside of family, she'd never trusted any man. And the possibility of what that could mean was scarier than being stalked.

9

"WHAT?" MORGAN ALMOST screeched next to him.

While Nick did enjoy the melody of Morgan's voice, he was pleasantly surprised by how comfortable the silence between them had been for the last forty-five minutes. Morgan had stared out the window since their heart-to-heart about his flashbacks. He wasn't sure why he'd talked about them with her. He wasn't shocked that he'd told her about the flashbacks. Like he said she had a right to know. Just like Seabass knew about them, and Nick knew about his. When you worked with someone, and depended on them, they had to know. She was going to be depending on him for the next week, so they had to wade through some shit together.

But he'd never talked about details. Still, if she had sat there another five seconds, he'd have told her the whole story. And he didn't have the damnedest idea why.

"What do you mean a *sex* resort?" she demanded, bringing him back to the present. He couldn't help but chuckle again. She was damn cute, especially when her eyes shot fire and her voice got all screechy.

"Nick?"

Yeah, he had to answer the question. They were less than two miles from Love Canyon, and she needed to know the truth. Once again, he pulled the car over.

"Well, doesn't this seem like a bad sign?" Morgan asked, but by this point, it seemed like she was talking to herself.

"Love Canyon," Nick said and flipped open the red folder that sat on the console between the seats. "Home of round rotating beds, mirrors for every angle, and naked pools."

Morgan's mouth hung open until she looked at the information in the folder. Then her eyes narrowed, and she glanced at Nick.

"This is a romantic retreat," Morgan corrected. "Champagne bubble baths, personal fireplaces, heart-shaped in-room pools. It's meant to build romance." She glanced down at the paper.

This just proved that men and women didn't come from the same planet. He read the identical information Morgan was currently reading, and he saw *sex retreat*. Everything encouraged it. They designed every moment of the day at this place to make men think about sex.

And Morgan saw *romance*.

"I think I'm saying Poe-tay-toe and you're saying Poe-tah-toe." Nick smiled.

"Oh my God, look at this little log cabin where you can get hot cocoa and watch the reindeer," she said, pointing to another page. "And they have ice skating and nightly dancing."

"And a sports bar, pool tables, basketball courts, and never-ending booze," Nick added, but she wasn't listening.

"You made this place sound freaky, but it seems cute."

Hey, if she was cool with it.

Originally, when he agreed to figure out how drugs were getting onto the resort property, Bex said she'd come with him. The two of them would play married. He could do his job, and she could float in the heart pool and relax.

He and Bex weren't going to be having sex at the resort that was made for it. No matter how many people thought they were headed down that road, it wouldn't happen. Bex was probably his favorite human on the planet. And if he had died in the roadside bomb instead of Lewie, Lewie'd be watching out for Bex for Nick. Because Bex was the one person in life he wanted taken care of.

Maybe it said something about him that he hadn't picked his sister. But truthfully, his sister was taken care of by his six other brothers, as well as her tool of a husband. Bex's family, not that they sucked, were all focused on themselves and they forgot that they needed to watch out for her.

It was probably because Bex was like him. They were both *get it fucking done* type people. He and Bex weren't sitters. They didn't wait around and see. They weren't listeners. They were live wires. And somewhere in the last ten years she'd become family, like another sister. And the thought of hooking up with her kind of made him sick.

So he hadn't planned this trip to be about sex—even at the sex resort. His eyes glanced at the woman in the seat next to him. The one he should think about as a sister. Exactly like he thought about Bex.

Because Morgan was Lewie's baby sister and *off fucking limits.*

But as he stared down her shirt, at the swell of her breast, he knew that nothing about what he was thinking was brotherly. And at the moment, he had the perfect excuse not to be brotherly.

"Freckles," he called, and her eyes narrowed as she glanced up at him. She must hate that nickname, which made him like it all the more.

"What?" she asked. Her satin curtain of red hair fell across her cheek, and he reached out.

It was strange to see the silver band on his ring finger reflect off the light as he tucked the hair behind her ear. This wasn't the first time he'd had to fake being married for a job. Normally, he used Bex as his wife, mostly because she wasn't a distraction and she was capable as fuck. This woman was neither of those things. She distracted the hell out of him and he didn't get the sense from her family that she'd be any help at all if shit went south.

It seemed as natural as breathing to rest his hand along the soft skin of her pale neck. His thumb rested above her pounding pulse, and he smiled as he felt her swallow. Her eyes met his before dropping to his lips as she leaned in closer. Her breath skated across his face, sending a burn through him like the best shot of whiskey.

He shifted, and her breathing hitched. The darkening of hazel eyes from an aqua blue to an almost turquoise sucked him under. His fingers pulled lightly on the back of her neck. The words he'd planned to say wouldn't leave his mouth. The need to claim her was too strong, especially as she moved willingly toward him.

With the smallest amount of pressure, he pulled her lips to his. Nick had intended to keep the kiss light, the kind they would need to pull off in public to pretend to be married. But intentions be damned because the moment his lips met her lush mouth, intentions, good sense—everything—went out the window. And he coaxed her to let him in.

Her mouth opened with a part-sigh, part-moan and his tongue dove in, claiming her the way he'd been dying to since the moment he'd seen her. His heart raced as his hand skimmed down the soft skin of her neck. His being was screaming to pull her over the console and onto his lap, slip that all too short skirt up, and press into her.

There were a lot of reasons this needed to stop. *A million fucking reasons.* But when her tongue danced with his, he couldn't think of one of them. His palm moved lower, skimming the side of her breast and down to her waist. He wanted so much more. But slowly she pulled back.

Her eyes flitted open and her exhale brushed against his lips. Her eyes dilated, and he knew if he leaned in, she would give him anything he wanted. But they were in a car, and this woman deserved better than that.

He shook his head as he remembered exactly who she was. *What the hell, asshole?*

He pulled away, forcing himself against his own seat. "I figured we should get that out of the way. Don't want it to be awkward the first time we have to kiss in front of people."

She blinked once, and those warm pools of Caribbean Sea turned hard and cold.

"*Right.* Wouldn't want to make this awkward." Her eyes rolled as she turned away from him.

Yup, he'd definitely fucked that up.

10

GOD, SHE WAS dumb.

Dumb, dumb, dumb.

For a few minutes, she thought he might be different from every other hero she'd met. But he wasn't. He was driven by the same things as all the others. Food, sleep, sex. And the need to do the job perfectly—every time.

She crossed her arms and glared, watching the trees pass. Nick had said nothing since he brushed the kiss off.

The kiss *that had branded her soul.* No one had ever kissed her like that. It turned her inside out. It flipped her stomach and stole every thought from her head. A kiss that made her believe in the kind of love that existed in the books she wrote.

A kiss that, for Nick, was nothing more than getting it over with so it wasn't weird the next time.

She gritted her teeth. Like she'd let him kiss her again.

Three deer glanced up as the car rolled down the street. Nick slowed. Whether to keep from scaring them or to be ready in case they ran in the road, she didn't know. Because she wouldn't look at him.

She forced in a breath through her nose, telling herself to calm down. They were playing a part. What was the big deal if he kissed her? They were pretending to be married—he was supposed to, and now that she knew it meant nothing? Well, she'd make damn sure it meant nothing to her too.

"Pretty sure new brides are supposed to be happy," Nick said as he pulled into a parking lot. The building in front of them looked like a log cabin. Morgan attempted to steel herself against the cuteness of this entire place.

It looked like something out of a storybook. Even the deer that speckled the area by the small lake and the second log cabin added to the ambience.

"Pretty sure grooms are responsible for the smile," Morgan countered. Nick turned her way, his eyes focused on her with a deep intensity that flipped her stomach. The corner of his mouth ticked up. Man, he was sexy as fuck. In one blink, though, his eyes went from smoldering to business. Just like right after he kissed her.

"Sit tight till I get around. Remember, from here on out you stick with me. Copy that?" he asked, picking up the sunglasses from the console and putting them on before heading around the car.

"Thanks." She took his offered hand and got to her feet, attempting to ignore the shiver down her spine as his hand settled onto the small of her back, guiding her. She hadn't noticed how tall Nick was before, but her eyes were almost even with his chin when she stood next to him. He pushed his sunglasses up onto his head, then pulled open the door to the log cabin.

Just as she stepped into the cozy lobby, Nick flicked out his phone, sending off a message before turning to her.

"Your friend Haley's calling your cell. Remember, she can't know anything that's happened." The fact that all of her calls routed through Nick's office before they connected to her phone to keep her off the grid was annoying. And she gritted her teeth as her own phone buzzed. "If you want privacy, you can go over there." Nick tipped his chin to the corner of the room. There was an enormous fireplace and a few overstuffed chairs just to the left of the concierge desk. The other side of the small building had windows looking out into the snowy woods. "No farther than the first chair."

She nodded and took the four steps away to the fireplace before hitting the accept button.

"Hey chica, what's up?" Morgan asked, dropping into the chair as Haley appeared on the screen, her eyes narrowing.

"Where are you?" she asked. "Wait, did Stew take you skiing or something?"

Morgan tried not to frown at the reminder of the idiot, but she hadn't been allowed to tell Haley about the fire or the possible stalker. She was lucky Haley didn't watch the news because then she might have had a question Morgan couldn't answer.

She didn't know what to say, so she shrugged.

Haley snickered. "You're really at a ski lodge? You must really be into him to freeze your ass off in the *snow*."

It was true. Morgan normally pretended to be allergic to snow. "The things we do in the name of love."

Haley's eyes popped wide and Morgan wished the flippant words back. "Did you really just say the big *L*-word?" Before Morgan could respond, Haley's head whipped to the side, showing Morgan a view of James's BMW. "I'm getting there, hun."

"Where are *you*?"

"On the side of the road. James has a flat. We were kinda hoping you could walk him through the whole change the tire thing because AAA said it was going to be like two hours." Haley's tone held a note of apology. "But I totally didn't know you were away—I mean you didn't even tell me it was that serious." Accusation had replaced any remorse in her tone but she turned away from the screen again. "No hun, I know it's freezing, but Moey just said *love*."

Morgan couldn't hear his reply, only Haley's scoff.

"Pass him the phone," Morgan said, and waited until she could see James's flushed face. "We can add change a tire to the list of things you can't do, huh?" she teased.

"Hey you can't cook either. That's on both our lists," he reminded, and she chuckled. "Where under the car does this thing go?"

Morgan laughed again and explained where the jack went and how to loosen the lug nuts.

"Like a star, really? Why does it matter the order I tighten these bolt thingies?" James asked as he finally got the spare into the wheel well.

"So the wheel doesn't shake, fuck nugget," Nick mumbled from behind her, and Morgan turned to him. He was shaking his head, probably at James's use of the word "thingies." That wasn't what gave Morgan pause—she'd already heard James call the jack a whatcha call it and thing-a-ma-bob.

Fuck nugget, though, was Lewie's term for an idiot. And Nick had just used it exactly like her brother would have.

"What?" Nick said. "I know not everyone can change a tire, but *come on*."

Morgan bit back a smile.

"Seriously, Morgan, like a star? Or is this like the time you told me my blinker was out because I didn't have any blinker fluid?" James asked. Morgan couldn't stop the laughter that burst out. That had been funny.

"No, you really need to do it that way. If you don't, the tire could shake." Morgan walked him through tightening the bolts and then lowering the car off the jack before hanging up.

"Did he actually try to buy blinker fluid?" Nick's eyes danced with a light she hadn't seen before, and he couldn't fight his grin.

"Oh, it was worse." She laughed. "He went to his mechanic and told him he was out of blinker fluid. He was pissed because he'd just had an oil change but all the fluids clearly hadn't been topped off."

He chuckled. The sound vibrated through her like a shock.

"You know cars?" he asked. It wasn't surprise on his face; that would have been insulting. It was closer to respect. The same look he gave her when they'd first shaken hands.

"Not by choice." Morgan rolled her eyes when Nick grinned. "Trust me, my dad insisted that no child of his would be the dumbass waiting for AAA."

"I would have thought it was L—" A laugh seemed to die in his throat and once again his face closed off. He swallowed hard. "Your brother."

Louis *was* the one who taught her how to change a tire, change the oil, replace the bulbs and filters. But Morgan also was getting a strong feeling that an *L*-word Nick couldn't hear was Louis.

She should have made the connection already. Nick was too young to have served with Donald or Howard, and yet he knew the family. He probably served with the youngest

Johanson brother. Which meant the "or something" that had set off his flashbacks this week was her. A part of her wanted to ask him, because she hated secrets, but at the same time, she understood triggers. Before she could decide if she had the right to demand an answer from Nick, he was on his feet again.

"We shouldn't hang out in the lobby," Nick said, pulling her from the chair. His hand rested once again on her lower back, guiding her.

Even though he didn't talk as he started the car, he was very much on duty, his gaze bouncing from one thing to the next while his finger tapped again on the wheel. Her eyes trailed up his wrist. His black sleeves pushed up to his elbows, revealing the corded muscles of his forearms. If there was a photo that represented arm porn, it would be of Nick's arms. Every slight movement caused a ripple of tight muscle across his skin. His biceps stretch the material of the black Henley.

What would he look like shirtless? She closed her eyes, letting her imagination draw the picture. The cut of tan skin flowing over each curve of thick muscle. Her teeth pressed into her bottom lip. He was Navy, so she knew that under all those black clothes were some serious tats.

Her eyes shot open. What was she doing fantasizing about him? This was a job to get done. She wasn't buying into anything else. She crossed her arms and glanced out the window.

He pulled down a narrow road that led to more buildings. Morgan's eyes caught on the gazebo lit with white twinkle lights that sparkled off the snow covered ground. A woman leaned against the railing looking up at the man whose arms caged her in. He leaned down, and she tossed her head back, laughing. If they had been closer, Morgan knew she would have seen the adoration in the man's eyes, as he watched his girl.

"What are you looking at?" Nick asked.

"Inspiration." She needed to start a new story. Deadlines beyond the final edits for her new release were looming. But writing was hard lately without having Haley to bounce ideas off.

"The place or the couple?"

She hadn't noticed Nick looking at the couple, but it didn't surprise her that he noticed. His eyes never settled. In fact, his body didn't seem to either—his fingers tapped, his shoulders twitched, his leg bounced—all the time.

"Hopefully both can shake something loose."

"Having trouble?" he asked. "I thought your new book comes out in a couple weeks?"

Wide-eyed, she turned to look at him and his hand came up to pull at the back of his neck as, once again, that ruddy pink colored his face. Would he back pedal?

"Am I wrong?" he doubled down even as the blush was becoming clearer.

"No." This only confirmed the idea that he knew Louis. Her brother was her biggest supporter. No matter where he was, he was always talking her books up. He'd claimed multiple guys on the teams had read them, but Morgan never knew which ones.

Louis was weird about bringing his teammates around. Morgan always assumed it was because their dad was technically the boss, and hanging out with him would be weird for any of his teammates.

"The one releasing should be done, right?" Nick asked.

"Almost. Just final proofing, and approving the formatting."

"Are you struggling with the edits on that, struggling to finish the next one, or are you struggling with books four down the line that no one even knows exist?" His gray eyes flicked to hers quickly before looking back to the parking spot he pulled into.

"All of the above," she admitted. She hadn't written a lot in the last year.

"Well, we got a week with not a lot going on. That will give you plenty of time." He shut the car off and slammed the door behind him.

Time wasn't her issue. She had tons of time in New York. The struggle was finding the words.

By the time he opened the door for her, he already had both his and her bags in his arms.

"It's 1742." His chin tipped up in the direction of the sidewalk leading to the row of doors in the building in front of her.

Five rooms were in the strip. And there were buildings on either side, each a different color: red, navy, hunter green. All with the same number of doors. He stayed right beside her as they made their way to the room and opened the door. It wasn't until he was inside and the door shut that he finally relaxed.

"Gonna sweep the room?" she asked.

He frowned. "Of course, but this room is random. I refused the first four."

"What?"

"The first two had the number three in it. I told 'em no threes. Then I had a problem with eights." Nick shrugged.

Morgan's eyes widened. No way in hell was Nick superstitious.

"I needed to not be in the first two rooms they picked. Telling people I can't stand threes works as well as anything else."

"Did she call you crazy?" Morgan asked. His eyebrows raised up as his lips formed a tight line. "Oh right. She was instantly drawn into all the hotness and didn't care that you sounded crazy."

"Hotness?" His lips twitched.

"Whatever. Claim you don't know you're hot if you want." She rolled her eyes, and he laughed.

"Morgan, the resort had so many empty rooms they were able to offer me five different options without issue. It was about the business needing me to stay here desperately enough that the *dude* checking me couldn't call me crazy."

She felt the heat creep into her face. What he said made sense—but—the concierge was a woman.

"The phone rang. While the woman was dealing with the call the manager helped me," Nick said.

She hadn't noticed, but she'd been busy with James and the tire. She shrugged and finally turned her attention to the room—her mouth dropped open.

"My God this is adorable," she said, heading straight toward the two-story stone fireplace. Her fingers ran along the back of the heart-shaped lounger as she glanced around.

The large TV was above the mantle, and she could envision a couple snuggled in front of the fire laying on the gray and pink cushions watching a movie.

Or—she thought as she leaned into the back of the chaise, resting both hands along the top ridge—maybe they would take a swim. The left side of the room was made entirely of windows that divided it from the indoor pool, which was, of course, shaped like a heart. The mirrors on the wall behind the pool reflexed into the water, making it seem twice as big.

She moved again, stepped toward the glass walls, and realized up the stairs to her right was the bedroom, which looked down into the pool. The entire suite was lined with glass walls and mirrors. A balance of all the sweet romance the brochure had touted and the sex resort Nick seemed to think they were headed to.

"I'll stay on the couch or whatever you call this weird heart thing," Nick assured, and Morgan turned to him. She hadn't thought about the sleeping arrangement, but seeing as she could see the entire room either in her line of sight or because of the reflection through the many mirrors, she understood his comment.

"You just want dibs on the TV, huh?"

"What?"

"The only TV is here." She pointed to the fireplace, "Everyone needs a TV to sleep and whoever gets this gets the television."

Nick snorted.

"What?"

The corner of his mouth lifted, and his eyes shone. "If you can't come up with something better to do in bed, than watch television, far be it from me to explain."

Her stomach flipped, and suddenly, she couldn't swallow as his gaze tracked down her body and then back up. His blue-gray eyes met hers, and a shiver shot down her spine at the intense heat reflecting at her. Without warning, all the desire in his eyes vanished—almost like he'd flipped a switch.

"But if you want the sofa thing." He shrugged with cool indifference. She spun away, annoyed that she'd once again fallen into the hot and cold game he was playing. Before she could say anything else he added, "No reason to pout or be overdramatic. I can always sleep on the floor."

Her jaw clenched. Really? She was being the dramatic one?

"That's right. Big bad Navy SEAL, 'we lay in the dirt, we long to jump out of planes, we like crawling through snow, we go after the bad guy, we are big, tough, strong, manly men, who aren't afraid to get *blown up*.'"

Nick said nothing, but she wasn't ready to turn back to look at him. Finally she gave in to his silence, but he was stone still when she looked at him. Staring straight ahead, unseeing.

It took a second.

Dammit, why had she said *that?*

Louis had died in a roadside bomb. Two years ago. In Syria. Half his team died along with him. Only three had made it to the funeral because the other three were in the hospital recovering from injuries from the same explosion. Nick wasn't at the funeral.

She was such an *asshole.*

Nick was in the same explosion that had killed her brother, and here she was making light of it.

She moved toward him quickly, but his eyes didn't track her movement. His body was rigidly still. Unmoving. So unlike the man she'd been watching all day.

"Nick," she said softly, but he didn't respond. He didn't even blink.

A shock would usually pull someone out of a flashback. A slap in the face worked wonders for her brother Howard when he first struggled with flashbacks. But she worried that Nick would respond aggressively. Lash out at her. Possibly attack her before he knew what he was doing.

She leaned closer and ran her hand across his face. The rough scruff of his day-old growth tickled her palm, but he didn't react.

"Nick," she said again, pulling his face down to meet hers. He said the smell of her lotion and sound of her voice brought him out of flashbacks. But the woodsy spice of his own cologne flipped *her* stomach. "Come on, Nick, come back to me."

He groaned softly as he leaned in closer—his cheek brushing roughly against hers. A shiver rocketed through her and for a second she forgot how to breathe.

"Morgan." His voice was a deep, needy whisper. His exhale danced against her neck, sending electric shocks tingling through her.

It was hard to swallow over the thick lump in her throat, but his eyes lifted to meet hers. Fierce, feverish need met her straight on.

"Fuck it," Nick said and crashed his lips onto hers.

11

ONE MINUTE HE was lost in the desert, and the next, he found himself lost in Morgan. Her silky skin pressed against his. Her soft, full lips right there—begging for his attention. Transported from hell to heaven—to her breath in his mouth and his tongue twirling with hers. He wanted more.

He *needed* more.

Spinning her quickly, he pressed her hard into the mirror behind them, and she arched into him. Full, round breasts pushed into his chest. His hand moved without permission, just the need driving him. The thin skin of her neck and shoulder was satin against his fingers as he danced his way down. Over collar bone, skimming the crest of her perfect breast. Finally, his hand possessed it. One flick of his thumb over her nipple, and she rewarded him with a breathy moan, causing a deep, hard ache in his groin.

They were so perfectly matched he didn't even have to bend to rock hard against her center. And she matched him—her kiss as wanton, her body as demanding.

Just as he dropped his hand to her skirt to give them both exactly what he knew they needed, a knock pounded on the door.

"Bro, you in there?" Seabass's voice shot through the haze of lust. One beat of confusion as to why Seabass was there before it was all crystal clear. He was here on the job. Nick was on a job. Protect the client—*not fuck the client.*

What the hell was he doing?

He glanced down, seeing Morgan's enormous eyes turn from warm with desire to hot with a different fire.

"Make sure you think about how close my knee is to your rod before you say something mean," she warned fiercely.

Nick couldn't help the chuckle that broke through his lips, but he stepped away from her as he asked, "Rod?"

Her chin rose just a fraction, and she adjusted her shirt. "I'm a romance writer. I can refer to your best friend in your pants by twenty names without even trying."

"Pleasure machine," Nick said, shaking his head. "That was your worst—pleasure machine."

Her eyes widened in delight. "You *do* read my books!"

Before he could answer and finally admit he'd been reading them for years and that they were actually good, Seabass pounded again.

"Nick, you got twenty seconds to get the door open before I'm doing it myself."

Nick sighed. "We have to talk about this later." She swallowed and gave a clipped nod, so he went to the door.

Seabass's eyes did a quick scan. A single thick eyebrow rose up. Nick ignored the unspoken question, opening the door fully to let him inside.

"Bex coming?" Nick asked.

"Right here," she called from the open door three feet outside their room. Seabass knew Nick's room. The plan was for them to get the one right next door. "I was getting my phone to call you. It's your honeymoon and all. I told Seabass it would be rude to just barge in." The sarcasm laced heavily in her voice. Although she thought she was giving him shit, if they had just walked in—"Where's Morgan?"

Nick spun around. He'd not even searched or secured the room yet. Where the fuck did she go?

"Bathroom. She was headed up when he opened the door," Seabass answered. That made sense. Of course she'd want a minute to regroup and, in this place, the only privacy was in the small three-by-three-foot space containing the toilet. "We should probably secure the side door."

Although it wasn't a question, Nick nodded.

"How long have you been here that you haven't *done that yet*?" Bex's voice rose, and her eyebrows shot up. Yeah, normally it was the first thing he did when he walked into a room. Scan the room, categorize the risks, secure the doors and windows. And he had all the shit to do it right in his bag. They knew the room's layout and had planned.

Yet after walking in, all he'd done was catalog all the places he could fuck Morgan. She'd shot off across the room to the weird-ass heart she'd called a chaise but looked like a bed, sheet included. The perfect height to bend her over, press against her, grab a fistful of her hair and take her hard from behind. And the mirrors. God, he wanted to slam her up against every single one of them. Grind into her, rub against her heat before he would slip inside her and have her screaming his name.

"Nick?" Seabass repeated his name. But Nick had missed what he said.

His head was a shitshow. It wasn't even his normal mess—no, this was a "he needed to get laid quickly" mess. A problem he couldn't take care of for at least a week. He swallowed, thinking about spending the next week with Morgan.

Shit.

He felt a hard slap on his bicep as Seabass grabbed his bag and headed for the side door. Nick locked the front before following Seabass into the glass room containing the heart-shaped pool. The door clicked closed, locking out the sound of Bex's chuckle.

Their boots hardly made a sound against the concrete surrounding the pool, but the wall of mirrors made sure Nick could clearly see the tight line of Seabass's grimace as he headed down the three steps and past the sauna to the side door. The purpose of the entrance was mechanical. The filters for the pools in each room sat in the six foot hallway just outside the side door. Both his and Seabass's suite had entrances from this hallway.

"Plan still to trigger both these doors to alert us every time they open and to set up video to record motion?" Seabass asked, and Nick gave a clipped nod. "Are we going to check out the guy at the gym?"

They had narrowed down the list of places the four guests who had overdosed on the grounds in the last few weeks had all hung out. Gym, dining hall, or sports bar.

"Donovan seemed pretty sure he watched him hand something off. I would have bet on the bar though," Seabass added, but Nick was only mildly paying attention.

He meant what he'd said to Morgan. They had to talk about what was going on with them. But what the fuck was he supposed to say? He was a professional. He'd done plenty of bodyguard jobs, protection, extraction. He'd never had an issue with getting involved with the person he was protecting. But every conversation with Morgan sucked him in deeper.

"Nick—bro." The volume of Seabass's voice said he'd called him a few times.

"Yeah," he cleared his throat. "Once we get this done, we'll hit up the gym."

Seabass smirked at him. "Want to talk about it?"

"What?" Nick asked, watching Seabass open the bag and grab the small black device. Nick turned, letting the door shut behind them, leaving them alone in the hallway. Nick bent down to ground level to set up the alarm.

"I get that it's Lewie's sister and it's probably making it hard. Ghosts hang on for a long time."

Nick's jaw clenched. Seabass was much more open about talking about his demons. He didn't hold back about the phantom leg pain that woke him, screaming in agony, some days. He didn't hide the fact that the flashbacks came on randomly. And if he thought Nick wasn't taking care of himself, he'd call him on it. Sometimes he didn't even bother to soften the blow.

"No, is an okay answer if you don't want to talk about it. But if the ghosts become too much, I got it. I can take Morgan to Florida."

Nick attached the second side of the alarm to the door jamb and clicked it on, letting an invisible beam move from one black box to the other. If the door opened, the connection would break and alert his phone.

"I'm fine," Nick assured him. "And I've got Moey."

Seabass gave a clipped nod. "I'm sure that's how Lewie'd want it."

But with exactly how Nick was feeling about her, he somehow doubted that to be true.

12

MORGAN WASN'T STUPID enough to think she could hide in the bathroom forever, so she had to leave this room. And she really wasn't hiding. She was just trying to cool off.

Holy shit, that kiss had been hot. Crazy hot. Which in itself wasn't bad. She'd done the hot one time hook ups in the past. But those men—none of them had ever had a haunted look in their eyes that cut into her soul. None of them blushed or showed weakness, lowering her defenses. And none of them could quote her books. Nick was dangerously different. And that made him definitely off limits.

She didn't need her heart crushed by a man who had no interest in anything but the adrenal rush of the chase. Made very clear by the randomness of when and how he kissed her. Nor did she want someone who was more interested in saving the world than being there for her.

When she opened the door, she did a quick mirror check, smoothing her hair and tucking it behind her ear before heading down the stairs. Instead of Nick and Seabass, a woman stood near the window looking through the blinds. It took Morgan a minute to remember that Nick's female friend was coming with Seabass, and Morgan braced herself. She doubted whomever was supposed to be on a weekend away with Nick was going to be happy to see her.

"They're in the back setting up cameras and alarms." The woman didn't turn, but her voice didn't sound hostile. Her long chestnut hair fell about a foot past her shoulders.

"Former military too?" Morgan asked.

"A mom. Eyes in the back of my head." The woman turned, and Morgan sucked in a breath.

"Rebecca?" she asked. The woman's eyes danced with laughter.

"I see he didn't bother to tell you—why am I not surprised?" The woman Morgan had met a few days ago with Haley smiled. Her smile was just as perfect as the last time. Less makeup today, but everything about her still screamed wealth. "Call me Bex. Pretty much everyone does."

Last time they'd met, nothing about this woman seemed intimidating to Morgan but now, knowing she was Nick's friend. The one who was coming away to the place he called a sex retreat with him, Rebecca—Bex—seemed all kinds of intimidating. Big honey eyes and chiseled features all tied up with that perfect complexion and a killer smile. Flawless, casual style in black leggings with her boots and the sweater that hung slightly off her shoulder. It was that slouchy look that Morgan couldn't get to work. Then there was the fact that Bex was that perfect height that Morgan towered over.

"If it makes you feel better, even though he knew I was nervous about meeting you and Haley for coffee, he never mentioned that you two were dating." It was supposed to be a joke delivered with a disarming smile.

Maybe that would have made Morgan feel better, but she and Nick weren't dating. They had never met when Bex had come out with her and Haley for coffee. But she couldn't stand here not saying anything.

"Men," Morgan said. "Can't live with them, but I'm not sure a life sentence for murder is the better option."

Bex laughed and moved to the heart-shaped couch sitting down. "So, Haley told me you're a hugely successful author."

Morgan paused. She was surprised Bex started with that. Not more about Nick. And not even with something Nick had told her.

Bex smirked. "I hate being cliché. Two successful women should be able to talk about something other than men."

"Damn straight."

The women spent the next ten minutes talking about books, authors, and trends. It turned out Bex liked reading romance as much as Morgan. They even shared two of the same favorite authors. One of whom Morgan beta read for and called a friend.

"What do you do?" Morgan asked.

"I finished law school and I'm clerking for Judge Macon for another three months before I start my job at the public defender's office."

"Criminal defense attorney?" Morgan asked.

She nodded.

"I don't know if I should be impressed or scared," Morgan said.

"I have a twin brother, Chuck. He's a prosecutor, and he constantly tells me I'm going to hate the PD office, but I really want to work with people who are in over their heads and just need some help to get a second chance." Bex looked down. Morgan watched her face, studying her. Bex looked like she was about to cry. She swallowed. "Sometimes people do things as teenagers or young people before they really understand the world, and it affects their whole lives."

"Like getting pregnant in college?" Morgan asked before she could stop herself.

Bex looked up and blinked twice. "Oh—I didn't think. No. I mean, sure it shaped my life. But James and I weren't." Bex stopped and took a breath. "James was too young to be a husband, and a dad all at the same time."

"You weren't?"

Her smile was harsh, and her snort answered the question better than the words. "I was five going on thirty. I was forced to be an adult long before I met James. Breaks of being a Carmichael."

"So, would you let James marry your best friend?" Morgan asked. And Bex laughed.

"Sorry, I'm sure that was a real question, but the thought of Nick marrying James—" She left that hang.

"Ohh" Morgan managed. Morgan didn't know how to swallow that answer.

"Nick and I are like family. He's my best friend, yes, but he's also like my big overbearing brother." Bex's foot shook, causing the sofa to vibrate just slightly. "Nick needed someone to write home to when he was away, and it wasn't going to be his sister or his brothers. His sister, Beth, she's a good friend of mine, but she had too much going on in her life, Nick would have never burdened her with his stress. And he loves his brothers, but he needs them to be his light, not his heavy. So he wrote to me. And when his brother Grant hit his rough patch, Nick needed someone to deal with the possible 'there's been an accident' call."

She tucked her long chestnut hair over her shoulder and sent Morgan a questioning look. But Morgan didn't need an explanation because she knew what call Bex was referring to. The one that explained how a loved one was hurt or not coming home.

"I guess I needed someone I could dump my complaints about my crappy marriage on too, and no that's not a dig at James as much as a dig at a loveless marriage. But even I can see how much he loves Haley, and I will not complain in the least because she is great. Our kids love her, and she's helped him grow up. So, it's all good."

Morgan watched Bex. She believed her, but—"Even after your divorce, nothing between you and Nick?"

Bex's eyes didn't leave Morgan. "Nick and I don't have that kind of chemistry, but even if we did—he didn't plan to settle down until he left the teams, and by that point," she swallowed, and the misery flashed across her face, "well, I had already decided I wasn't a relationship type girl."

Morgan knew that look—heartbreak. "I thought you said you never loved James."

"Not loving James doesn't mean I've never been in love."

Morgan waited, but Bex didn't continue. "You can't leave it like that!"

Bex laughed lightly.

"No, you don't get it. I'm *nosy*." Morgan assured. "The who, the what, the where, the how, I want to know. It's one of the reasons I became a writer."

"As long as you don't expect the why," Bex said and then swallowed. "A couple of years ago, there was a guy."

"Description, details," Morgan begged.

Bex rolled her eyes but gave into the request. "He had this penetrating deep gaze that saw everything. There was no way to hide from him." Bex smiled and her teeth bit into her lip. She crossed her arms. "He could have full conversations and most people wouldn't realize he hadn't said anything. Yet with me, he opened up, and he could get me to talk constantly because he listened. I spent a lifetime remembering to be a certain way, but with him, I always just. . . was . . . and he looked at me like it was enough."

Morgan's eyes stung, and her hands came up to her rest on her cheeks. "Holy shit."

"What?" Bex asked.

Morgan took a breath. "When I write a story, I always have a moment, where I have the hero or heroine describe the other without a single physical description but yet, the reader can feel how hot they are just by the love in the description. And you just freaking did that in real life."

Bex chuckled uncomfortably.

"What happened?" Morgan asked.

Bex shrugged. "We dated for a few months, then slept together, and I never heard from him again. I fell hard, he didn't. Simple as that." She cleared her throat and glanced away.

No way was it simple. This woman was gorgeous and nice. Classy and smart. And everything Haley had said about her was probably true. So, it couldn't have been simple that this guy never called her again. Bad marriage, heartbreak, Morgan thought when she met Rebecca Carmichael, her life was perfect. Haley thought she *was* perfect, but that wasn't the case and maybe Morgan needed to become less quick to judge people.

"How about you? You write all the big love stories, got one?" Bex asked.

"Me?" Morgan asked. "Well, I guess not, I mean, I keep

trying to, but it just doesn't work out. I don't know—maybe I'm trying too hard."

"Doesn't work like that," Bex said, her eyes glanced away. "It happens when you aren't ready and suddenly you're just whomped on the head. Like you and Nick. You know how you're married?" Bex's voice had a teasing edge to it.

"Oh, well—uh," she stuttered, unsure of how much Nick had told Bex.

Bex snickered and waved her off. "It's okay. Seabass already told me it was a cover. When it's just us, you don't have to pretend, but I am wondering how much is pretend."

"All pretend." Morgan shook her head now that she could be honest. "No military men for me, *definitely* no Navy, heroes aren't allowed."

"How come?"

The twenty-million-dollar question. Why was she against a hero? The world loved them. Multiple genres of romance were dedicated to the idea of hot hunky heroes who swooped in to save their women. Her agent even begged her to write a few. But she wouldn't do it.

"I've been around Navy men my entire life. They're fun, hot. Usually a good time, if you know what I mean." Her lips pulled up into a smile when Bex cracked a laugh but it wasn't funny. Morgan shook her head, thinking of all the women who ran through her father's life, her brothers' lives. All around her, the same thing. The women falling in love with the men but the men were married to the job. Their only love was the thrill of being a hero. "But *broken*."

"Broken?" Bex asked, but before Morgan could explain, an icy voice answered from behind them.

"Yeah, she's gotten a good look at exactly how *broken* I am."

Morgan spun, finding Nick standing at the door to the pool room. His jaw clenched but it was his eyes that sank her stomach. She expected anger, but it was crushing pain that reflected in them as he met her gaze straight on.

"Nick, I—"

"Don't." He cut her off, and his gaze bounced to Bex.

"Well, I'm going to go," she said standing up. Her lips pulled into a tight line and she raised her eyebrows at Morgan. Morgan wasn't sure if the look Bex sent her meant *apologize, talk to him, or what the hell is wrong with you?* But she hadn't meant broken because of his trauma or broken because he was fighting demons. She didn't want him to think that.

Morgan tucked her hair behind her ear before glancing to him. "I didn't mean—"

"There's a bag of clothes there," Nick interrupted. He moved to his black bag, searching for something, not looking her way. "Seabass and I need to check out the gym, and you need to come. Get dressed."

"Nick—" She wanted to get this out.

He raised his eyes from the bag to stare her down, but every emotion was wiped from his face. "Get. Dressed."

She stood to do what he ordered, but once again, she felt like an asshole, and she had no idea how to fix it.

13

IT WASN'T WRONG that he was fucked up beyond repair, but the idea that Morgan thought so cut deep into his chest because he didn't want to be that. And he definitely didn't want her seeing him that way. Hell, if he'd met Morgan two weeks ago, not knowing who she was, he'd have put most of his energy into getting her into his life.

During active duty, he'd kept relationships light. Always clear about his intentions and the reasons, and he'd never had an issue with a nasty breakup like some of his fellow teams guys. The danger, the travel, the secrets all made special ops a hard life for a relationship. And he knew that. So, he hadn't planned on marriage until he was done with his time on the teams.

Nick was a planner, and he always had one. Play football at the Naval Academy, graduate and apply to the BUD/S program, twelve years with special ops, then move up the line of command; follow a path much like Admiral Johanson. Once he was calling the shots from San Diego or Pensacola or Washington, he'd settle down. Marriage, kids, dog, pool—the whole shebang.

But with fifteen months left in his time as DEVGRU team leader, his plans all fell apart. He had to pivot. Life became—healing up and starting a new career. It wasn't the time to get involved with someone. He had to sort through his own shit first. He knew that. But for the last few months, his therapist had been constantly dropping hints that it was maybe time to open his mind up to the idea of more than just running NAE Securities. That the way Nick had shut himself off from people in the last two years might not be healthy.

His flashbacks had been under control. He hadn't woken up in a cold sweat in almost a year. He was in a good place. The idea that he was ready to move on was settling deep into his bones. But one phone call, and his entire well-being fell apart. He was right back in the struggle of trying to keep his fucked-up head in reality.

No such thing as better.

A demon to fight until death.

Forever broken.

Trying to fix himself never worked. The thoughts ate away at him as her reflection came into view through the last window while he attached the open/break sensor.

"Nick." Her soft voice was breathy as she drew his name out a bit too long. It would have been hot if he didn't know she was getting ready to apologize again. He'd brushed it off twice already before he'd sent her up with the clothes he made Bex bring.

Usually, he could appreciate Danny's sense of humor because it was very close to Nick's. However, it wasn't funny. His brother sending his intern out to get clothes for Morgan with the direction that she was going undercover as an office temp who was trying to lure the boss under her spell *wasn't funny*. It meant everything Morgan owned tempted Nick like candy to a six-year-old on Halloween.

Not that Bex's purchases seemed much better.

"Did you forget your shirt?"

Morgan glanced down at her body before lifting back to him. "Yup, definitely wearing a shirt."

"Where's the rest of it?" he demanded, wincing at his tone. Morgan's hand came up to rest on her hip and his eyes zeroed in on the smooth skin just above her tight gray pants.

"It's a crop shirt and again I didn't pick it. But you said we're going to the gym. This is what I have."

Her hand waved over the green skin tight tank top that stopped about an inch above her belly button, showing off her smooth tight abs. He forced his eyes up to her face. The green swirls in the tank top seemed to cause her normally aqua eyes to pop with flecks of green like the luminescent plankton in the ocean on a dark night.

Damn it. Was his head spitting out poetry like a sap?

His phone beeped, saving him from saying anything stupid, and he glanced down. His eyes narrowed at the group text Donovan had sent and Seabass's fast response.

"What's wrong?"

"Nothing." Nick's answer caused the very familiar burn of anger to flash in Morgan's eyes.

"Don't lie," she snapped.

"I'm not lying. We've been trying to find another shot of the unsub that set your place on fire—" Nick began.

"And you can't?" she interrupted.

"No, we found one," he corrected and then sighed.

"Is it another bad picture?" she asked and moved toward him as if she wanted to see the photo. But he tucked his phone in his pocket, not wanting her to see either Donovan's or Seabass's assessment.

He'd been told Morgan was a panicker. Not only had her father mentioned it, but Howard and Donald recently warned that she'd panic and break down. He'd need to handle her carefully. Even Lewie had always said she was a drama queen.

"The picture is of the back of the hoodie he's wearing. It's not a great shot that will help, but the thing is, the guy was waiting by the entrance to your building," Nick explained.

He watched her flip that over in her mind.

"Waiting," she drawled. Her teeth pressed gently into her bottom lip before she swallowed. It was a muted reaction but twisted Nick's gut more than full out panic would have. "You mean he was waiting for *me*."

He carefully balanced the need to reassure her with the need to make sure she understood the situation.

"That's our working theory. He was confirming you didn't get out or, more likely, planning to grab you as you left in the chaos. Although the fire escape fall wasn't comfortable, it probably saved you." Nick expected some reaction to this news, but Morgan simply nodded, so he went on giving her some reassurance. "It changes nothing. I still feel like we've lost the trail, and I'll keep you safe until my guys figure out exactly what's going on."

"I know," she agreed. "And this makes more sense." Her arms crossed over her chest, rubbing her hands up and down the skin, as if warding away a chill. It was the only sign she was unnerved. "I had felt like someone was following me for a couple of weeks."

Nick worked to unclench his jaw at that statement and he followed it up with the question he already knew the answer to. "You never told anyone, even when Danny asked you?"

Her head shook just slightly, causing a lock of beautiful red hair to slide against her pale cheek. The thick strand blocked his view of her eyes. "I thought I was being over the top."

He was starting to wonder if her brothers' constant claims that she was dramatic were complete bullshit and he definitely didn't want her afraid to admit things to him. His hand moved to push the lock of hair so he could look at her. She didn't look up at him, instead she leaned her cheek into his palm. Her soft skin warmed his hand, causing a current to move up his arm and zap through his body. Without permission, his free hand moved to her waist and pulled her into his arms.

"Never feel that way with me. If you feel something, you tell me." His voice came out gruffer than he intended, but it wasn't the result of anger. It was more the panic of the complete loss of self-control this woman in his arms caused. Her breath danced against his neck as she tucked her forehead against his cheek.

A war waged inside him. The need to be the detached hero who always kept her safe fought with the desire to be the man who got to hold her. It all clashed with the knowledge that with every passing moment, he was falling more helplessly under her spell.

"Moey," he whispered, and her body tensed but she didn't pull out of his arms. Instead, she tucked herself farther into him.

"You knew Lewie."

She laced the statement both with the accusation of him not telling her and the hesitance that said she knew this conversation might hurt him. But he owed her some truth.

"BUD/S." He shut his eyes, fearing what might come if he talked about Lewie. "I was in a group with this kiss-ass know-it-all. And the training instructor was such a hardass.

He gave us shit about everything. Even what shoes we wore in our free time. The guy had this list: no slides, no sneakers, no boat shoes. I was a dickhead. Instead of just wearing our Navy issued tact boots, which was the guy's goal, I fucked with him." Nick chuckled. "And every day, I tried to find shoes not specifically on the list."

He barely heard the laugh, but he felt her breath against his neck as the chuckle left her lips. It was like fire moved through his body in response. He swallowed hard and went back to his story but let his fingertips rub light circles around the soft, warm skin of her lower back.

"I pushed it too far the day I wore my snowboarding boots to the pool. The instructor said if I thought the boots worked, I could spend the next two hours treading water in them. After forty-five minutes, I was dying, not that I was going to admit it. Especially when the kiss-ass know-it-all dove in next to me." Nick could still picture Lewie's piercing blue eyes as he got in his face that day. 'Give me a boot,' he said. When I started to argue, he snapped at me. 'We're a team, and although you're apparently the token asshole, we sink or swim together. So give me a fucking boot.'"

The number of times they had laughed about the story was infinite. Lewie always said it never got old. Even more when Nick became his commanding officer. The ache stabbed at Nick's chest. Sometimes the happy memories were as painful as the bad ones. Two years, and there were still moments when the fact that Lewie wasn't there anymore cut as deeply as the day he'd died.

Nick swallowed the lump wedged in his windpipe, but he still couldn't get his voice to work. He cleared his throat.

"That's why Lewie called me Boots, to remind me that no matter where I got in life, I was still the asshole who thought he was funnier than he actually was."

Her intake of breath was sharp. Harsh. Yet her hands moved, and her arms snaked around his waist, pulling him close.

"You were his best friend."

"I *am* his best friend. He's not here, but that doesn't change anything. And that's the reason I'm going to make sure you're safe. Because I promised him I always would."

Morgan jerked out of his arms, instantly stepping three steps back wide eyed. Nick didn't know what he'd said, but whatever it was clearly upset her.

"Aren't we supposed to meet Seabass and Bex at the gym?" she asked coolly, crossing her arms.

What the fuck did he do?

14

"YOU WANT TO play one on one?" Nick asked incredulously.

"You dragged me to the gym and told me we had to do something. It's this or nothing because you will literally have to carry me if you expect me to get on that god-awful treadmill." There was only one sport Morgan played. One form of exercise she allowed.

Basketball.

Nick's eyes narrowed as she turned and walked onto the court. She heard the sigh before he moved.

"You take it," he said, bouncing the ball to her. He'd changed into gym shorts and a fitted black sideline athletic shirt, which clung to every curve of muscle on his upper body. She was sucked back to how it felt to be wrapped in his arms only an hour ago. Once again, she'd been falling into the idea that Nick was different.

Idiotic.

She knew Nick was attracted to her, but she thought there was something deeper happening between them. But the deeper wasn't about her. It was about being a hero. Fulfilling the duty to her brother.

It was ironic how she and Nick had finally met *after* Louis died. Louis talked about his friend constantly, and she knew that although Louis would joke around about Boots being an idiot, he respected the hell out of him. As far as Louis was concerned, Boots was his brother by another mother. On more than one occasion, she'd asked to meet him, but Louis always said it wasn't the right time.

"Change your mind?" Nick asked, bringing her back to the present. The basketball court and the hot guy with an anchor tattoo and chain wrapped around his left calf. The same one her brother had. Louis used to say it represented the fact that he would be forever chained to the Navy.

Forever chained to the Navy, *first and foremost.* It was a reminder of everything she hated.

She propped the ball on her hip and tipped her chin. "Normal half court rules. Outside the line is two points. Inside is one. We play to twenty-one and have to win by two."

"Whatever you want, freckles," Nick answered, and she clenched her teeth. She hated freckles. And by the way his lips quirked up in the corner every time he said it, she was pretty sure he knew it.

She checked the ball to him, and his eyes narrowed.

"Easy." Nick smirked and gently bounced the ball back.

Morgan dribbled while Nick put up a half-assed effort. She backed up, lifted to her toes and sent the ball up in the air. Nick turned and watched the nothing but net shot swish through the hoop before turning to her. The loud thunk of the ball hitting the high gloss wood floor echoed behind him.

"Lucky shot." Her shoulder shrug accompanied the mock innocence of her tone.

Nick's shoulders pulled back to tighten slightly as he jogged to the ball, still barely bouncing off to the left of the hoop. He checked it to half court and moved forward, neither protecting the ball nor blocking her out. In less than five seconds, she had the ball and another two points.

"Hewie," he said, crossing his arms and glaring at the bouncing ball.

"Well, he and Dad both played at the Naval Academy," she reminded him. Howard had taught her to play throughout the years. Anytime she followed him around, annoying him, he made her head out and do drills. By the time she was fifteen and five nine and counting, she could play. "Want to just play Horse or something?"

Nick scoffed. "No, but don't think I'm going easy on you anymore." He scooped up the ball, ran it back and before she could move to defend him, he had driven to the basket for a layup. "Kinda slow there, freckles."

"Yeah," she said. "So, four to one *me*?" Her finger tapped against her chest, making the point.

Fifteen minutes later, both were covered in sweat. It was no-holds-barred, and after a few elbows to the stomach, and one tripping claim by Nick, she hit the basketball that made it fifteen to fourteen.

"You're such a cheater!" Nick shook his head and stopped the ball with his foot, leaving it resting on the ground next to him.

"*That* I learned from Louis." She laughed. Her brother was such a sore loser that in any game, he'd cheat to win.

"Somehow, I very much doubt your brother taught you to rub your ass against my crotch to distract me." He pulled up his shirt as he spoke, rubbing the sweat off his face. But holy hell, talk about a distraction. Nick didn't have the body of someone who just worked hard in life.

Nope.

He had the body of a man who worked hard in the gym. Every. Single. Day. High, tight pecs that lead down to cut eight pack abs, and that male V that teased the brain into wondering what was lower. Like an arrow sending her straight to where she should not be heading. Her body clenched. God, the man was hot as sin. Her heart skipped.

"Something interesting?" Nick chuckled, but didn't drop his shirt.

Not willing to back down nor give him a compliment, she stepped closer, not stopping until she was just an arm's length away. "Lot of dates." Her nail ran along the spaces between his lower ribs, touching the dates inked on his skin. He hissed out a breath, and his already hard ab muscles popped impossibly tighter. Slowly, her finger ran along the hot, damp skin. Month, day, year, followed month, day, year. Maybe twenty between the rib bones on that side of his body.

"You're going to be the death of me, Moey." Nick's groan sent a ripple of heat down her spine, settling deep into her stomach.

He moved fast, backing up slightly, angling straight into her stomach and suddenly she was flipped over his shoulder, ass in the air.

"Nick," she screeched as she pressed her palms against the hard plains of his back, pushing to angle herself up. "You're all sweaty."

Nick laughed. "That wasn't an issue when you needed to push up into me to make your shot. Just hold still. It's time you get some of your own medicine." He squatted with an ease that didn't match her weight, grabbed the ball, and dribbled with his free hand toward the hoop.

"Put me down," she demanded as she squirmed, but he ignored her, heading to the hoop to toss up a shot.

"Tie score," Nick said, dropping her back on her feet.

"That absolutely doesn't count," she scoffed. He was crazy if he thought she'd let him have that basket.

"You make a much cuter sore loser than Lewie did." Nick smiled at her as he gave a slight tug on her ponytail resting over her shoulder. It was a teasing gesture, but the second she felt the pull, her breath hitched. The smile fell off his face, and his gaze dropped to her mouth. She took one step, closing the distance between them. His throat bobbed as he swallowed thickly. "I need to keep you at a distance, Moey, but you make it impossible."

His hand came to rest on her back right above the curve of her ass.

"I feel the same way, Nick," she agreed even as her tongue slowly wet her lips making him groan.

"*Moey!*"

They both spun as the door to the enclosed court slammed against the back wall and Haley barreled in.

"Haley?" Morgan's eyes widened and she spun back to Nick, who was frowning past Haley to James, who was standing in the doorway.

"Do *not* Haley me," she said. Her hazel eyes had that crazy look she got right before Haley dropped any pretense of southern charm and *lost* her shit. "Tell me that ring on your hand is a lie, and you did not run off and get married. And what the hell happened to Stew? Four days ago, you had a date with him. But now you're married to *Nick*?" Haley's voice had taken on that screechy sound and even Nick winced.

"You didn't tell her about the whole misunderstanding?" Nick asked. His hand came up to rest on Morgan's hip, giving it a squeeze. "It's actually a funny story."

What the hell was he talking about? Morgan looked up at him, but his face gave nothing away. The second squeeze on her hip woke up Morgan to the fact that she needed to play along.

"What story?" Haley asked, and the door for the court slammed shut.

Morgan glanced back to see Seabass, Bex, and James at the door.

"Babe," James said. "Bex was trying to tell you."

Haley whirled on him. "My best friend will tell me how and why she got *married* and didn't mention it to me, not your *ex-wife*." She sounded like she was speaking through gritted teeth, and Morgan instantly felt like the world's biggest bitch. She'd never hurt Haley. If she had really gotten married, Haley would have been the first to know. But this was fake, and Haley wasn't ever going to find out.

Nick sighed.

"Haley, relax. We're not married," Nick said. His hand fell away from her hip as he took a step back. His face had hardened and Morgan recognized the all business face Nick could switch to at the drop of a hat.

"You're not?" Haley's eyes jumped from Nick to Morgan and back to Nick.

"No," Nick assured. "But when I needed to come check out James's family resort—"

"Wait," Morgan threw a hand into the air. "This is your resort?"

"We'll talk about me later," Haley said. Her hands both hit her hips and her don't mess with me voice ran out of her mouth. "We are *definitely* still on you."

Morgan rolled her eyes. "Fine."

"I'm sure Morgan told you how she met Stew." Nick said.

"Yeah, at the coffee shop." Haley's eyes moved to Morgan.

"I was on assignment, using one of my cover names—Nick Stewart."

Nick's eyes flick to Morgan quickly, and finally, Morgan got on board. Nick didn't know the story Morgan had to take over.

"You know how I told you the barista called the drink order and Stew and I both grabbed for it."

"Yes, you'd both ordered the same drink, but it had his name on it. Stewart." Haley finished the story.

"Right," Morgan agreed. "So, I assumed it was his first name. I started calling him Stew."

"And I let her," Nick finished, and sent Morgan a smile. "It was *shitty*." Nick smirked down at Morgan as he said it. "And she was furious when she found out who I really was and what I did for a living."

Morgan snorted and whacked him in the stomach. That wasn't even a lie.

"You were," Nick teased. "But I convinced you to get over it."

"Hm, it's funny—*I* remember it differently," Morgan countered.

"Yeah, yeah, you two are at the adorable *we have to flirt and banter stage*, I get it. But why are you both wearing rings?" Haley demanded.

"Because *my wife* and I were scheduled to check in today. But we had the whole this is serious talk." Nick's statement wasn't exactly a lie. He and Morgan talked about the seriousness of her situation. But he was implying something different. "So, after Thursday night, there was no one else who could play my wife but Moey." Haley's eyes widened at the fact that Nick used Moey because besides Haley, Morgan only let family call her that. But Morgan focused more on Nick's words—true and yet a total misrepresentation of the situation.

It was everything she hated about highly trained special ops. They all talked out of both sides of the mouth. They didn't *lie* even while lying.

Haley's eyes bounced again between the two of them for a second before she smiled. "Actually, this makes sense. And before I saw your massive diamond flash, I was saying how cute you two were. Sorry I wrecked the game."

"That's okay; she was already pouting. And look, as soon as you mentioned the game, she got all mad again," Nick teased.

She should say something, join the teasing banter, but the words weren't leaving her mouth, so she just rolled her eyes and shrugged.

An attraction was sparking between the two of them constantly, and for moments, like during the game, she could forget that Nick was the adrenal-chasing man full of secrets and lies. Until the truth came back, slamming her in the face. If she couldn't keep herself at a distance from Nick, she was terrified she would end up hurt.

15

"ARE YOU KIDDING me," Seabass snapped. And Nick pulled the phone a bit away from his ear.

Nick glanced up at the sound of running water before looking back at his sneakers. He and Morgan hadn't finished their game, because something Haley said had upset her. None of the conversation seemed to Nick like something that would cause Morgan's reactions but she didn't want to talk. Silently they'd come back to the suite and now she was showering.

Only twenty feet away, naked and wet. *Fuck.* He was doing his best not to think about it. And trying not to look. But the mirrors reflected everywhere. The steam was fogging up the mirrors upstairs in the loft area that had the shower and the bedroom, but Jesus, this place needed some doors. If he turned around he could see straight upstairs without any issue. His free hand pulled at the back of his neck.

"Or quit." Seabass's voice blasted through the phone.

"What?" Nick asked.

"Do I actually have your attention?"

"Of course."

"Don't even fucking say that—you've heard nothing I've said for the last five minutes."

Nick would argue, but he really hadn't. "Look, I know you're mad I broke cover."

"Mad? I'm not mad, I'm dumbfounded. It's not like you said, 'Haley, this is not the time and place. Let's go somewhere else rather than the gym that we are investigating to talk.' What the fuck?"

The answer was simple. Morgan had looked like she was going to cry when Haley approached them. And Nick would do anything to make that not happen, even something stupid. Seabass was right. He'd never put an op in jeopardy before, but at the time, his head was focused on Morgan not his job. And now, weighing the pros and cons, he'd say Haley knowing hurt nothing. Still when he'd made the decision, he hadn't taken the time to think it through, he'd simply reacted. Morgan had jumped in and went along with the story well enough that it worked. As far as Haley was concerned, he was the asshole Morgan had been dating for weeks.

Which made Nick want to pound the real Stew into the ground. But analyzing why he felt so mad at a guy he'd never met bothered him, and he didn't like where those thoughts might lead.

But regardless, it worked out.

"Look, you don't have to like it, but I made a call."

"Pulling the 'it's my business' card?" The shock was obvious in his voice.

"I've never done that. You know me better than that Seb." Nick didn't hide his offense to the statement. "And Haley knowing what's going on chilled everyone out instantly. I'd told James to stay away this week, and I already reamed him out for showing up. He agreed he and Haley would keep their distance while they're here. But he's the client, and he's paying us. And even if he wasn't, Bex wants me to help him."

Seabass didn't answer, and Nick heard the shower shut off. His gaze moved up to the loft automatically. Although the mirrors in the shower area were steamed up, the bedroom mirrors were not and he saw the pale skin of a wet arm reach out from behind the curtain for a towel. He turned his back and stared at the closed blinds.

The idea of Morgan wet and naked was bad enough, if he saw her—

He reached down and adjusted himself because his shorts weren't hiding his current train of thought.

"Nick, if the flashbacks are getting this bad, I think you need to head home." Seabass's statement checked Nick back into the conversation.

"What?"

"Listen—two in a ten-minute conversation is a problem. Maybe your brother was right and your head wasn't ready for this. And that's fine. If Morgan's affecting you, I get it."

Nick pulled at the back of his neck again and took a deep breath. Lilac hit his nose like a sledgehammer. But the smell wasn't comforting anymore because now he associated it with his face buried in her hair. With her body pressed into his.

"Danny wasn't right. I'm not having flashbacks." Which, at the moment, was true, because he was too turned on and focused on how much he wanted Morgan spread out beneath him to be lost in the past. "Morgan isn't affecting me at all. She's not even in the room, for God's sake—she's in the shower."

Seabass snorted. "Oh, *huh*."

"Huh what?" Nick snapped.

"Focus. Anyway, at the gym today, I overheard the personal trainer we're watching say his girl worked at the sports bar as the bartender." The change of subject threw Nick for a second, but Seabass went on. "If he's working with her, the drugs could come out of both places. That would be why the staff and guests are getting hit hard, so fast. I was thinking Bex and I would check that out tonight."

"Okay, we can all go—"

"No," Seabass interrupted. "Haley thinks you and Morgan are a lovey dovey couple. If you don't want her asking more questions you need to play the part a little bit."

Morgan was unhappy she still couldn't tell Haley about the fire or the person waiting outside her building, but Nick wanted to keep Morgan's issues quiet. On the off chance whoever was after her wasn't part of the drug cartel from Florida, then it was important that the circle of people in the know was extremely small. There were very few possibilities. She didn't have tons of people in her life; a couple of friends, a few ex-boyfriends, her agent and the small staff that worked in that office, and her editor. Although he couldn't discount a random guy from the grocery store or something else he hadn't seen yet. But his guys, along with Danny and the bureau, were working on it.

"You telling me to put on a show for Haley?" Nick asked.

"I'm saying you and Morgan eat in the dining room, but *not* with the *owners*. It makes more sense to split up. I'll take the bar, you take the dinner. At least until we have something solid."

Nick was tired and didn't feel like arguing, and dinner sounded better than the sports bar.

"Fine."

"I checked in with Danny. He's tracing the chemicals for the fire starter; he doesn't have a solid lead, just a few possibles. But he pointed out it hasn't even been a week yet. I mentioned the stalker angel and sent him the photos."

"Yeah, I talked to him," Nick said. Danny was good. Nick trusted him to be working it out. Plus, he had Donovan and his team back at the office double-checking everything.

"And Nick," Seabass added. "I'm clear on your problem now, but hell, keep it in your pants. At least until her trial is over. Because if you screw around with Morgan, you're not only going to mess with her case but also your relationship with Admiral Johanson. And considering how close Haley and Morgan are, probably this case, and maybe your firm's reputation. Think before you do something stupid."

"Fuck off, Seb," Nick snapped. "It's all under control."

But twenty-four hours later, Nick felt no more in control as he watched Morgan through the reflection in the mirror over the desk where he was working. She sat across the room on the weird ass heart bed staring at her computer screen, frowning. Last night they had gone out to dinner, just the two of them. Like Seabass suggested. Keeping space between the owners of the property and Nick. But Morgan had been quiet, not her usually sassy self. And today he basically let Seabass take over so they could hang here and she could stare at a computer screen. Not talking.

For all the jibes about Morgan being dramatic, she wasn't. Competitive, feisty when she was mad, but she handled shit without an issue. And the fact that she'd yet to panic over her stalker was impressive.

He'd spent the last few hours going over countless footage from different angles of the area around her apartment the night of the fire and the week leading up to it. He'd gotten no-where. Whoever was after Morgan, stalking her, was good at it, or they blended in really well in New York. The only times they'd found him on any camera were because a program Wyatt created to scan the photos picked up a unique design on the hoodie the guy was constantly wearing.

Morgan sighed again and her fist punched the blanket next to her. He finally turned away from the desk to look at her.

"What's wrong?" He couldn't stand not knowing what *her* problem was because he needed to solve something. Fix something.

Blue-green eyes flicked from the computer screen to the mirror so she could see him before she dropped her gaze to her screen. "You've read some of my books." The statement had the air of a question and a hint of accusation, much like every time she called him out for some fact that he hadn't yet gotten around to share. Hedging and half-truths were part of his life every day, but he was getting the sense that Morgan hated them.

He could attempt the full truth, when possible, with her. There would always be half-truths, because some things he could never share. But growing up with her father, she had to realize Nick couldn't spill government secrets just because she was cranky.

"I've read all of them."

She glanced over her shoulder at him. "You've read all eight of my books?"

"Yes, on the kindle app on my phone, because *yes,* I would get shit for reading a book with a half-naked guy on the cover. But you make me laugh. I love the characters you create, and you write a hot sex scene. Mock me if you want, but I've read all of your books."

She'd spent most of the day sitting on the heart-shaped couch-bed she'd slept on the night before in the same shorts and tank top she'd tortured him with at Grant's.

He reached up and pulled on the back of his neck, waiting for her response.

All day her back was to him. But she moved the computer off her lap and spun so she was facing him, giving her a view that didn't require a mirror.

"So, you know what a meet cute is?"

That was a test.

"Couple meets under unique circumstances, sometimes funny, sometimes sweet, but the idea is to grab the reader."

Her deep aqua eyes flashed.

"Want to talk about pinch points, character arcs, or black moments?" Nick added with a smirk.

"It's unfair you read all my letters with Louis. What did you do memorize what I'd tell him?" She pouted and spun away.

He chuckled and stood up from the desk chair he'd been working and moved around the front of the heart to sit next to her. She turned, adjusting to make room as he sunk onto the huge pink sofa bed beside her.

"I only read some of them, freckles," he promised. "But Lewie wanted help when he was giving you advice."

"Was it all you?" Her voice cracked, and her eyes sparked with pain.

"No," he assured quickly. "Lewie loved helping you. A lot of times, I'd just tell him his idea was solid." He chuckled, thinking back. "Other times I'd tell him it was garbage." He paused. "Oh man, I wonder if he sent this to you. You were asking about the happily ever after. He had this idea about tacos—"

"Oh my God, the tacos." She reached out and let her hand rest on his thigh. Nick watched her face light up. Her eyes sparkled, and her cheeks lit with a smile. The woman was beautiful, no question.

"I forgot about that. It was bad," Morgan added, a cute little snort of laughter coming out. She shook her head and lifted her hand away from his leg to tuck a stand of that red hair behind her ear, exposing the soft skin of her neck. Nick would've loved to lean in and press his lips under her jaw. To taste the pulse that pounded in her neck. Run his tongue across and nibble on her ear. God, he wanted to taste every inch of her.

But she was Lewie's little sister, the Admiral's daughter, and his current assignment. Nick's business was finally getting off the ground, finding the groove, and touting a serious reputation in the industry. He didn't need to toss that away. Especially when Morgan had made it clear she didn't want a future with anyone like him.

"A lot of his ideas were bad," Morgan said.

"He might have sucked at helping, but never doubt he wanted to," Nick added. "And he definitely was your biggest fan. He made all of us read your first book."

"He talked about you a lot too. So much that I kept asking to meet you, but I think you were always busy or something." She glanced down and picked at the blanket tucked over her long legs.

"Busy?"

"Yeah, he always said it wasn't a good time." She shrugged but still wouldn't look up.

"Moey," he said. But when she still didn't look at him, he reached out and tipped her chin up. It was strange to see her look vulnerable, but that's exactly what reflected back at him.

Almost like his next sentence had the power to crush her. "He never asked. If he asked me, I wouldn't have said no."

"Sure, you'd have wanted to hang out with your friend's baby sister."

"You're all woman. Beautiful, talented, and the more time I spend with you the more you impress me. So don't assume I wouldn't have wanted to meet you."

Her breath hitched as her eyes moved down to his mouth. She swallowed. Nick had never in his life wished for something as much as he wished to reach across and kiss her right now. Lose himself in her. But her stalker was real, and what she needed from him was protection. Not a quick fling.

So instead of reaching for her, he forced himself off the sofa toward the hearth to restock the fire. He tossed a log on before he said.

"So, the meet cute issue?"

"Meet cute?" Morgan whispered. Her voice sounded unsteady and Nick knew if he turned around, he'd see the desire still in her eyes. His control had limits. Her begging, even without words, would be it, so he just poked uselessly at the fire. Unwilling to risk the temptation of even looking at her.

"Your book, the meet cute. What's the issue?"

"Oh." She cleared her throat, disappointment in her tone, and Nick felt like an ass.

But she'd thank him in the end because the truth was, he wasn't good enough for her. Or anyone long-term. Her comment to Bex about him being broken was still forefront in his mind. And a quick fuck would end up leaving them both hurt.

"It's not the meet cute, it's the nickname. The meet cute's great—bartender is stuck in a beer cooler at the bar she works.

Hot, very Brooklyn delivery guy comes to drop the keg—she scares the crap out of him. I had him call her bunny—"

Nick scoffed. "Bunny?" He spun around to look at her. "Really? That ranks up there with pleasure machine, Moey."

Her back stiffened as her eyebrows rose. "She hops out of the reach in, like a rabbit. I thought bunny worked, but everyone has flagged it as crap." Her arms crossed over her chest as she flopped into the pillow behind her and the pout flooded her face in full force. "Now everything else doesn't work. I want her to hate it, but it to be cute for reasons she doesn't get."

Nick paused, thinking. "By him being 'very Brooklyn,' do you mean Italian Brooklyn? Like a stereotypical New York Italian?"

"If you tell me that doesn't work—" Her voice was full of all the competitive feistiness he'd met on the basketball court.

"Stop," he said with a laugh. "I'm saying lean in to that. *Cara mia.* If he's Italian, he'd use that."

"How did you know her name is Cara?" she demanded.

"No." He shook his head. "I didn't. But not Cara. *Cara mia.* Exactly translated it means my dear but if you use it as a term of endearment it means something similar to *beloved.*"

"Carmya, carmy, oh my gosh—that's perfect," she said and reached for her computer. "She can think he's mocking her. She'll hate it as much as bunny. Then, after at the happily ever after..." She probably would have finished the thought, but she was typing furiously.

"He'll tell her he knew from the moment she hopped out and scared the crap out of him, that she was his forever," Nick finished.

"Exactly!" Bright excitement radiated out of Morgan in a way he hadn't seen before. It was passion and joy rolled together. And it looked good as fuck on her. "Oh my gosh, this is perfect. It's all I wanted with bunny, but didn't work."

"Glad I could solve one problem today," he said and walked to his chair when it was clear she was once again engrossed in her computer.

"Nick?" Morgan called when he sat down. "You speak Italian?"

"Yup," he agreed. "The girl I wanted to date in high school spoke Italian. I learned it to impress her."

"Just Italian?" she asked. It was the tone she'd given him about the meet cute. All test.

"No," he said. This was a truth he could give her. "I was recruited into special ops because I was good at languages. I learned I could put the TV on SAP as a kid, and it annoyed all my brothers that they couldn't understand the Spanish. I had to sell it to my mom as I wanted to learn Spanish. Otherwise, I'd be in trouble. I was an asshole kid, so I did it enough that by high school, I spoke passable Spanish. So, my mom made me take French. Like I said, I learned some Italian to impress Gianna. And then at the Naval Academy I learned Mandarin and Russian. German and Arabic came during BUD/S and on the teams."

"Howard and Louis both spoke Arabic," she said. Yeah, he knew. "They used to speak it to annoy me, say things in Arabic that I couldn't understand just to make me upset."

"It's SAP on the TV all over again. I was at my brother Grant's place over Christmas, and I put the news on but changed the TV to Mandarin. Grant got so pissy and because he sucks at technology, he couldn't fix it. I told him it's good for his kids to be diverse. He wanted to throat punch me." Nick laughed. "We all torture our siblings, right?"

"What's the fun in having siblings if you can't make them insane?" she asked with a laugh. Odd that she could appreciate his humor. His sister and sister-in-law told him he was being a jerk. But the fact that Morgan got it was fun.

"Exactly."

Before she could say more, his phone rang. He glanced at the name and stood up. Morgan went back to her computer, and he headed into the pool area because the door suppressed the sound.

"Yeah?" he asked Seabass.

"Got anything?" Seabass asked.

"Watching footage all day, but apart from the small clips Donovan sent of the guy in the black coat and hoodie following her all week, I got shit. Tall, thin, but I've yet to get an actual shot of his face." Nick frowned. "Lucky isn't right. This guy is smart. Smart as fuck. I can't see him being part of the drug ring down in Florida.

"You think she picked up a stalker in New York?" Seabass asked.

"That seems like a crazy coincidence, but I'm struggling to believe this guy is part of the idiots Dewie is taking down."

"Yeah, I know," Seabass said. "But Wyatt's on his way out tonight now that his dad's thing is over and good. And Donovan is on a mission to find this guy's face." None of that made Nick feel better. "But I did find something for the resort—maybe. Bex got the trainer to give her an invitation to the club tonight for some 'special' fun. That girl is the shit. I get why you always bring her."

"Yeah," Nick agreed. Bex was always good at getting someone to open up.

"You think you and Morgan can come?" Seabass asked.

"Sure, we'll meet you at nine."

Four hours later, Nick leaned against the wall and watched with angry eyes as Morgan and Bex stood at the bar chatting with the woman serving drinks. They were maybe ten feet from him and Seabass, but Nick didn't like it.

"No one is going to approach any of us if you don't get rid of the glare," Seabass reminded him again. "We separated a bit to increase the odds, because the girls look like they are out for a good time, and you look like you're ready to murder someone. But if you can't stop threatening to kill anyone who looks at Morgan, it won't help."

Blend in was all she was supposed to do tonight. He told her to wear something for a night out, but the dress she picked was too much. Every male in the room couldn't pull their eyes off the deep purple lace that wrapped her body tightly. Nick's eyes skimmed down her backless dress, over the perfect curve of her hips to the well cupped ass. He swallowed. He ran his hands over his face, turning away from the bar.

She was making him nuts, completely fucking nuts.

Damn it, he needed a drink. And he couldn't drink on the job anymore, than he could fuck the protectee.

"You under control?" Seabass asked.

"Why the hell wouldn't I be?" he snapped. His eyes scanned the room, taking in the couples standing at high tops, the ones on the dance floor. Random singles from the area who came to this hot spot at night.

The idea of opening this part of the resort to non-guests brought in revenue but it coincided exactly with the overdoses on the property. It also meant there were a ton of single men standing around, staring at Morgan.

Nick growled at Seabass's chuckle as the ass-wipe took a sip of his water, hiding his smirk.

"Usually when that vein pops on your forehead, you're about to rain down a massive amount of piss off." Bex added helpfully, and Nick's gaze shot to the bar. Morgan stood alone now chatting with some buffed up idiot from the gym they were investigating.

"You were supposed to stay with her," he snapped. "Buddy system?"

"The trainer seemed way more into her than me, and she wanted a minute to see if she could get anywhere. He's not the guy stalking her, and maybe she'll get somewhere with him. What's the issue?"

Nick glared at Bex, who was smiling. They found his misery all too much fun. This was the exact plan he'd worked up driving with Wyatt to Grant's to pick up Morgan. Come to this place, have Morgan move around the resort with him. Watch her, while he figured out who was handing out heroin to the guests. But fucking hell. Nothing had gone the way he planned.

When Morgan laughed and rested her hand on the guy's arm, Nick shot off the wall straight at her. She tensed for one second as his arm wrapped around her waist, pulling her back against his chest before sinking into his embrace. In the heels she wore, her ear was almost even with his mouth as he leaned in. A shiver racked her body. He gritted his teeth and gave the guy a fuck off frown before turning his attention back to Morgan.

"Wanna dance, freckles?" As soon as she nodded, Nick guided her away. His eyes met Seabass's, silently telling him and Bex to work the guy at the bar. Once they were on the other side of the room, he pulled Morgan into his arms.

"I thought you said earlier you didn't dance." Her voice all mock innocence, which Nick didn't believe for one second, as she rocked her hips against him. His muscles clenched, and he pulled her tighter.

"Don't start something you can't finish, Moey," he grunted.

She looked him right in the eyes. Desire pooled in the aqua depth, cutting the breath out of his body. "We both know I'm not the one who wouldn't finish it, Nick."

Slowly, never breaking eye contact, she leaned in, brushing her lips against his. His heart sped up as his eyes flitted shut. Soft, plush lips pressed against his briefly before her mouth opened slightly, allowing her tongue to dance along his bottom lip and he was done.

An electric current like he'd never felt before shot through him, and with a groan he sunk into the kiss. He invaded her mouth the way he wanted to claim her body, owning her. The slight moan that echoed from her only drove him on. But finally, she pulled away, and it cut at his heart that he saw her brace herself for what he might say next. But the words that he should have said didn't come.

"Want to get out of here?" Nick asked.

16

MORGAN WATCHED AS Nick locked the door behind them. She could tell he was at war with himself, and half of her wondered if, by the time they got to the room, he'd push her away again. He'd been doing it all day, turning her on and then pulling away. And she couldn't take it anymore.

She wanted him. One hot night to get it out of their system would be perfect.

He turned and his eyes ran up her body, over her legs, past her hips and waist. His breath sped up as his gaze ranked over her breasts and it felt like an actual caress. He paused at her lips before meeting her eyes.

"Don't change your mind again, Nick." She sounded breathless even to her own ears, and she stepped forward. She took his hand in hers and closed the last space between them.

"I'm not good for you, Morgan," he whispered in her ear.

"I know," she agreed and rested her forehead on his shoulder. He would always be married to the job, to his former military buddies, to his secrets and half-truths. But she wasn't looking for forever. "I can't ignore this anymore. I want you."

His arms tightened around her as he shook his head before he said, "It's a bad idea."

The rejection stung hard. She shut her eyes, taking a breath, unwilling to cry. And he pulled back, forcing her head off his shoulder so he could see her. His eyes were too intense. Desire and heat hit her hard.

"I'm not saying I don't want you. Don't think that," he said.

"I never know what you mean Nick. You do hot and cold better than anyone I've ever met." Pain flashed in his eyes at her words, but she continued. "I feel like there is something going on here, but one minute, your eyes light up like a fire, and the next, they shut down completely. What do you want?"

His gaze tracked down to her lips and then farther before lifting again.

"Come on Nick. Stop fighting this—you won't hurt me. I know this isn't forever, but it can be one hell of a for now."

His hands came out, cradling her face and pulling her to him. His lips slammed down, hot and demanding. Fingers tipped her chin up, deepening the kiss. She opened, willingly begging him for more. But he pulled back, resting his forehead against hers. His hot breath danced around her face.

"I want to be very clear. I want to turn you around, press against you, move inside you. Pull your hair until you feel so good you can't think of anything besides my dick making you scream."

She wet her lips. "I want that."

With a groan, he backed her up until her calves hit the heart-shape chaise. In a blink, she was flat on her back and he was above her.

"One time deal. Get it out of our systems, right?" he said above.

"Yes," she agreed.

He leaned down again and claimed her mouth. His tongue wrestled and teased hers and she pulled needing him closer. His weight fell, pressing every plane of his tight body against her as her arms circled his neck. She arced into him.

"Slow down, freckles." He chuckled, letting his breath tease her lips. "If we're doing this, it's going to be slow and we're both going to enjoy every second." His finger ran lightly along the sweetheart neckline. Goosebumps broke out along her body. "This dress, were you trying to kill me?"

"Just get your attention."

His finger dipped between her breasts. "You always have my attention, Moey. Since you stepped out of the SUV at Grant's farm, I can't see anything but you."

He dipped his head again, kissing her lightly before moving lower, peppering kisses along her jaw, moving down her neck. Her heart pounded in her chest.

"Nick," she moaned, and her hands shook as she worked the buttons on his black shirt. He pulled back, reached over his head and in a swift motion, both his T-shirt and button down were on the floor. The lack of barrier gave her hands the ability to run over the hard muscles of his chest. The dusting of chest hair tickled her palms before she grabbed his shoulders to pull him back to her.

Their mouths crashed together, releasing all the pent-up lust that both had been running from. It was the hottest kiss of her life. Lips, teeth, tongues clashed. His hand roamed along her side to her thigh, squeezing hard before lifting her dress to her waist.

"This needs to go. I need to see you, Morgan." His hot breath flooded her face as he hissed out the words.

"Zipper's on the side," she said, lifting her arms over her head to make access easier.

Nick paused, staring down at her before running his hands from her wrists down her arms, down her sides, teasing the edge of her breasts, stopping when he reached the zipper.

His fingers moved torturously, slowly lowering the zipper, letting his rough pinkie brush lightly against the exposed skin.

"So soft," Nick said, and pulled the dress over her head. He laid her back possessively, taking her in. "You're my fantasy, so get ready because I love a slow torture." Dropping his head, he ran his tongue lightly over the curve of her breast, flicking the front clasp of her bra as he moved, letting both free. Without removing the bra, he zeroed in on her taut nipple. He groaned, taking it in his mouth making her gasp. But he was in no rush, lightly teasing her, switching from right to left and back. Before letting his tongue run between the two again. Her stomach tightened as a moan left her lips. She arched up, needing the pressure of his hand lower.

"Getting inpatient again?" His eyes met hers as his thumb brushed lightly just below her breast. He flipped his hand over so the back of it danced across her stomach, making slow waves down her body. Each line the slowest torture she'd ever felt, teasing that he might touch her where she needed him most but never reaching between her legs. Her heart pounded in her ears as need flooded her core. Finally, he rubbed the line of purple lace resting along her hips.

"Mmm, you look good in purple, Moey," Nick groaned. "So fucking good."

When his hand made no move to slip inside, her stomach tightened and her hips thrust up

"Please, Nick," she begged.

Her breath caught as his finger dragged slowly along her lace panties, not pressing nearly enough.

"Please what?" he asked, but dropped his mouth again. His tongue circled her nipple slowly, causing a whimper to leave her throat. "Please worship your body? Because trust me, I am."

"Please make me come," she begged.

He chuckled but kissed his way down along her ribs to her hips, removing her panties and settling himself between her legs. His nose brushed along her leg and his hot breath danced against her. Her core clenched in anticipation. Her stomach jumped when he switched, running his hot breath along her other leg, placing wet kisses on her skin. Her legs quivered. When she couldn't take it anymore, he finally let his mouth softly run along her slit. But it wasn't enough.

"Just as perfect as everything else about you," Nick said, and each word caused a throb at her center. She was close, and the man had hardly touched her.

"Nick, I need you t—"

"Hell, yeah you do." He dropped his mouth to suck hard on her aching clit. The buildup had been tortuously slow, bringing her achingly close that the sudden burst of pleasure swamped her. Overwhelming her. When he pinched hard on her nipple just as his mouth took another powerful pull, the bundle of nerves exploded. She lost it. She was coming almost instantly. She arched up into his mouth as he lapped at her, driving her higher. Until every cell of her body tingled with the most incredible shaking thrill she'd ever had.

"More," she moaned as his tongue circled her clit, lightly revving her up again.

"Christ, I wanted this to be slow, but there is no fucking way. I need to be inside you now." Nick's eyes burned into her like molten lava. "I want to bend you over the back of this stupid heart and finally give us both what we need."

His voice was desperate. Once again, that veil of control he wore disappeared, and she was staring at the desperate man beneath. The man who needed her. And she wanted to give him exactly what he wanted.

She moved, leaning on to the back of the chaise, spreading her legs just slightly before glancing over her shoulder. "What are you waiting for?"

"Fuck, yeah." His deep rumble shot through her like lightning, making her quiver with anticipation.

Turning, she watched in the mirror as he pulled the condom out of his wallet and dropped his pants. Their eyes met as he rolled the condom on his long, hard length. Using his hand, he guided himself. She felt the pressure, but her eyes stayed locked with his in the mirror.

Erotic and intimate, watching in the mirror added something extra to the pressure of his entrance. His hips rocked until he pressed into her completely.

"What a perfect pussy," he mumbled before he started to move. She saw his hand snake up before she felt his fist wrap her hair tight. The pressure of his tug arched her back slamming her hips tight into his. She watched their bodies move together, adding to every strong, swift stroke.

"That's it, baby, yes," Nick said. "So hot, so wet, so fucking tight. I want to feel you come all over me."

Each thrust of his hips pressed deep inside, lighting everything inside her. It was like she'd come alive under his hands. Every pound was driving her higher, bringing her closer to the edge.

"Moey," he groaned. "*Fuuuuck.* I need you to come." He yanked harder on her hair and snaked his hand around to rub tight circles against her.

At his mercy, she was pinned by her hair and pussy. The complete domination just on the edge of pain sent her higher until she burst in a surge of unstoppable pleasure. His orgasm followed hers almost instantly.

He dropped her hair, and his arms came around her waist, pulling her tight against him. His lips pressed into her shoulder. And she almost felt cherished for one moment before he pulled away.

"That was good," he said, immediately lifting his pants and walking away from her.

An icy chill remained in his wake; molten lava and glacier freeze. The man did it better than anyone she'd ever met. And she was going to tell him just what an ass he was when he came back. She scooped up his shirt, untangling the white T-shirt from the black button down, and tossed it on. Yup, when he came down those stairs, they were going to talk. Something very strong was happening between them, and she would not let him act like it was nothing.

17

THE WATER SUCKED down, taking the condom with it, but Nick just stared into white porcelain, unsure how to feel. Morgan was much more than he expected. She was fucking perfect. And he was a complete ass. He shouldn't have walked away like that, but he needed a minute to get his shit together.

He'd never lost it like that before. He hadn't even taken off his shoes before slamming into her from behind. But hell, every time he thought she couldn't get any better, it was like she knew and needed to prove he hadn't seen the best yet. The way they clicked was crazy, and that sex had been off the charts. Fuck, she blew his mind. When his lips pressed into her soft skin, a deep ache in his chest told him to hold on to that forever. But the fading bruises on her back were like a slap in the face, reminding him of exactly what he was supposed to be doing with her.

Protecting her was his responsibility, and objectivity made him more effective at that job. And with the amount of contacts Admiral Johanson had that could crush his business, staying professional should have stopped him from crossing a line, but none of that mattered. The only thing that mattered was he wanted her, in his arms, tucked into his side, under him, over him.

But he had no business getting involved long term with anyone. What could he offer her?

There was nothing stable about his life. He moved around for days at a time when he was working. And for the last week, he struggled to keep his head in reality. Yes, she was pulling him out of the past, and even talking about Lewie was easier with her. But what right did he have to dump the burdens of his fucked-up head on her?

He left the small space of the bathroom and paused. It almost sounded like a steam kettle was running, like someone was making tea. Nick's gaze bounced around, using the mirrors to check the room with a quick shift of his eyes. Maybe it was coming from outside. He should text Seabass to go check it out. He reached into his pocket, but his phone wasn't there. It must be on the floor. He glanced in the reflection down at the sofa.

His gaze landed on Morgan, already asleep on the heart-shaped sofa thing. Damn, she fell asleep fast. He shook his head at himself as the pride of wearing her out made him smirk.

He should leave her there and sleep on the floor, like he'd done last night, but although it should, it wouldn't happen. As soon as he left the loft, he would climb in and pull her right against him because even now, standing upstairs, he longed to be holding her. Make up for the fact that he'd just walked away before her legs even stopped shaking from her orgasm.

And really, being close to her wouldn't stop his ability to protect her. The more important she became to him, the deeper she pulled him in, the more vital her safety became. Why couldn't he keep her safe and keep her in his arms?

He stared into the mirror as he washed his hands. His own gray eyes reflected back at them, but he imagined they were a brighter blue. Lewie's. The thick knot tightened in this throat. The unspoken rule was to stay away from a buddy's sisters. They protected each other's families; they didn't hurt them. And they definitely didn't put their brother in arms in the middle of drama. He wondered what Lewie would say about him and Morgan. Even if Nick wanted to have good intentions with her, with all the shit, wouldn't Lewie want someone better for his sister?

His hand went automatically to Lewie's dog tag in his pocket of the cargo pants he hadn't even snapped. He flipped it between his thumb and middle finger.

But the hiss stole his focus again. It wasn't loud, but too loud to be coming from outside. What the fuck was it? It sounded like someone was letting air out of a balloon, slowly. Was it something with the vent? Turning, he glanced up, trying to place it, but it almost seemed like it was coming from behind. He spun again and moved into the bedroom area. He did a quick glance before he realized.

Fuck

It was coming from downstairs. He turned and flew down the stairs. On the third step, instinct kicked in and he stopped breathing, but instincts didn't stop the panic bubbling up in him as he saw light white fog coming from under the door. He couldn't see it in the air beside the concentration forced under the door, but he knew it was there.

Morgan.

His knees threatened to give out on him with the idea he might be too late for her. He had her in his arms in seconds. Her chest lifted slightly in a breath and the double-edged sword ripped through him. Knowing he wasn't too late while also knowing she was breathing in whatever poison was being pumped into the room.

His actions became robotic. Through the pool room, out the back door, across the hall to Seabass's room. He lifted his foot and slammed his heel into the door with enough force to crack the door through the deadbolt, slamming it open and moved into the pool area of Seabass's room.

His gaze landed on Bex floating in the pool, wide-eyed confusion on her face. The door behind her flew open, and Wyatt and Seabass moved into the room, guns trained in his direction.

Wyatt lowered his gun first. "Legend isn't good enough—auditioning for Superman now, boss?"

"Poison." Nick said the words as he took his first breath in probably two minutes. The words sent a new jolt of action through both Wyatt and Seabass. "Under the door." He swallowed, glancing at Morgan out cold in his arms.

His brain was firing too fast. If whoever did this knew the room, they could be outside. Waiting, like with the fire. He spun back to the back door. If they knew about that door, they might be there setting a trap. How would he get her out of the resort? He spun again. What was the gas? Where was the closest hospital? Should he drive or would eventually whatever was in the room get him too?

The tight bite of the slap snapped at his cheek, pulling him back. He blinked. Seabass and Wyatt were gone, but he didn't know how much time had passed. His heart pounded in his chest.

"Look at me, breathe," Bex demanded, standing in front of him, clothes thrown over her wet suit. "Focus, stop panicking."

Panicking? Is that what he was doing? He was trained not to panic. Was whatever gas had been in the room affecting him? Even still, he'd been trained to get the job done under any circumstance. He needed to pull it together.

He forced himself to take a slow breath in and then slowly release it.

"Good," Bex said, watching him. "Seabass checked it out. It's a sedative. Stronger and less stable than nitrous oxide, but it won't kill either of you. Wyatt and Seabass just went back out to clear the area. Since Morgan's out cold, Seabass will need to check on her. He's the medic."

Nick nodded and moved, carrying Morgan out of the pool area and down the three steps into the living room, setting her down on the heart-shaped sofa in Seabass's room.

"Put these on her." Bex handed him black sweats. His hand trembled slightly as he slipped them over her legs before looking at her. Her dark eyelashes fluttered against her pale cheeks. Beard burn marred her jaw and brushed across her neck.

If he hadn't been so focused on sleeping with her, he would have noticed the noise at the door. None of this would have happened if he had simply been paying attention. Protecting her, like his job required. Instead, he lost focus and she'd paid the price.

The parallels between his sister's wedding, the long flights, and the bomb that killed Morgan's brother spun in his head. Both times he wasn't doing his job, life and fun impeded what should have been important.

The bag slamming to his feet pulled him out of his thoughts again. He shook his head, trying to clear the haze that seemed to fog his mind.

"Seems clear. We can't find anything, but there are over thirty rooms, and we don't have time to clear them all." Seabass nodded at Nick's feet. "Go bag—laptop, phone, wallet." The way he frowned at the word wallet told Nick it was still on the bed, probably with the condom wrapper. "Wyatt's in the car. I'll check you both and then you need to go. Call Danny from the car. I'll secure the scene until the FBI gets here."

Nick nodded.

"And get a fucking shirt," Seabass added. Seabass might be pissed, but as Nick looked down at Morgan, unresponsive on the bed, Nick knew Seabass couldn't be as mad at him as he was at himself. He couldn't make another mistake. He needed to take a step back.

18

MORGAN TURNED, AND the comforter shifted around her. Her body felt strange, almost like the gray bedspread weighed her down, but it didn't seem heavy. She paused, realizing she wasn't on the heart-shaped sofa anymore. Shooting up quickly a wave of vertigo spun her head. Her stomach flipped, and she teetered.

Strong hands guided her back down to the pillow.

"Morgan, you're in my bedroom. It's not where you fell asleep. I know it's jarring, but you can trust me—you're okay." Nick's voice was a whisper in the dark room. She felt the mattress sink as he settled next to her. But he didn't lay down or touch her now that she was back on the pillow. A cloud of confusion fuzzed her mind. She couldn't quite focus. There were questions floating right out of her reach.

"What—" She didn't know what to ask. They'd been at the resort, out at the club. Then they'd gone back to their room. The details flashed through her brain, hot and heavy memories. His kisses, the feather light touches, the teasing, the mind-blowing sex. The way he'd walked away and left her. She stiffened.

"What do you remember?" he asked.

"I was lying down waiting for you to come back to tell you what an ass you are."

"I know I am," Nick agreed too fast, almost as if they'd already had the conversation.

"I—" She wasn't sure what to ask. "Nick, I just. I mean, what happened?"

He sighed.

"I'm sorry. I feel like we've already gone through this, but I can't remember."

"*You* have no reason to be sorry, and we'll go through this as many times as you need to be comfortable and remember. While I was in the bathroom, someone set off a canister of gas into the room that sedated you."

She sucked in a gasp of air as her hand lifted to cover her mouth. "The same person who set my apartment on fire?" The words were jumbled as her hand pressed into her lips. The concept of someone following her, trying to hurt her, was hard to wrap her jumbled head around.

"That's the working theory. But we don't know. As soon as I saw the fog coming under the door, I got you out—"

"You came into a room full of gas and got me?" The idea that he rescued her shouldn't be a surprise. That's who he was, but there was something uncomfortable about him putting himself in danger for her.

"Of course." His tone indicated it was an absurd question. "Seabass checked you out. It was decided that it wasn't safe to check you into the hospital, and you were stable enough to come here." His voice was rough.

She turned to look at him, but he was staring across the room. His face unreadable, the mask of professionally-trained special operative firmly in place. The man she'd been getting to know wasn't in the room. She didn't understand.

"You don't want me here?" she asked.

"I want you *safe*," Nick replied, which might be true, but didn't answer her question.

"And I'm not safe here?"

"I'll make sure you are safe here," he said fiercely. "The alarm is on. Wyatt is downstairs and will stay with us twenty-four hours a day until we figure this out. I have my guys all on shifts outside, three at a time, watching the house. You *will be* safe. I know I don't deserve it, but you can trust me."

Her hand came up to rest on his thigh, but he didn't react to her touch.

"I trust you, Nick," she assured him and squeezed his leg.

He turned, and his eyes flashed, the mask slipping for one brief second before he turned away.

"Good. How's your head? An hour ago you woke up uncomfortable," he asked back to business.

Her body was heavy, her head felt achy, but she didn't want to complain. "I'm just tired."

"Sleep. I'll watch over you. You're safe." He lifted himself off the bed and moved to a chair, leaving her cold and alone and confused about what exactly happened because it had to be more than he explained, but she drifted off.

She shifted, and this time, her body moved easily. Like the weight was removed, and she had control again. Sitting up, now alone, she took in Nick's bedroom lit from the sun shining in the window. It was what she would have expected. Streamlined. White walls, dark wood dressers and nightstands. Gray bedding hardwood floors. Blinds. Curtains. Not sterile.

There were two family pictures on the dresser, and a dish that held coins and Nick's wallet. A charger sat on the side table by the bed for his phone and smart watch. It was set for efficiency rather than decoration.

The exact opposite of everything she'd pick for a room.

She pushed the blanket back and stood from the king-size bed, letting her feet sink into the plush carpet. The unfamiliar black capris sweats fell just past her knees. Saying they weren't hers, at this point, was absurd. What did she own?

Not much. Some stuff in storage in Florida. A few things that would be shipped to her father, which were salvaged from her New York apartment. But she owned very little. Because someone was trying to *ruin* anything she owned. Or maybe they were trying to get her? Or kill her? She didn't know, and that made her teeth clench.

Until this point, no one had told her much. But she was over that in a big way. She needed to find Nick and demand some answers. And not only about her stalker but also about them. She glanced around again.

The room had three doors. One led to a large bathroom, the other must be a closet. She paused, hearing angry voices. Following the sound, she opened the door to a long hallway with multiple doors. Carefully, she moved down the hardwood floors to the staircase.

"I don't know what you want from me, Nick." It took Morgan a minute to place Nick's brother's voice.

"Danny, it's been five days, and the best you can tell me is that you've got nothing. In fact, the only solid lead came from my people."

"Fuck off. That's grossly unfair and you know it. I've been busting my ass to chase the chemicals all over the US. I don't have a team of twenty-five. This isn't a movie where I can snap my fucking finger and create a lead."

Morgan moved slowly down the stairs, trying not to make any noise, stopping halfway down to listen to the fight.

"I'm not asking you to create one. I'm saying get your entire team on it. Do the legwork. Get some answers."

Danny scoffed. "So—step one, talk to the victim. You gonna allow that yet?"

"Fuck you, you had plenty of time at the hospital," Nick snapped back.

"Whoa," said an unfamiliar voice. "Nick, Danny, chill."

"Wyatt," Nick snapped, "butt out."

"No," Wyatt answered. "Look, you know I respect the hell out of you. So this is hard as fuck, but Nick, I agree with Seabass. You're too close to this. This is the hospital fight all over again."

"Are you kidding me?" Nick seethed. Morgan could imagine the daggers shooting out of Nick's eyes. She didn't know Wyatt but she winced at the thought of Nick's ice-cold anger directed at the poor guy.

"No, Seabass was right," Wyatt continued. "Morgan's fine. Taking her to the hospital last night would have been a massive issue because she would have needed to use her ID. And our unsub is way too smart to miss that. It'd be like waving a banner that said *find me here*."

There was a long, drawn-out pause, and Morgan almost moved before the conversation started again.

"I'm well aware of the fact that you being willing to walk into a hospital for the first time in two years means this chick is important to you." Danny's statement flipped Morgan's stomach. The hospital was another trigger for Nick, and the idea he was willing to plow through it for her gave her a hope she didn't realize she wanted. Maybe this thing between them was more than just a fling.

"Of course she is. She's Lewie's sister. And it's my obligation to make sure she's safe." Nick's words crashed down on her like a rockslide. Her heart plummeted into her stomach and she shut her eyes to take a breath. One night, one time, scratch an itch, get back to business. He'd said that. Clearly. And that was the space he'd put up when she'd woken up earlier. She couldn't be hurt that he acted that way when she'd agreed to it going in.

She missed Danny's reply, but heard Nick snort.

"We need to figure this out before she goes back to Florida in two days for the trial," Wyatt said. "Because whoever this is will know exactly where she's going to be on Monday morning. That's going to make our job a hundred times harder, and his a cakewalk."

Morgan swallowed as the panic rose in her throat. But she couldn't panic, not until the crisis passed. And from the sound of it. Nothing was over. She needed to get it together.

"Maybe you should get on your shit then, Danny."

"Nick, Danny traced the thermite back to the plant in Passaic, New Jersey in five days. He rushed the lab testing, and then strong-armed the plants into turning over the chemical compounds. He's tracking employees and is on top of the Feds in Florida, back tracing any tie to the drug ring on the panhandle. He's done work that should have taken weeks in days. And last night, we added a second crime scene with medical grade chemicals. Give your brother a break." Wyatt's voice was calm.

Morgan knew what she needed to do. She descended the last few stairs and turned into the huge, open room. Kitchen, dining room, and living room all rolled into the space. The three men stood around a large empty slate island. Like a triangle, each stood braced in their corner. Holding their position against the others. Nick looked, as fierce as ever, dark eyes scowling at the tall young blond who looked like he should be surfing in Hawaii, not discussing the case. Danny Evans towered over both, but at the same looked the least intimidating. Almost like Danny had a bubble of happiness around him. And that was who she approached.

"If talking to me would help you figure this out, I'm happy to do it." Morgan announced to the trio. "Plus, I'd love for you to answer some questions for me, Agent Whatta Waste."

"Morgan, you don't need to talk to him right now." Nick moved, but she shook her head and he froze.

She crossed her arms and glared. "Nick, I'd like him to solve this case. So you can be relieved of your obligation to watch me."

Nick flinched at her words.

"Miss Johanson, I'm Wyatt Cross." The man she didn't know took the four steps to meet her halfway and held his hand out to her. "I work for Nick."

"Morgan," she corrected and then said, "Huh, I thought all his guys were Navy, but you're not."

"Marines," Wyatt said.

"What happened to high and tight?" She joked at the hair that almost covered Wyatt's eyes. He cocked his head to the side, and his mouth lifted at the corner.

Nick scoffed. "Drop the charming as fuck pretty boy attitude."

Wyatt looked at Morgan. "I'm going to live to regret this." Everything about Wyatt's demeanor changed. His jaw clenched and he aged ten years in front of her eyes as he turned to Nick. "Take a walk, Nick."

Nick walked right up to Wyatt, staring him down from an inch above Wyatt's frame. "You want me to fire you?"

But Wyatt didn't back down. "Take a walk, Nick, or I'll call Seabass, who has no beef, calling the admiral," he repeated.

Finally, Nick spun on his heel, slamming the back door behind him.

When the vibration of the door stopped, Wyatt turned back to her. "Excuse me, I'm going to throw up."

19

NICK SLAMMED OUT the door and pulled on the back of his neck. He wanted to kill Wyatt, but at the same time, the fucker had finally stood up to him. He'd been waiting for this moment for almost two years. It might be shit timing but Nick couldn't help but admit he was glad that Wyatt was getting over his hero worship, because that served no one well.

But the problem was, Seabass had been clear when Morgan woke up for good that she'd need some fluids and a small dose of salt. Not to mention her stomach needed to be tested. And Danny wouldn't do shit for her. His entire focus would be on the case. On the questions. Morgan's wellbeing wouldn't matter because his obligation would be to the case. Which is exactly the way Nick wanted it, so it shouldn't annoy him now. And he didn't want Morgan to be Danny's obligation anyway.

He winced at the thought of his comment earlier.

He hadn't meant Morgan was an obligation, even if he had—kind of. Putting her in a box was impossible. He sank into one of the six chairs that surrounded his unlit fire pit. The January cold cut through his long sleeve black shirt, but he hadn't thought to grab his jacket.

He caught motion out of the corner of his eye. It took a second to realize it was just one of his guys doing a yard check. Nick's eyes track the man through his entire circle of the yard before he disappeared back to the front, probably to his car to warm up.

Nick crossed his arms over his chest as he heard the door open behind him.

"Since I've pissed you off already today, this is probably going to slam the last of the nails into the coffin." Wyatt's voice got closer as he spoke. "I'm going to give you the update. You're going to lose your shit, then we're going to talk, okay?" Wyatt swallowed, moving to sit in the chair next to Nick.

Nick raised an eyebrow. "Are you using my method of bad news?"

"Yes." Wyatt didn't hesitate. "You're going to be pissed. Because this was a fuck up on all of us."

Nick's jaw clenched. How many times could they fuck up Morgan's case?

"Social media." Wyatt's hand shot up before Nick could interrupt. "Wait. I know Morgan hasn't been on it. But Haley tagged her in a post that also tagged the resort."

Wyatt passed Nick his phone. Nick stared down at the photo. The picture was ridiculously idyllic. Morgan and Nick sat at a dining table in front of a massive window. Behind them, the sun set in a flow of oranges and reds, reflecting off the snow and contrasting with the evergreens. Hell, if he was a publicist, he'd tell the resort to use the photo on everything. Because not only was the setting picture perfect, but so was the couple. Morgan's red hair tucked over her shoulder, a half-smile on her lips as she leaned toward the table. Like a magnet was pulling her toward Nick. He sat raptured, like the most beautiful sight he'd ever seen was playing out in front of him. But he wasn't gazing at the sunset. He was watching the girl.

It was hard to look at the picture and even attempt to claim he wasn't emotionally involved in this case.

The tag from Haley.

'Happy to see my bestie finally found the right man.' At LoveCanyonResort.

Nick's head dropped back, and he shut his eyes.

"She didn't mean to cause an issue. She said she has a private account with less than two hundred followers who are people she knows and had no idea posting anything with Morgan was a big deal. Apparently, she posted photos of Morgan in December at her wedding, and then again at New Year's. But I'm sure you don't need to be told how this is like gasoline on a fire for a stalker," Wyatt said.

"Yeah." Or the perfect trap if they had known. He saw how this could have played out right. But a small twist where the right hand wasn't talking to the left created a shit show.

"Seabass talked to Haley and James about the stalker situation. The whole story, not whatever story you all told her. No way around it with the FBI there."

Nick nodded but didn't open his eyes. He didn't want to fuck up something important, but the more important it became, the more it got fucked up.

"On the good news side of things, they caught the bartender passing off something to a guest on tape. Danny helped pull her in for questioning before he left the resort this morning, and turns out, her boyfriend was supplying her with the heroin to pass to the guests. So, they're both in custody."

Nick grunted. His brother had gone out to the resort last

night to look at the room and the canister of sedative himself. Three hours' drive each way was more than Danny had needed to do. Then he'd helped with Nick's other case and Nick thanked him by telling him he sucked. He hadn't meant it, but he was frustrated and working on no sleep in the last thirty hours. He was getting too old for this shit.

Nick glanced over at Wyatt. He didn't look the least bit tired. Wyatt hadn't slept either, but being twenty-seven had perks that didn't exist ten years later.

"Figured one case closed would be good."

Nick gave a clipped nod. It was. At least one problem was eliminated. NAE had a few other open files currently. But nothing major, which was good because he had his guys all taking rotations sitting outside his house.

"So, one more thing before I go in because it's cold as fuck out here," Wyatt said, standing up jamming his hands into the black cargo pants that were the standard NAE Securities uniform. Wyatt rocked back on his heels and sighed. "Look, I know you think you're a machine, and I mean dude, you are most of the time."

Nick's eyes narrowed, and Wyatt swallowed, but didn't stop.

"But man, you're running on fumes here. You keep saying you're fine, but fifteen hours ago you were *drugged* with a heavy sedative. You haven't slept in days or eaten in at least twenty hours; you've been on one call after another, pushing yourself and everyone else."

"What's your point, Wyatt?" Nick didn't need a recap of the last day and a half.

"You had me bring groceries, so make a sandwich and then take a nap. You employ the best people I've ever worked with. Go be a human and let us be the machines for a little while."

When Nick didn't respond, Wyatt sighed and walked away. The door opened behind him, but Nick didn't turn to watch him go in.

"For the record, I don't think your girl needs a hero today," Wyatt added. "But she might need a hug." And then the door shut, leaving Nick alone.

His hand lifted to rub his forehead, the slight tremble in his arm shocking him. He pulled back, opening and closing his fist, trying to work the tired muscles. He didn't think of himself as a machine or a robot. Just someone trained to handle shit. But he wasn't as young as he used to be, and there was a reason guys left the teams in their late thirties. And Wyatt wasn't entirely wrong. Now that he thought about it, he was starving, and Morgan should eat too.

Nick stood and headed back in straight to the fridge. He grabbed a bottle of water and found Morgan and Danny sitting around his poker table. He held the bottle out until Morgan finally pulled her gaze from Danny.

"Seabass said you needed liquids," Nick mumbled.

"I'd really like coffee," Morgan said. "Is that allowed?" Her tone had a bite of sarcasm that he flicked back to the obligation comment.

He pulled at the back of his neck. They probably needed to talk, but if she wanted coffee, he'd get her some. He moved back and grabbed a mug before filling a cup. It might be almost one in the afternoon, but everyone in this house had been up all night, and no one was letting the pot get empty. He added the milk and set it in front of her on a coaster.

Aqua eyes glanced from the cup to him.

"It's milk, not cream," Nick assured her. And she glanced away.

"Any chance you might get me a refill, Nick?" Danny asked.

Nick frowned. What was he, the butler? Low man on the totem pole did this shit. Before he could move, Wyatt grabbed the craft, bringing it to Danny as Morgan took a sip of her coffee.

"How is your stomach?" Nick asked. "Seabass said you should eat. How about I make you some toast?"

"Fine," she replied.

Nick scrambled up some eggs and toast as he listened to Danny question Morgan. They went over her past two years of relationships. Nick tried not to frown as she talked about the men. Four men.

"We already talked to Chase, who works with your agent, Erica. When we spoke to her, Erica mentioned that you two dated briefly."

Morgan sighed. "He was nice. We were both busy and never made time to see each other. It ended mostly because we weren't actually seeing each other ever. But I don't think he has any hard feelings, and he's definitely not obsessed with me enough to stalk me."

Nick looked over as he plated the eggs, watching Morgan's pale hand come up and rest on her throat. Dark circles shone under her eyes. She needed to sleep. Seabass had said the drug would probably take about thirty-six hours to leave her system completely. And she'd spend most of the day drowsy.

"Joe just moved away. And again, no bad blood, no intense feelings for either of us."

"That leaves Reed and Stewart?" Danny asked.

"Well, I doubt Stewart blew himself up, especially since he cried about it. And he hasn't even tried to reach out since the fire." Morgan's tone expressed exactly how Nick felt about the idiot.

Nick carried the two plates of eggs and toast to the table, placing one in front of Morgan before pulling out a chair next to her. She turned to him, her eyes full of so many questions.

"You should eat something," he said, nodding at her food.

Danny's gaze ticked between him and Morgan

"Just pretend I'm not here," Nick said, picking up his fork and grabbing a large bite.

"Reed?" Danny asked, turning his attention back to Morgan. "He was the guy that left you alone in the bar shootout, right?"

Morgan dropped the coffee cup back onto the felt of his poker table. Nick automatically grabbed a coaster, putting the mug on it, but Morgan didn't seem to notice. She picked at the green felt in front of her.

"That ended poorly," she admitted as she picked up a piece of toast, taking a bite.

"Haley mentioned something about having to block him on all your social media?" Danny prompted. Morgan swallowed her second mouthful of toast before she spoke.

"Yeah, he said I was being dramatic for breaking up with him. After like a ton of messages, I just couldn't take it anymore. He wanted closure but I was done. I blocked him, and that was the end of it. He didn't try to bother me again." She sighed, but Nick's eggs caught in his throat.

He swallowed harshly, and his gaze swung to Wyatt. He'd said this Reed guy was blocked, but he didn't mention he'd been harassing Morgan. Every instinct in Nick's being said start yelling, figure out how the fuck they missed this. But Morgan set down her toast and fisted her hand on the table.

She doesn't need a hero, but she might need a hug.

The statement echoed through his head and he reached out to wrap his hand over hers, giving it a squeeze. She immediately spun her hand, interlacing their fingers and clinging to him. Although his hand was wrapped up like it was in a vise, the knot inside him loosened. His gaze jumped back to Wyatt who was typing madly on his phone. By the buzzing going off in his pocket, Nick assumed he was on the group thread with Seabass and Donovan. Wyatt had the job aspect of this covered. But as Morgan's jaw clenched, he realized he could help with the comfort part.

He gave her hand a small squeeze, and she finally continued talking.

"But that was back in April. I blocked him by like August, and the first time I remember feeling like someone was following me was New Year's Eve," Morgan said. "I'd gone to Haley and James's party at their apartment."

"With a date?" Danny asked, and Nick tensed.

"No, Stew and I had met before Christmas, but he was out of town for New Year's." Morgan frowned, but Nick's entire body relaxed. "I remember leaving Haley's, and that was the first time I felt like someone was behind me. I ended up flagging a cab."

"But you didn't mention it?" Danny asked. "Not to your brothers or your dad?" She sighed and Nick gave her hand another squeeze.

"It was one o'clock in the morning. On a night in New York, when the crazies are all out. No, I didn't think anything of it."

Danny cleared his throat. "But it continued?"

Morgan didn't answer, just swallowed. With his free hand, Nick nudged the coffee mug toward her. She picked it up and took a sip.

"Morgan? Did it continue?" Danny pushed.

"Almost every time I went anywhere, until the night of the fire, but I never saw anyone. *Ever.* I thought I was getting paranoid because of the trial coming up. I thought I was being dramatic." She took a breath, which turned into a yawn.

Nick met Danny's eyes silently sending a wrap it up. Danny's head barely moved acknowledging him.

"I think that's good for now," Danny said.

Nick looked down at her half-eaten eggs and toast. "You done?" he asked, and she nodded. Now that he'd gotten some food in her, he wanted her to rest. But if he told her she had to, he knew her well enough to know she'd push back. "How about you take a shower? Then maybe we can watch a movie or something?"

She shrugged.

Nick released her hand and took both their plates to the sink. He turned to head back upstairs, grabbing Morgan's suitcase that Danny had brought back from the resort. He took her into the bathroom and grabbed a towel out of the cabinet.

"Soap, shampoo. It's all in there." He tipped his head toward the glass enclosed area. Her eyes flicked that way and then back to him before she nodded again. "I'll be in my room."

He turned and almost had the door shut.

"Nick," she called, and he paused. "Thank you."

He smiled and then headed to the hall bathroom for a quick shower before settling on his bed. He propped up a couple of pillows as he sat against the headboard to wait for her. Once he got her settled, he'd go downstairs. Maybe take that power nap Wyatt suggested.

The door opened, and a small burst of steam entered his bedroom before she appeared. Her damp hair hung past her shoulders, and she had on another torturous tank top and short combo, this one in green. Her long legs moved toward him and the scent of lilacs flooded his senses.

His entire body heated with the memories of getting to touch every part of her silky skin. Of her moving against him, her moans as she came.

She stopped a foot from the bed and her tongue snaked out to wet her lips. He fisted his hand, not letting himself reach for her. Her eyes were wide, and something about them seemed vulnerable.

"Can I lie with you?" she asked.

He wouldn't be able to say no, but he knew exactly what would happen if she got into this bed with him.

20

NICK GAVE UP fighting his ability to stay away and shifted over, making room for her. She settled next to him, sitting up against the headboard, mimicking his position. He turned to the nightstand and pulled out the remote.

"What do you want to watch?" he asked.

Her gaze shot around the room, not landing on the television. "Where is it?" she finally asked.

Nick pressed the power button, and the mirror over the dresser turned on.

"Huh, I would have never realized," she said, turning an accusing glare on him. "I thought you said there were better things to do in bed than watch TV?"

He chuckled. "I'm an asshole, aren't I?"

Her beautiful aqua eyes flashed. "A lot of the time."

Nick sighed. He owed her some words. The big, hard kind.

"Look, the way I walked away last night was shitty. I'm sorry." Her mouth lifted at the corner as her gaze softened, encouraging him to continue. "But my head's a mess. And I'm not a guy who should start a relationship," he admitted.

Instantly her eyes turned hard as aquamarines, and she

crossed her arms. "That's good, because I don't want a relationship with a Navy SEAL."

"Former SEAL," he corrected automatically. "And I'm aware. Because you think we're all broken."

She flinched. "I didn't mean it like that."

He didn't want to talk about it. Instead he added, "And I didn't mean you were just an obligation, either."

"Good thing we aren't in a relationship, because we seem to be crap at communicating." A soft chuckle forced past her lips. Her arms crossed under her chest, and his eyes zeroed in on the curve of each perfect mound.

His hands twitched, wanting to run his finger along each one. Dying to cup the weight in his hand. He swallowed, unable to glance away, even as he felt her watching him stare.

"In the interest of full disclosure." He cleared his throat to get rid of the hoarseness. "I might be crap boyfriend material, but I don't think last night was a one time thing either, Moey."

His eyes flicked up to see her teeth sink into her bottom lip.

"If we're going to be stuck together until next week, it'll probably happen again." Her breathy voice shot through him.

"Probably more than once."

She shivered at his words, and he leaned in and brushed his lips against hers before pulling back. His body pounded with need. But he knew no matter how they both felt at this moment, she needed to rest, and absolutely nothing about what his body was demanding fell into the resting category. He pulled deep into his own willpower and simply wrapped his arm around her and tucked her into his side. "But right now, we're going to watch a movie."

She groaned against his chest.

"What do you want to watch?" he asked.

"You pick." Her tone was innocent, but Nick wasn't an idiot. Statements like "I want you to choose," or "whatever makes you happy" out of a woman's mouth sent off all the "warning, warning, trap approaching" alarms.

She was a sucker for a romance, but he had something else in mind.

"You have Disney Plus?" she asked when he clicked over to the app on the bottom of the screen.

"How else would I watch all the Avengers?" he asked with a smirk.

"Of course, action movies. All about the heroes." She didn't look up, but he swore she was rolling her eyes.

"Who doesn't love the captain? Given the chance, I'd love to be the test subject for the super soldier serum." As he spoke, he clicked on the Disney Studios Animation and started a different kind of movie.

"Wait? You want to watch the Little Mermaid?" she asked, turning up to look at him. There was something in her face. It was the same thing that reflected when she talked about writing.

Nick laughed. "Freckles, this isn't about me, but I heard Prince Eric is quite the catch."

"Shut up," she said and moved her hand to pinch him, but his body instantly jerked. "Oh my God!" she shrieked, and he locked his muscles, trying not to move, but as her fingers hit just the right spot above his hip, he flinched again. "*You are ticklish!*"

Fuck, he hated being so ticklish that he couldn't help but squirm and laugh as she attacked him. There was power in size, and it didn't take him long to flip her over, straddling her body and locking her arms above her head.

Damp red hair fanned his white sheet and her blue-green eyes danced with a laughter he didn't get to see nearly enough.

"Let's see how ticklish you are?" He smirked as the pointer finger of his free hand moved along her side and down to her hip. Her response wasn't the one he was expecting, and her eyes heated. The moan that parted her lips hit straight into his gut. "Fuck, Moey," he said as her hips thrust up, cradling his cock that went from semi to ready to go in seconds.

"Please do," she replied. Her gaze dropped to his cock, and slowly she rocked against him once more. His control snapped like a single thread and he dropped his mouth to meet hers. She tasted like toothpaste and temptation as his tongue invaded her mouth, staking his claim.

Her back arched up, lifting her perfect tits to him, begging for his attention. Releasing her wrists, he complied with the unspoken request, flicking his thumb over her nipple. Her answering moan vibrated through his body, straight between his legs, increasing the pounding need to claim more than just her mouth as his own. Sliding up the thin tank top, he let his palm run along her silky skin. Goosebumps broke out across her ivory skin as his thumb brushed the bottom of her full breast, causing her breath to catch. Wedging her legs apart, he slipped his thigh between hers dropping down against her body. Needing more, he broke the kiss, to remove the material that separated them until her full breast pressed tightly against his chest.

Fuck. He was in heaven. His body ached with a need to slam into her tight heat. But he wanted her wet and ready, begging for him.

He shifted, forcing his throbbing dick into the mattress because she came first. His hand snaked lower, teasing the elastic of the too short shorts she'd spent days torturing him with. Her hips rocked up into his thigh, and he gritted his teeth. Control was his forte, but she always managed to leave his steel will in tatters at her feet.

"Nick." The breathy moan tingled against his ear and his fingers moved lower, spreading her sinking deep inside her. She rocked against his hand.

"Damn, you're already wet."

"I need you," she answered. Her back arched up; her taut nipples pressed against his chest. He dropped his head one more time, meeting her lips before he reached into the side table for the condom. He stood, dropping his sweats and boxer briefs in one motion, freeing his cock. Her eyes zeroed in on him, and she lifted off the bed, removing her own shorts.

"Let me," she said, taking a condom in her hand.

His teeth gritted at the feather-light brush of her fingers along his length.

"Morgan," he warned. But the temptress kneeling in front of him just smirked as she wrapped him in her hand and squeezed. "Fuck." His hips shot forward, pressing his cock deep in her fist before she finally slid the condom up his full length.

Her hands danced up along his stomach, over his ribs to his shoulder, pulling his mouth down to hers. Their tongues tangled as she spun them, pushing him flat on his back and, in one swift motion, settling herself fully onto him. His hands rested on her hips, but she didn't need to be guided in the motion.

His vision swirled as she rocked against him, pulling him deeper into her tight liquid vise of heat. His hips pressed up, meeting her every move enthralled as her head fell back. He rose to take one tight nipple into his mouth for a hard pull.

"Yes, Nick," she moaned, rocking faster. His stomach tightened and his legs locked. He thrust hard, losing his control. But she needed to be first. His fingers moved, finding her tight bundle of nerves and pressing in a circular motion.

Her orgasm clenched against him and he snapped, hips slamming up faster and harder until with one last thrust, his world exploded. Everything disappeared, and euphoria filled his senses. His heart clenched and then exploded in an eruption of emotions that he couldn't and didn't want to place. She collapsed onto him. He buried his face into her neck enjoying the feeling of her soft, warm skin against every part of him.

MORGAN WANTED TO ride the high of Nick's mind-blowing orgasm, but a piece of her braced for what he would say.

"Give me a second to get rid of the condom," he whispered into her ear before kissing her forehead and lifting her off of him.

He moved quickly to the bathroom. The toilet flushed and the water turned on.

The loss of his heat left her cold, and she buried herself into the soft comforter. Nick came back in, moving toward her with something in his hand. He yanked the blankets off her before she was ready, and a chill shot through her body.

"Nick!" she shrieked, trying to grab the comforter he'd flung out of her reach. When something wet pressed against her leg she jumped.

"What? You do this in every single book," he said as a warm wet cloth moved from her inner thigh and carefully wiped her off. "If it's important enough to keep repeating, it must be a big deal. And I will not be the asshole who messes this post sex thing up again."

Even his sweet always hit ridiculously, and yet she couldn't help but smile. He flung the towel into a hamper to his right with a precision that didn't seem fair before he settled himself down, tucking her into his chest and covering them both.

"Well, we're going to have to rewind." He sighed as he reached for something on the nightstand. "I mean, this chick was a fish when we started this. Now she's dancing around on legs. You definitely distracted me through some important stuff."

Morgan laughed. "I can't believe you have never seen this movie."

Nick shrugged as he started the movie over. "In a house with seven boys, princess movies weren't a thing. I mean, Mom had some of her athletes stay with us—"

"Athletes?" Morgan asked.

"She was a gymnastics coach. Really good. A lot of her girls made the national team," Nick replied as he rewound the movie. "I think she always wished she had a daughter. That's why she had so many kids. But she brought a lot of her athletes into the house."

"Don't you have a sister?"

"Yes and no. She's not my biological sister, but Beth is my sister in every way that matters."

Morgan wondered if she was one of his mother's athletes, but Nick didn't say. "I'm surprised your dad allowed it. My dad only had four of us, but the idea of more definitely would have made his head explode."

"My dad always indulged my mom. He used to tell me all the time that it's a man's job to take care of his woman." Nick paused. "He said every woman needs to be taken care of in different ways, and you have to pay attention. But it doesn't change your job. Take care of her." He chuckled. "My mom always said she didn't need to be taken care of. My dad would laugh that she was fine until it snowed—then she needed someone to shovel. But the truth was, they fit each other in a million ways that I look back on and realize how lucky they were."

"Were?"

"They died almost fifteen years ago. Kinda like swans. My mom died, then my dad died six months later. Almost like he couldn't live without her."

Morgan saw the first date on his ribs, and her finger ran along it.

"Yeah, the dates they died. My mom and dad are first. Grandparents." His finger pointed out dates. "Some guys from the academy." He moved to the next row. "BUD/S." Then dropped another rib. "My brother."

"You lost a brother?" Morgan asked.

Nick nodded. His hand moved lower, and he pointed to two small dots that scarred his lower abdomen. "Gallbladder deformity runs in the family. I took mine out because it was prone to infection. He said he didn't want unnecessary surgery, but his got infected, and ruptured. The infection went to his heart."

Morgan's finger moved from the lines of dates to the scars from surgery. "So not battle scars."

"Not those," he said. "This was an in and out, when I was twenty-six. Shot as I was almost on the helo for the extraction. Stupid rookie mistake." His finger moved to another scar just over his hip. Her fingers moved next to his, and he jumped again with a small chuckle.

"I can't believe you're ticklish."

"It's a national secret. Almost no one knows."

She rolled her eyes and glanced back at the tattoos on his ribs. Six dates exactly the same finished the bottom line.

"Lewie's," he said as his finger moved along the first of the six. "And the rest of my team. And the scars on my thigh from the same day."

"Were you in the car with him?" Morgan asked hesitantly. She knew some details, but not many. Roadside bomb Lewie died on impact.

"Yeah." Nick's answer was clipped, and Morgan would not push. But he started talking. About the supply run, how Lewie took a route Nick wouldn't have taken, following orders that were supposed to help keep the peace. How they had just gotten out of town when the bomb went off. "I didn't get hurt in the explosion. Neither did the reporter traveling with us. We were fine."

Nick paused, but Morgan felt him swallow.

"What happened?" she whispered.

"We're trained not to leave anyone behind. You take your fallen with you. But even if we weren't when you live through something like that." He paused for a long time, staring at the ceiling. Her ear rested against his chest and the only sound was the steady thump of his heart. "Watching your friends die in front of your eyes." Nick's chin brushed against the top of her head slowly. "You leave so much of yourself in that broken Hummer. You can't leave anything else behind."

That squeezed her heart in a big way, and she tucked herself further into him, wishing a hug would cure the demons she couldn't understand.

"Car two was bad. Not stable. It was rough getting the guys out. Just as we got the last body, it rolled. Pinned my leg under the chassise." Nick sounded robotic. "If it wasn't for the reporter, I don't know if we would have figured out how to get it off me." His entire body shook, and she squeezed tighter.

"It's okay, you can stop," she said.

"No," he said fiercely. "You need to understand. This was all on me."

"On you?" she asked.

"I should have been driving. I should have changed our course. I should have done something. These men counted on me. And I let them all down." Nick swallowed.

She sat up, forcing him to look at her. "No."

He blinked.

"Nick, you don't get to blame yourself."

"Moey." The painfully drawn out whisper crushed her. But he didn't need pity in this moment.

"No," she said fiercely. "You all were doing a job. An assignment. You followed *orders.* And when shit went south, you got your men out and brought the bodies home. You did your job. You're a hero."

He gave a clipped nod. "But the job meant I needed to be more than just a hero."

His words cut through her as she turned them in her mind. This man had been through so much loss, had many things he couldn't ever share, had seen so much. And yet could laugh and joke. Tease and let someone tickle him. He could bark orders and read romance books. He loved his family. And would watch princess movies for her. "You are so much more than a hero, Nick. Don't doubt that."

His smile was sad as he pulled her back to him, tucking her into his side.

"Damn it," he said, and she glanced up at him. "We're going to have to rewind again because this chick has legs, and we missed it."

She scoffed. Nick kept proving to be more than she expected, and her heart was in so much trouble.

21

THE LIGHT PEEKED through the blinds as Morgan opened her eyes. She didn't have to look to know Nick wasn't next to her. Last night, after the Little Mermaid——take three—Nick threw on some clothes and made them grilled cheese. Then he'd insisted on watching The Hating Game and proceeded to blame her because they had to rewind that one too.

His sex drive was never-ending, and he'd reached for her a few times. She was definitely sore this morning. In all the best ways.

She glanced around, seeing a pile of clothes on the end of the bed. The chuckle escaped her lips as she read the note.

For my sanity, please.

Fifteen minutes, a shower and a toothbrush later, she was standing in the kitchen in gray sweats and a Naval Academy hoodie. Neither Nick nor Wyatt looked up. This morning the poker table that sat in his kitchen was covered with laptops. Three in front of Wyatt as he moved between the keyboards on two different machines.

"There's coffee and bagels on the counter. Give me a second, Moey." Nick's eyes, shielded by the thick black rimmed glasses he wore when reading or using the computer, were focused intently on his screen.

Morgan moved to the counter and grabbed a coffee mug, filling it up. It was almost eleven, but even with the time, she wasn't hungry. Food never appealed to her first thing in the morning. So, ignoring the bagels, she glanced for the milk.

"Wait—right there—pause it." Nick got up and moved behind Wyatt. "Do you see it, D?"

"What the hell are the letters, though?" Boomed from the third computer in front of Wyatt.

"I might have an answer for that." Nick's penetrating gaze finally flicked up to her. The corner of his mouth lifted just slightly before he pushed off the back of Wyatt's chair, heading her way. His only pause on the way was to grab the milk from the fridge. He topped off her cup before smiling at her.

Slate-blue eyes burned into hers, and her stomach flipped as his left hand came out to rest on her hip.

"Morning," he said, and his gaze never left hers. Something about their connection seemed more intimate than if he'd kissed her.

"I like this look," she whispered, letting her finger run along the stubble on his jaw. "With the glasses, it's like 'sexy librarian,' male style."

Nick chuckled.

Wyatt cleared his throat. "Need a few more minutes with the machine, and then you can human the fuck out."

Nick growled as his eyes cut to Wyatt, but he guided her back to the table with a hand on the small of her back.

"Shouldn't you put the milk away?" she asked as she carefully took a sip of her coffee.

He shook his head. "You usually have two cups first thing."

Her eyes shot back to him over the lip of her mug. It had only been a few days, but he held on to the details about her that ex-boyfriends hadn't picked up in months. Was it because he was being paid to watch her or because she mattered?

"Hey Morgan." A voice called from the screen, and Morgan looked down to see two faces.

"Grumpy." She nodded to the dark-haired frowner she recognized. The second man on the screen chuckled and pulled on his thick brown beard.

"Donovan, our resident hacker," Wyatt introduced.

"Says the guy that just cracked the firewall himself." Donovan's brown eyes twinkled.

Wyatt's eyes widened playfully and he shook his blond head with a chuckle. "Dude, I'm West Point criminal justice. I'm the dumbest guy in the room."

"Sure you are, Hawaii." Donovan snorted.

Morgan raised her eyebrow in question.

"My dad was stationed on Oahu until I graduated from high school," Wyatt said with a smirk. "I know all the good beaches if you want a personal tour." Nick's hand shot out, and smacked the back of his head before she could respond. "I meant both of you, like you *and Morgan*."

"Be professional, please," Nick mumbled, shaking his head.

"Sometimes it's clear how you and Grant are brothers." The guys on the screen both laughed at Wyatt's statement.

Morgan shook her head with a small chuckle. It was like being with her brothers—the give and take of shit being passed around like chocolate on Valentine's Day.

Nick sighed. "Pull up the graphic, please, Wyatt. I want Morgan to look."

She glanced at the screen, seeing the black-and-white image. Reaching out, she ran her fingers along the multiple infinity symbols. Eight of them tied together in the center. On the loop, a letter. An initial.

"Where did you get this?" she asked, looking away from the screen to Nick.

"You know what it is?" Donovan asked

"Yeah, it's a mockup I was going to use for an author graphic for my website and social media. But no one thought it looked romancey enough."

"*A–D–E–L*. Addison, Dylan, Emma, Liam. Characters names," Nick said beside her. "The letters are your characters' names."

She nodded. "Eight infinity symbols together making a loopy circle or a flower, but each symbol has the two characters' initials inside it. The couples from each book."

"How would Reed have gotten this?" Nick asked and nodded at Wyatt, who clicked off the graphic and opened a Facebook page. Her frown formed when she heard Reed's name, but she gasped when she saw the photo.

"Wait," she said, making Wyatt pause. "He photoshopped a picture of us?"

"What?" Nick asked.

"That asshole." Her jaw clenched. "That was a picture of Louis and me. It's at Howard and Rain's wedding. The last photo I have of us." She glared at the screen. "Right there." She pointed to the nautical compass on his forearm. That proved her point, but no one said anything. Instead, she glanced up at Nick, who was looking at Seabass on the computer. Neither man looked happy.

"Wyatt," Nick said. Wyatt clicked to another photo. This one of her graphics. Then a second photo of Reed standing on a beach. Morgan's eyes widened as she saw the design on his shirt just above his heart.

"He could have asked someone to make it or drawn it himself." She paused. "I mean, I was trying to pick graphics when he and I were together. I showed them to him. But I never thought—" The words died, and she swallowed as Wyatt opened another folder on the computer. This one full of photos. Too many photos of a man wearing hoodies in multiple colors with her design. She took a step back at the sheer number of photos of Reed around New York City.

"Oh my God," she said, and Nick's arm came up around her. She turned to him. "I can't believe he was following me. He's a chemist—he set the fire—*he tried to drug me*?"

Yesterday, when Danny was asking questions, she hadn't really believed it could be Reed. He'd been crazy, demanding she talk to him. Saying he'd gone by her house. Not understanding where she'd gone when she left Florida, but to imagine a guy she dated tracked her to New York and set her apartment on fire seemed unbelievable.

"Where is he?" she asked before she realized. "Oh—you can't find him."

She swallowed.

Nick tucked her close and dropped his mouth to her ear. "Moey, listen to me. This nut job won't get within a hundred feet of you. Ever again." The promise was a fire-breathing oath. And in his arms, she believed that truth. "I have every one of my guys on this. This is our only priority, but we need your help. And so does Danny."

She pulled away and looked into his eyes. Fierce determination raged in their depths. She dropped her head against his strong shoulder. And she felt his lips press into her head. She had to get it together. No panicking until the crisis was past. She leaned into his strength.

"What do you need?" she asked.

Two hours later, she still sat at the same table in front of the computers. Danny, Seabass, and Donovan were on the screens. Wyatt and Nick sat on either side. They all peppered her with questions over and over, similarly worded, differently. All about Reed. Anything that would help them find him. But she knew by their expression she didn't know enough to be helpful.

"Guys, let's take a break," Nick suggested, and he paused the audio and video on the feed before shutting the laptop. His eyes cut to Wyatt, who stood up.

"I'll see if the guys outside need coffee." He rose to his feet and headed through the living room and out the front door.

As soon as it shut behind Wyatt, Nick reached out, pulling her toward him. She settled onto his muscular thigh and rested her head against the top of his. His thick black hair brushed against her cheek as a powerful arm wrapped around her.

"You have nothing to worry about. We'll find him," Nick said.

"I just don't get it," she admitted. "Why is he doing this?"

Nick's eyes narrowed, but he didn't answer, just pulled her tighter against him. She lifted her head. His gaze didn't move from across the room.

"What do you know?" she asked. So many times, she thought they were past the secrets, but then, in moments like these, she remembered exactly how many Nick had.

"Every time I can, I tell you things," Nick said, and his eyes skated over her face before they moved away again. "But sometimes I need some trust."

Those words were like lead in her gut, and automatically she tensed, shifting away. Instead of pulling her back, his arm dropped from around her. She moved back to her own seat. Nick turned and looked like he might say something, but the phone on the table buzzed.

He picked it up. "Yeah?" His eyes flicked back to her, but they were guarded in a way she hadn't seen before. "Sure." He dropped the phone. "Haley's here. She's been bugging us all to see you since yesterday. I told her she could swing by."

He stood up and moved to the door to open it before Wyatt and Haley followed him back into the kitchen.

"I feel like every time I see you lately, the conversation needs to start with *what the fuck,* Moey," Haley said, and although she crossed her arms, she sent Morgan a sympathetic smile.

"Finally, understanding where my dad was coming from?" Morgan joked since that was her father's go to conversation starter with all of his kids. Wyatt laughed, and Haley rolled her eyes as she set a large container on the slate island in the center of the kitchen.

"What's that?" Morgan asked.

"Soup," Haley answered. Morgan glanced from Wyatt to Nick, silently asking if they'd told her to bring it. "I mean, you bring soup for sick people and surgeries, right?"

Nick glared at Wyatt as he snickered.

Haley tossed her hands into the air. "I don't know the etiquette for visiting your best friend after she gets blown up and drugged by a stalker she didn't tell you about."

Morgan winced at the not quiet "bless her heart" Haley had just tossed into that sentence. She hadn't talked to Haley much this week. But everything, from the time she'd had coffee with her and Bex in New York until today, had moved like a flash of light. She blinked, and it was over. Yet as she watched Nick's eyes narrow, knowing something had upset him, it was hard to imagine she hadn't known Nick forever.

"Well," Haley added, waiting for an explanation.

"Haley, don't. She was following my orders. You want to give someone shit for not talking to you about it, give it to me." Nick crossed his arms and moved between Haley and the table. Almost like he was stepping between them. But that didn't make sense.

Haley just smiled. "Interesting, very interesting. But where can Moey and I talk?"

"We can move this stuff," Wyatt said, and headed to the table.

"Without the testosterone?" Haley added. Morgan laughed.

"It's pretty empty, but it's got a door." Nick walked to the small sitting room off the great room and opened a door. "Go ahead." He moved back to his own computer at the table and picked up his glasses. It was the seat he'd been at when she came down the stairs hours ago. All his energy focused straight back on what he was doing before she came down this morning.

Morgan watched him for a minute with a sinking stomach, but he didn't look up. Finally, she followed Haley into the other room. He was mad; she knew that, but she wasn't the one with the secrets.

"Does he have kids?" Haley asked.

Morgan shut the door behind them. "No, he says he bought this house from his sister."

This must have been a playroom at some point because besides shelves labeled with tags like *Legos, books, cars,* and *buddies*, the small loveseat was the only other thing in the room.

"I think I somehow missed the details of your week?" Haley asked as she sat down, crossing her arms with a frown.

"Abridged version." She sighed and went through it for Haley.

"How did Nick know Louis?" Haley interrupted almost immediately.

"Oh, he—" She stopped. Normally she'd tell Haley they were on the teams together or Nick was Louis's commanding officer. But Nick hadn't even told his family. "They were stationed together."

Haley's head tipped like she might ask a follow up question, but before she got the chance, Morgan continued on with her story, finishing up with everything she'd learned today.

"I never liked Reed." Haley lifted a finger to her lips in thought before she shook her head.

"Really?" Morgan raised her eyebrows. "That's it?"

"I already knew most of that. After the issue at James's place, one of Nick's guys came over and told us the entire story. And I even get why Nick and James kept us apart at the resort."

Now it was Morgan's turn to cross her arms and stare.

"I know what you're thinking. Why didn't I tell you about the resort?" Haley nodded and tucked her blonde hair over her shoulder. "I know you want to know and we'll get there, but I want to talk about Nick first."

Morgan shrugged. "I told you he's the bodyguard that's being paid to watch me." She thought back to the conversation right before Haley got here. "Full of his secrets and lies, and lives to be the hero."

Haley rolled her eyes. "I knew it." Then she pulled out her phone and played with it for a minute before she passed it over to Morgan. "Look at this."

It was a photo of Nick and Morgan at James's resort. Dinner. Nick had been asking her about how she came up with her stories. She talked through appetizers and dinner almost without pause about how ideas struck her, how she plotted, or didn't. And he sat, engaged the entire time. The man who normally couldn't stop focused on her the entire time. She'd felt like the only person in the room. And in the picture, he looked captivated—about how she came up with ideas for romance books.

"I've met Nick multiple times, and James talks about him a lot." Haley took her phone back. "He has a lot of those traits that are typical Navy."

Morgan snorted.

"But he's also totally different from what you'd expect," Haley said. "He came to James pissed when he left Bex."

"What?"

"According to James, Nick confronted him. Told him you don't leave your family. James expected a lecture on commitment. But it didn't come. Apparently, Nick thinks marriage isn't supposed to be easy. That it takes work, and that love is a verb, not a feeling. And if you're not feeling it." Haley paused, smirking.

"If you're not feeling it, what?" Morgan asked.

Haley smiled. "Then you're doing it wrong, because your job is to take care of your woman."

Morgan sucked in a breath. Nick had said that same thing last night.

"I know you hate that he's Navy," Haley said. "But don't miss out on this." She flashed her phone with the photo at

Morgan once more. "Because you're jumping to conclusions about something he can't change."

Morgan looked at the photo again, unsure of how to feel. "Why didn't you tell me about the resort?"

Haley rolled her eyes. "Okay deflect, but truthfully, Moey, it goes together."

She glanced up, unsure what her best friend meant.

"We had this entire plan about what we wanted in our future husbands," Haley said and shrugged. "And shit, I'm not going to lie and say the fact that James was married before and has kids hasn't added stress to our relationship. But I'm willing to deal with that stress for him."

"I know," Morgan agreed.

"But here's the thing." Haley glanced down. "It's the first thing you see about him. And you hold that against him. So, he and I both feel like he has to prove to you he's not awful because he's divorced."

Morgan's eyes widened. "Wow." That stung. She teased James, but she always thought she was nice to him.

"No," Haley said. "Wait, that sounds worse than it is. I get why you feel that way. After your mom died, your dad just randomly ran through women, and your brothers can't settle down either."

"Going to leave out your story?" Morgan asked.

"No, that's the thing. I know my dad was the nail in the coffin, because we both thought my parents had the perfect marriage."

"They did until he deployed and cheated on your mom. And everything got fucked up."

"Yes, between their divorce and the move, it was a lot. So when we were sixteen we made the list to make sure we never ended up like any of those women," Haley said.

Morgan nodded. "No heroes. Only boring, average, steady men."

Haley nodded. "Who weren't too good looking or too rich—like owning a resort type rich . . ."

Morgan froze. "You didn't tell me about James owning the resort because you thought I'd just add that to the reasons he wasn't good enough?"

"I was going to tell you—eventually. I promise I was. But I wanted you to see him before you checked anymore of the 'he's not good enough' boxes." Haley said. "Because he's not a match to our list, but he loves me, Moey. And I love him."

"I know," she said. "I'm happy for you."

"But he doesn't check our boxes," Haley admitted.

Morgan stared at the ground. She remembered her conversation with Bex, and her realization that she'd judged her. Now, apparently, Haley thought she was doing it to James, too.

"I'm sorry, Haley. I just want you to be happy," Morgan said.

"I know you do, and I love you for that. And the thing is every time you spend time with James, you become more team James. Because you see him for him, and that's all I wanted, which is why I didn't tell you about the resort," Haley admitted.

Morgan took a deep breath. "Well, I kind of already decided to be more open-minded and I guess I should work on not judging everyone by a checklist."

"Good," Haley agreed. "Start with Nick, because he might not check all the boxes, but holy shit, if you let him, he could check all the ones that mattered."

Morgan opened her mouth, but then slammed it shut again. Because what could she say? Haley was right. Nick was more than a checklist. But the problem was, even if she let go and trusted him, with his secrets, and her heart. He'd been pretty clear he didn't even want her past the end of the stalker problem.

And she couldn't change that.

22

"CAN WE GO through the timeline again?" Seabass said from the video chat on the screen. "He sees pictures of Morgan in New York, and he comes up here."

Nick gritted his teeth, hating to think about Reed's level of obsession. He'd quit his job two days after Haley posted pictures of Morgan at her wedding. He got on a flight to JFK airport and checked into the Marriot a few blocks from Haley and James's place for three days. Now that they knew what they were looking for, he was easy to track.

"City's huge. He realizes he can't find her. But he knows where Haley is, which is why, for the next two weeks, he's outside Haley's apartment building, on and off." Wyatt flipped to the photos of Reed around Haley's apartment in December.

"He realizes this is going to take longer, so he gets a job," Donovan started.

Nick stood and paced behind Wyatt's chair.

"Or my theory, which makes more sense, especially since he moved to an extended stay under a fake name. That's sketchy as fuck and says I'm already planning something," Wyatt pointed out.

"Probably, it's also why he doesn't approach Haley, even if he believes Morgan's in the apartment staying with her. So, he wants chemicals to start a fire to get her out," Nick agreed. Morgan was a homebody; she didn't go out a lot. Especially when she was writing. It made sense for Reed to expect she might not leave the apartment.

"Yeah, because he probably believes Morgan's hiding from him personally now." Wyatt raised his eyebrows before continuing. "Like I said, he gets the job in Jersey at the Passaic chemical plant. He's over qualified for it, and they hire him without question. And he immediately starts to skim off chemicals."

"It's smart as hell that he skimmed it slow enough over the course of weeks that it didn't flag as a theft, just general loss," Donovan said. "We have pictures of him outside Haley's house on New Year's Eve, but we don't know why he didn't approach Morgan that night."

"Typical stalker MO says it's because he's pissed at her for avoiding him," Wyatt said, and Seabass grunted.

"But he followed her, just not fast enough. He must lose her when she gets into the cab, or he follows her back but Morgan's building with a doorman scares him from going inside. Until finally, he sits outside the coffee place the night of the fire. He follows her back to her place, and wants her out of the apartment."

"Or he's pissed Stew was up there with her," Seabass suggested. Nick gritted his teeth; he didn't love that reminder either.

"He sends his home-made fire bomb into the bedroom when he knows she's in the living room. And waits for her," Wyatt added.

"But she goes down the fire escape. And once again, he loses her. Until Instagram and the resort." Seabass sighed.

"He breaks into the small local lab and makes a mess, claiming animal testing, which the lab has had constant issues with, causing them to overlook the canister of sedative missing," Wyatt explained.

"Again, smart. We need to figure out how he's getting around." Nick pulled at the back of his neck as he paced. Reed had to have a car, but the Honda he'd driven in Florida was still sitting out in front of Reed's apartment, and there wasn't a single record of him renting a car.

He listened as the guys went over next steps and plans for moving Morgan to Florida to testify in the drug case tomorrow morning. Nick had already talked to the Admiral, and he was sending a private plane for them so they could land on a base about an hour outside of Tallahassee.

After the video call ended, Nick just stared at the screen but he wasn't getting anywhere. His head was replaying his conversation with Morgan. Maybe he should have told her about Reed's sealed record. It was a gray area, something he knew about, but shouldn't. But could he tell her?

"You good? 'Cause I'm going to need to move to the counter if you don't stop shaking the table. I'm trying to code, and the lines are jumping like I'm in a boat," Wyatt said.

"What?" Nick asked, but he stopped his leg from bouncing.

"Man, you sat here with Morgan for two and half hours, holding her hand through the questions without an issue. Not once did I feel like I was riding the backroads in Afghanistan."

Nick focused back on his computer, scrolling through the traffic cam shots near the resort, hoping to flag Reed's car.

Wyatt sighed and started to stand up.

"Sorry, I just…" Nick paused working out how to ask the question. "Think Morgan needs to know about the juvie record?"

Wyatt leaned back in his chair and smirked at Nick. "You asking me if our protectee needs information or if you should keep secrets from your girl? Because those are two completely different questions."

"Forget it." Nick shook his head. It was ridiculous to think Wyatt wouldn't read more into the question. The kid was the smartest person in every room.

"No man." Wyatt shook his head. "Is she a 'a girl' or she a 'the girl'?"

Nick turned and raised his brows.

"Come on, you know what I mean."

"No, I have no fucking idea what you mean ninety percent of the time, Wyatt." Nick pulled at the back of his neck before resting his elbows on his knees.

"'A girls' come around all the time. You like 'em, it has potential, but if it doesn't work out well—you tried." He shrugged his shoulders before kicking his feet up on the chair next to him. "But '*the* girl' only flies into your world once, and she kicks your ass, makes you rethink everything you thought you knew, and the idea of her not being around tomorrow is a gut punch. And that girl, she gets all of you, no secrets, no hesitation." Wyatt smirked. "Which one is Morgan?"

Wyatt never ceased to amaze him. The kid seemed like a complete tool half the time. And the other half he came up with things like this.

"Don't look at me like that. After watching your brother Grant's entire world turn around when Trish walked into his life." Wyatt shook his head. "Shit, man—I know 'the girl' is a thing."

Not that Wyatt was wrong. No one in the family questioned the idea that Trish was the best thing that happened to Grant. But those two were a natural fit: same interests, same goals. If that's what forever looked like, then Morgan definitely wasn't his forever. Maybe she was right, they were just a hell of a for now. So he didn't need guilt about keeping things to himself.

Wyatt's boot thumped against the hardwood floor as he shifted in his seat to pull something out of his pocket.

"Hello?" His brow wrinkled before his eyes cut to Nick. "Yeah, he's sitting right next to me." His head tipped. "Uh, sure, man, hold on." Wyatt held out the phone. "It's your brother-in-law."

Shit. Nick was actively avoiding his family's messages, but if Marc had resorted to calling Wyatt, his sister could be in labor.

"Pretty boy." Nick forced his tone to be light, and Wyatt went back to his computer.

"She's texted you fourteen times about tonight. I know this is not reasonable. I get it, trust me. I live with it. But women who are almost eight months pregnant with twins aren't expected to be reasonable."

"Shit, Marc, I'm working a case. You know this."

"And as Beth has pointed out, this is Clayton's last game of his college career, and it's the BCS National Championship. She can't go to Cali because she can't fly. You promised to watch this game with Danny, Corey, and me. You know what she's like."

Nick groaned. His youngest brother's football game was tonight, and his sister's legendary ability to nag the fuck out of the Evans men was the reason he was ignoring her. "Yeah, I know, but I have Lewie's sister."

"Bring her. My house is Fort Knox. You know that."

Wyatt cleared his throat. "Family night definitely separates an 'a' from a 'the.'"

"Eyes open, mouth shut, Wyatt," Nick snapped. "But fine, we'll come. Not for long because she has a zoom call for prep on her testimony tomorrow on the drug case until six. And we can't stay late because we're flying to Florida at four am."

"As long as you're here," Marc said, and then hung up.

"I love your family," Wyatt said. "Can I come?"

"If you go through these traffic cam photos and find what Reed's driving before we go." Nick chuckled, knowing it was an impossible mission.

"Oh, I already coded the program to search all the traffic cam footage for a forty-mile radius of Love Canyon for the last sixteen hours. I just got it running. Give me an hour, and I got you." Wyatt turned his computer to Nick. The photos flicked through at a speed the eye couldn't catch. "Sometimes the nine years between us, feels like a million, huh?"

"Fuck off." Nick shook his head. But twenty-five minutes later, when they had a license plate, and the make and model of the car Reed had been driving, it was hard to be mad at him. Especially when Danny had APBs out before they even walked into Beth and Marc's place that night.

"Why does your sister have secret service?" Morgan asked as they walked through the large entryway of Beth and Marc's house. Morgan had come out of her conversation with Haley in a better mood, almost like she'd forgiven Nick for his silence in a way she hadn't before.

Although her focus was on the trial prep, Nick could see she was nervous about it. But even still, it didn't come across as dramatic as her brothers described. It was quiet and focused. Almost as if she was scared to mess up more than she was scarred by what happened. In fact, with everything Morgan had been through in the past year, she didn't seem scarred at all. Or dramatic. It impressed the hell out of him.

"The secret service is because her dad's the vice-president." Wyatt responded to the questions before Nick could answer.

"VP Campbell," Morgan said. "Oh— Elizabeth Campbell. She *was* one of your mom's athletes."

Nick nodded. "And she married my oldest brother. They had two kids before he died."

"How long have she and Marc been married?"

"Two years," Nick answered before walking into the living room. Danny, Marc and Beth were already on the sectional. "I made it, and I brought extras."

"Don't get up," Wyatt said quickly, as Beth attempted to rock her enormous stomach into a standing position. He made his way to greet all three.

"Thanks, man," Marc said, giving Nick a fist bump. "Beer's in the fridge."

Morgan shook her head slightly, and they both sank into the couch.

"Clayton plays for USC, right? I'm going to root for them, but I'm an Alabama Alum, so I mean roll tide is in my blood. Don't hate me if I cheer wrong." Morgan laughed, and Nick rested his arm on the sofa behind her. He watched Beth and Marc's eyes zero in on his arm and braced for a reaction.

"It's okay, our daughter, who is at the game with her uncles, normally roots for the prettiest colors even if they aren't Clayton's." Beth laughed and the conversation moved on.

Nick was surprised how easily the next half hour went. Beth and Morgan chatted about everything from house decor to baby shit. And even Wyatt seemed to behave.

Corey walked in with a blue plastic bag, dropping it on the counter, and sending Nick a nod. He pulled his arm from behind Morgan and stood up, walking across the huge open concept great room to the marble island in the kitchen. Nick stuck out his hand for a fist bump.

"Thanks for getting that for me," Nick said.

Corey Matthew had been a part of the family for so long Nick thought of him as another brother.

"Bringing a date to beer night, huh?" Corey asked. His two-tone brown eyes bounced from Nick to where Morgan sat on the far side of the large open area. Morgan and the others were far enough away they couldn't hear Corey but Nick still wasn't confident this should be labeled a date.

"It's not beer night, it's Clay's game. Beth freaked out, and Marc whined."

Corey snorted a laugh. "He asked me how to get you here. I said beg."

"You're an asshole. But anyway, the job had to come." Nick's gaze rested on Morgan as she chatted with Wyatt. Her long, thin fingers lifted to tuck a strand of red hair behind her ears. They had to be talking about her books; her face was lit up like that every time her work came into the conversation. He felt that pull of desire settled deep in the pit of his stomach. Man could Moey get him going, and her passion for her writing was an immense turn-on for him.

"So you're not into her?" Corey asked, and Nick turned back. "Because you just sent me an 'SOS help a bro out' text."

"She's Lewie's sister, and a job. She's going back to Florida when it's done." Nick's eyes flicked back to Morgan. But even as he said it, he frowned because the idea of her leaving sucked.

"Can I give you some unsolicited advice?" Corey's sudden serious tone had Nick turning his way again. He popped off the top of the beer and offered it to him, but Nick shook his head.

"When has anyone in this family ever *not* shared an unwanted opinion?" Nick raised an eyebrow at Corey, who chuckled as he took a swallow of his drink.

"Don't lie to yourself," Corey said. "Don't say it's nothing and let her leave, if it's not nothing." Corey cleared his throat, and cracked his neck left and right before continuing. "Because when she's gone, you just have to live with it because you didn't stop her."

Corey lifted his beer and downed the rest in one long chug. Nick had no idea what was up with him, but at the moment, Corey definitely seemed off.

"Hey you good, man?" Nick asked.

Corey shrugged. "When it rains, scars ache, right?" For the first time, Nick saw a crack in the "I'm good" vibe Corey always threw off.

"Corey-"

But he shook his head and grabbed another beer from the fridge. "I'm chill."

That was the word Corey always used, but Nick finally realized it didn't mean good or even okay. Nick opened his mouth to argue and then shut it again.

"I mean it, if you and Lewie's sister have something real— say it. If she's just your fuck buddy..." Corey shrugged and took another swig of beer.

Nick growled.

"What?" Corey asked, too innocently.

"Fucker, it's not like that," Nick snapped, and Corey full on smirked.

"What's it like?" It was the question Wyatt had asked earlier just worded differently.

But this time Nick figured out Corey's game, and he didn't spit out the first thing in his head. Corey was good at working people, but Nick wasn't ready to lay everything out yet. Mostly because he didn't know.

"No idea," Nick finally said.

"What are you two whispering about?" Danny asked, heading to the fridge.

"Nick needed me to get his girl some White Claw," Corey chuckled. "Imagine that, White Claw on beer night."

Danny shut the fridge, three beers in his hand. "Yeah, Beth's switched to ginger ale, club soda when Trish is here, White Claw for Morgan. Beer night's going to need a new name. But bubbly shit water night doesn't have the same ring to it."

Nick shook his head and grabbed a White Claw out of the bag before heading back to the sectional.

"Here," he said, passing it to Morgan as he settled next to her.

"You got this for me?" she asked.

"Anything for you, freckles."

Her eyes shot to him with the statement. Almost like she was asking if he meant it. But he didn't know how to respond. Should he tell her that, yeah, he thought he meant it? But he kept his mouth shut. Just because she was feeling like "the girl" to him didn't mean she thought of him as anything more than "a guy."

23

THE SUN HADN'T even risen above the horizon as Morgan settled into the soft gray leather. Private jets, even the government-issued ones, had a comfort that commercial air didn't allow. She wasn't sure if it was her dad or Nick that had pulled the strings to get them on this plane, but she wasn't going to complain.

"You okay?" Nick asked for the third time as he settled in the seat next to her in the first row of the small plane.

She'd told him she was okay a few times already, but she nodded. She turned her head. The first two rows of seats faced forward like a typical airplane. Rows three and four faced each other with tables between, more for a working situation than simply travel. Wyatt, Seabass, Donovan, and three other guys she didn't know settled into the seats set up around small dark-wood tables like the pro travelers they all were. No one seemed stressed.

Well—apart from Nick.

He had assured her, although they had yet to track down Reed, she was safe. But yesterday hung between them. Neither had addressed the fact that Nick wasn't telling her something.

Morgan was trying to let it go, because what Nick had said was true. When he could, he'd shared with her. More than he needed to. About himself, about her brother, about the case. If he wasn't saying something, it might be classified, or illegally obtained, or maybe it was just something that would scare her for no helpful reason. So, she'd decided to trust him. But she didn't know how to tell him that either.

They should have talked last night, but when Haley left, she had to get on a Zoom meeting with the district attorney and Donald about the court appearance today. And then Nick had rushed her out the door to his sister's. Once they got home, the second they were alone in his bedroom, he'd kissed her. And lust took over. Sex, sleep, no words. A part of her knew that was wrong, but at the same time, today, he was bringing her back to Florida.

The plan was to go to the courthouse, and then move straight to the base in Pensacola and stay with her father. It made sense because the base was safer than anywhere else, but she was pretty sure that Nick would become *just* her bodyguard the second they walked through her father's door.

She glanced out the oval window onto the tarmac of the small airport. Lines lit the path of the runway, and the skyline of New York shone behind it. But not even a sliver of the morning sun was peeking up yet.

"I swear you can hear a person think," Nick said. "Almost like their mind racing has its own sound."

"You can hear everyone think?" she asked. Her question was flippant because he was asking her why she was quiet without saying the word.

"No," he said, and she turned away from the window. His slate eyes met hers, and once again, they seemed to burn into her. Almost like they wanted to say things his mouth didn't. But she didn't know what they were. "I don't pay enough attention to hear most people think, Moey. But you, I hear your silence almost as loud as your words."

Her heart fluttered, and Nick leaned in to press his warm lips against her forehead. His breath danced along her skin, and she melted into him.

"I trust you to tell me things when they're important. I believe you know the difference between secrets and sensitive information. And it wasn't fair that I assumed you were hiding something." Morgan rushed the words out before she stopped herself from saying them.

Nick pulled back slightly and then forced her to look up at him.

"He dated a girl named Danielle when he was sixteen," Nick mumbled. "She broke up with him after a few months, but he wouldn't leave her alone. Kept showing up at the house. Her parents called the police a few times, but they did little until he finally broke into her bedroom window. The family moved away after that, but he continued to stalk her on social media until she stopped using it." Nick's eyes swept over her face. "Red hair, green eyes, freckles. He called her Danny."

Morgan sucked in her breath and glanced away, staring down at the swirls of gray on the carpet below her feet. The seat jerked as the plane moved.

"I know you said he called you Gany. But the way these guys work—"

"She and I have become the same person in his mind." Her hands quivered, and she fisted them together in her lap.

"Probably. After counseling and community service, his record was sealed when he turned eighteen." He placed his large palm over her hands, giving them a small squeeze. "But we'll get him, trust me." The growl of the statement vibrated through her.

"I know," she said and turned to the window as the plane sped up, lifting off the ground. The New York area got smaller as the plane rose farther into the air until finally, she couldn't see any of the details of the houses or streets below. It should feel good getting away. But he'd follow her.

"Hey," Nick said. She turned his way. In his hand was a book. She recognized the lake on the cover instantly. Her favorite small town romance series. "Get your mind off things for a few hours."

She took the book out of his hand. "How'd you get it? It just came out this week."

He flashed a smile that made her heart skip. "I have my ways."

Just like the Blackberry White Claw last night, something she hadn't asked for but he'd made show up. The way he paid attention to what she mentioned liking in passing and then pulled it out later made her feel special. Important.

"You're kinda great, Nick," she said quietly.

Nick shook his head. "I'm always going to be a fucking mess. Don't forget that, Moey."

Before she could respond, he unbuckled and moved back to sit with his team at the table, leaving her alone with the reminder that even if she was trying to be open to the idea of something between them more permanent, he wasn't.

She turned the last page of the book, smiling at Jackson and Ashley's happily ever after. Enemies to lovers was a favorite of hers, and the banter between these two had her laughing out loud. It definitely made the plane ride and drive go fast.

"Five minutes out," Howard said from the driver's seat. Her brother had met them with two SUVs at the airstrip on base. He was driving them over to the court house.

She was squeezed between Wyatt and Nick in the middle of the black Escalade. Seabass was up front next to Howard.

"This entire thing makes me feel way more important than I am," she mumbled to no one.

"No shit, Moey. Who would have thought you'd ever need a two car line of bodyguards?" Howard laughed.

Nick grunted beside her.

"Can't be too cautious," Wyatt replied. "Not when everyone who's after her knows exactly where she'll be."

Just the idea that anyone was waiting at the courthouse to hurt her flipped her stomach. She was trying to stay calm, to do all the things the prosecutor had told her yesterday. Relax, breathe, don't overthink. But she was nervous. And the edginess coming off everyone didn't help. The guys had all been laser focused since getting off the plane. Even the normally light-hearted Wyatt was only sporting serious today.

"You're clear on the plan?" Wyatt asked.

"Yes, you and Seabass will get out to clear the steps. The guys from car two will get Nick and me out and inside. I don't stop, no matter what happens. I move inside." Morgan rolled her eyes. "No tornado, earthquake, or massive amount of gun fire will keep me out of the courthouse."

"Not funny, Moey," Nick said. His leg bounced against her, and she reached out, resting her palm on his thigh. He stilled instantly and his warm hand covered hers and his fingers wrapped tightly.

"I still think the vest is overkill." Her free hand banged

against the bullet-proof vest her brother handed her before she'd even walked down the airplane steps onto the tarmac.

"You do realize the two guys you're about to testify against came into a bar with guns, planning to shoot you, right?" Howard snapped from the front.

Morgan shivered.

"Ease up, Hewie," Nick said calmly. "She's handling this better than most people would. If she wants to bitch about the vest, she can."

Howard's eyes shifted to Nick in the rearview mirror. She looked up to him, but his eyes were on a swivel. They bounced out each window, latching onto nothing, just seeing it all.

"What the hell?" Seabass said as the courthouse came into view. "Isn't Dewie supposed to wait inside for Morgan?"

"That was the plan," Wyatt said.

Howard pulled up to the curb and rolled his window down.

"Don't lose your shit," Donald said as he leaned in the car window. "I know you just drove hours from the landing strip, and it's three hours back to Pensacola, but they just pleaded guilty."

Sighs echoed through the car. But Morgan wouldn't complain. Even doing the witness prep online yesterday afternoon was nerve-racking. She was glad to not have to testify.

"What?" Howard asked.

"They were hoping she wasn't going to show," Donald said. "When she was on the list for today, they pleaded. Judge is going to sentence them in an hour."

Seabass pulled out his phone, firing off a text as Howard rolled up the window before pulling away from the curb.

Morgan expected some sort of reaction from Nick, but even when she glanced up, he gave her nothing.

"I'm confused." Everyone seemed super calm about this.

"Don't be," Nick said. "For the first time since I met you, something just went the easy way."

"Hooyah!" Seabass answered with a smirk.

Wyatt chuckled next to her and it was like the fog of tension rose away, almost like the entire mood shifted.

"It's only coming from one side now, freckles." Nick leaned over and whispered in her ear. "And I got that side covered." His lips pressed lightly into the side of her head. But what she saw was Howard's eyebrows raise and his mouth silently form four words.

What the fuck Moey.

24

NICK REACHED IN and grabbed his and Morgan's bags from the trunk. Not having to deal with moving her in and out of the courthouse had been a nice reprieve. But until they found Reed, nothing was over. So, although they were spending the night with the admiral, Nick and Morgan were headed back to Nick's place tomorrow. Truthfully, if they weren't all tired as hell from the thirteen hours of travel already, he probably would have insisted they go back tonight.

Although the admiral's house was on base, and somewhat protected. Nick always felt better on his own turf. Plus, he and the admiral had never talked about Lewie. At some point, they were going to have to, but it wasn't a conversation Nick was looking forward to having. Add into the mix the very unlabeled thing going on between him and Morgan, and the idea of facing the admiral became even less appealing.

Nick dropped his bag on the driveway and hit the button to shut the hatch of the SUV.

"What's up, Hewie?"

Howard stood on the asphalt in front of the closed garage door. He was heading out with Donovan and some of Nick's other guys for dinner. Since they were on base, Nick didn't need seven people hovering. Wyatt and Seabass would be enough for the night.

"What's the deal with you and Moey?"

This could go a lot of ways, but the truth of it was that until he and Moey figured shit out he didn't need other people weighing in.

"The part that concerns you is that she's being stalked by her ex-boyfriend, and I'm going to be damn sure he's arrested and she's safe." Nick crossed his arms and looked Howard in his blue eyes.

He nodded once. "Okay."

But Nick froze. The hair stood up on his neck and his eyes moved. Using the windows and mirrors, he checked his three sixty in less than a blink. Houses, lawns, one trash can still left out on the street from the morning pickup, same empty six cars. Nothing. They'd already cleared this. Nothing was there. He did another scan before actually turning to check full circle. Normally, he wouldn't doubt his instincts. It was that sense he got that said pay attention. But his head was such shit lately. Could he even trust that?

"Hawk?" Howard called him, and Nick looked back his way. Howard was as trained as he was. And Donovan and three of Nick's guys, all of whom Nick trusted with his life, had eyes on him and the area. "You okay?"

The doubt in his tone rankled Nick. "I'm good. Guess its ghosts."

"We all got 'em," Howard said and climbed into the car.

Nick picked up the bags and moved toward the house.

"Hey." Howard rolled down the window and Nick turned. "I heard the *fuck off* loud and clear in your statement, but that never stopped me before. As far as keeping her safe goes, you better. But the rest."

Nick's eyes narrowed, waiting.

"She could do worse, probably a lot better too, but, just saying, it could be a lot worse," Howard said and with a two-finger salute, drove off.

Nick chuckled as he walked up the path, then through the front door.

"What are you laughing at?" The admiral's tone warmed Nick's heart and flipped his stomach.

"Your son." The words left Nick's mouth and his gaze shot to the admiral. Those same words had come out of Nick's mouth probably a hundred times before, but they'd always been about Lewie. The man's bright blue eyes flashed, and Nick's chest panged with guilt.

"Hey Daddy, do you want me to stir this chili?" Morgan called from the kitchen.

"*No!*" he shouted before adding under his breath. "You and I should talk at some point. But heaven help us; if she touches dinner, it won't be edible." He spun, heading into the kitchen.

Nick's shoulders slumped in relief. Glad to put off the conversation even if the admiral's tone implied it wouldn't be a bad one.

"Oh my God, I can't ruin a meal by stirring it." The eye roll Nick couldn't see from the front door was loud and clear in her statement. "One time, that happened *one* time."

Morgan stormed into the room, red hair flying. She stopped short, seeing Nick still standing in the doorway.

"So, you can't cook?" he asked.

Her jaw clenched as her hand flew to her hip. "I make up for it by being really good in bed."

Nick smiled, a reply on the tip of his tongue.

"I did not hear that," her dad yelled from the kitchen and Morgan turned the most adorable shade of pink as she stood frozen and wide-eyed. "Nick, come eat."

Nick set the bags down on the floor and moved toward her. "You definitely do, freckles," he whispered as he headed into the kitchen.

Wyatt and Seabass both sat at the large island wearing shit-eating grins, but Nick ignored them. The sun was setting in the large picture window above the sink. He paused, looking at the view of the water he hadn't seen in a long time. It felt like a lot of his life was spent on a boat watching the sunset on the ocean.

"Miss it?" The admiral handed Nick a bowl.

"Always and never," Nick replied, and the man's hand came to rest firmly on his shoulder giving him a squeeze.

"The only answer. Beer, boys?" Richard Johanson asked, dropping his arm to move to the fridge and pulling one out for himself. After a round of *nos*, he turned back to the door Nick had just come through. "Pouting, embarrassed, or eating?" he called as he stood across the island from Wyatt and Seabass. Nick moved around to sit next to Wyatt.

"Eating, I guess." Morgan came in and slumped onto the stool next to Nick.

He leaned over toward her and in a stage whisper added, "I finally am seeing some of this drama I've heard so much about."

Just as the words left his mouth, Nick got that tingle again. This time, he stood up and moved to the window. His eyes scanned the dock that ran just past the grass. Behind that was water. A fence, neighbors' yards. But it was all nothing.

"Nick?" the admiral asked. Nick turned to meet his eyes

silently conveying to the man who'd been his boss for years that Nick's internal warning alarms were ringing. Richard gave him a nod before turning back to say something to his daughter.

Seabass moved next to Nick. "Want me to check the front?"

"I'm with you," he said before turning to Wyatt. "Watch her."

They headed out the front door and separated. Nick moved to the driveway and scanned the area, but saw nothing. House, grass, one trash can, six cars. One man walking his dog. Something felt off. But he couldn't find the difference, nothing was different.

He moved to the admiral's two-door black Acura and pulled out the side mirror that someone must have tucked in when the SUV was parked beside it.

"I'm paranoid," Nick said as Seabass came up beside him.

"Never known that to be the case. I'd bet my ass he's here," Seabass said. His eyes scanned everything they had both already checked.

"Where?" Nick asked.

"I have no fucking idea, but we need to call the guys to come back and sit on the house."

"Yeah," Nick agreed with a nod and headed back in. Although Donovan agreed to come back, Nick didn't feel better. He still had the itch.

"False alarm," Seabass said. Nick watched both Wyatt and the admiral's eyes narrow, almost like they didn't believe it.

"It was nothing." Nick dropped back onto the stool next to Morgan. He picked up his spoon.

But his brain wouldn't stop. Something was different. Something had been off when he scanned the neighborhood. But his mind raked back over it. The houses. No blinds were different. No door open. The lawns and bushes all the same. The same empty six cars. Not even a van or SUV. No, they had clear views. Nothing was different. The trash can.

"Nick?" Morgan asked.

"What?" he barked.

She tilted her head. She must have said something. Ask something.

"I got it." Wyatt grabbed the container of sour cream sitting on the island and handed it across Nick to Morgan.

But his mind was already back on the street. Something was nagging at him. The cars. The lawns. The trash can. The man with the dog. Not odd to walk a dog, and not the right build to be Reed.

Nick gritted his teeth. What the hell was he missing? He took another bite of the chili, not tasting it as he swallowed.

"I need the lid," Morgan said.

"The lid," Nick repeated. His brain whirled; his heart pounded hard as the pictures cleared in his mind. The difference that he'd missed.

"Yeah, it's right there." Morgan pointed.

"No," Nick said as it clicked. His entire body went ice cold. "The lid."

"Fuck, the trash can lid was closed," Seabass muttered as spoons clattered to the table. "And open when we got here because trash had come this morning. He's in the trash can."

Both men were on their feet, moving again. "Watch her," Nick called over his shoulder again. But he knew they'd be too late. Not shocking, the trash can was on its side, tipped over onto the road. Seabass moved to check it as Nick once again scanned the yard.

The hair stood up on the back of his neck as he stood in the driveway. The fucker was here. Nick knew it.

"Gone," Seabass said, coming back to his side.

"No," Nick said. He wouldn't leave. A conversation with his brother scanned through his mind. A stalker wants two things: the victim and whoever touches her. Nick took a few steps away from Seabass. "I'm here. And this is the best chance you get." Nick spun slowly in a circle. "Unarmed, and right in front of you."

Seabass's eyebrows shot up as he realized what Nick was doing. But Nick moved farther into the center of the yard, communicating silently with two hand gestures to Seabass. If Reed was here, Nick could draw him out.

"Come on, Reed." He raised his voice, making sure no matter where in the yard Reed was, he could hear him. "Get me now. Because in five minutes, all my guys will be here. But right now, you're not nearly as outnumbered. So, it's now or you lose."

The scoff came from his right and Nick whirled toward it.

"Lose?" Reed stepped out from alongside the house. "Don't you know I've already *won*?"

25

HIS LONG BLOND hair hung matted around his jaw that was covered in an untamed beard. Crazy eyes darted as a manic smile lit his face. Every fiber of Nick's being wanted to smash him so deep into the ground he'd never see the light of another day. Reed's statement had Nick expecting him to pull Morgan out from behind the house with him, but as his tall frame moved away from the structure, Nick realized she wasn't there.

She was inside, safe with Wyatt.

Thank God.

"I won't lose. Everyone always underestimates me, but I don't lose." Reed laughed. His hand, black with dirt, rose and wiped against his forehead, leaving behind a small streak of what must be mud. Unkempt and unhinged, often the two went together in a psychotic break. Unpredictable usually filled the trio, but Nick needed to get control of the situation.

His jaw clenched. He didn't see a weapon, but the baggy clothes hanging off his sickly thin body could hide one fairly easily. And if he was armed, someone could get hurt. He took in a calming breath and let years of training take over. He'd done this before, talked down a crazy and this was no different. Tell him what he wanted to hear.

"I hear you. Not a huge fan of losing either. And I know you didn't really lose her. She left suddenly because of the bar issue," he said calmly.

"That wasn't my fault," Reed said quickly. His eyes darted around again, stopping on Seabass, who was moving toward the far side of the house.

"I know," Nick assured, drawing Reed's attention back, hoping to give Seabass a chance to move away. "We all know. Those guys in the bar, they were the problem."

"Yes," Reed said, and he blinked. Almost like his brain was clearing, and he glanced uneasily past Nick toward the driveway. But Nick needed his focus if he was going to let Seabass move around behind the house to get Reed from his blindside. Nick took two steps closer to Reed. Nick's eyes burned a bit at the scent of dirt and foul body odor. Something else, harsh, and bitter wafted off Reed.

"It's not your fault." Nick took one more step.

Reed's eyes hardened as his hands twitched at his sides. "Just like the last time."

Seabass came into view at the far back of the house behind Reed. Just give him thirty more seconds. He could keep him talking that long.

"Last time?" Nick asked.

"Yes, her parents thought moving would keep Gany and me apart. We lost years. And now again she's gone." Reed ranted, his eyes shifting, unfocused. "But this time, I got her." He laughed manically just as Seabass hit in low from behind. Reed fell with almost no fight, continuing his manic laugh even as Seabass put a knee in his back, forcing his wrists together and securing them with a zip tie. "I win." The excitement in Reed's voice put Nick on edge. It was too easy.

"Ignore him," Seabass said over the laughter. "Go check on your girl."

"It's too late, I win. I'll always win." Reed lifted his head from the grass and glanced past Nick, almost like he could see someone else standing in the driveway that he was calling out to. "If I can't have her, no one will."

Nick's body tingled with that *something's off* edge. Almost like, once again, he was missing something.

"*Go*, Nick. By the book. Let me deal with it," Seabass said as the black SUV pulled up and Donovan jumped out.

Nick glanced at Reed once more before looking across the lawn. No one was there. Just the driveway and the black Acura, but nothing was different or off and they'd searched the car already. Nick turned and headed inside, knowing in his gut something wasn't right.

"NICK!" MORGAN CRIED as he walked into the kitchen. She wanted to throw her arms around him, but she was aware of her father's eyes, so she didn't. Nick had only been outside for maybe ten minutes. But both times he'd jumped up from the table had Morgan's heart racing. Watching him go was both painfully familiar and yet strangely different. She lost count of the times in her life that she'd sat at the window watching her dad or brothers get in a car and drive away for a deployment. That ache of "would they come back" that never went away until they walked back in the door stuck in her throat. She knew the life. She was used to the feelings, but this was different.

There was more to it this time. The way his eyes flashed as something lit inside him was hot. The "I've got this covered" swagger that draped over him came with a weird feeling of pride. He was good at his job, and she felt a strange happiness watching him love something. It didn't make the fear go away, but it made it different.

Even the relief of him coming back inside safely was more potent.

Nick's eyes cut straight to Wyatt, and he tipped his head to motion him to the door. Wyatt left without a word. And her father began to stand.

"Admiral, I suggest you stay in here. We want this by the book."

"What?" Morgan asked and spun to her dad.

"So, you got him?" her father asked. Morgan's stomach jumped at the idea that Reed was outside. But if they had, that meant she was safe.

Nick gave a clipped nod, and for a second, relief flooded her body, knowing this was finally over. But one glance at Nick stomped any ember of relief out of her system. Her heart skipped a beat not knowing what she'd missed.

"What's wrong?" Morgan asked. Her voice shook just a bit and she swallowed hard.

"It was easy," Nick answered. His gaze narrowed. She leaned forward, trying to catch his eye.

"Isn't easy good?" she asked.

Nick blinked and turned to her. His hand lifted and settled over hers on the granite counter. Wrapping hers in the strong, steady assurance that was Nick Evans.

"Simple and straightforward are good. Easy—" Nick looked at her dad.

"You think you got something wrong?" Her dad frowned.

Nick didn't answer. It was like earlier; he was sitting here with them but his mind was somewhere else. She would swear he was going over and over something in his head, like he was putting a puzzle together.

"I've got to check something." He stood and walked out the front door.

Everything felt wrong. She didn't know if she should be relieved they had Reed or scared of whatever was haunting Nick. She wanted answers from him. But Nick was distant since they'd gotten to her father's house. Like he'd already pulled away. It shouldn't be a surprise. She expected him to be nothing more than a bodyguard. And if it was over, he'd leave.

She wrapped her arms around herself, trying to heal the crack at just the idea of Nick leaving caused in her chest.

"He'll figure it out, Moey, don't worry," her dad said, and she turned back to him.

"Did you know he's Louis's best friend?"

Her father raised his eyebrows and picked up his bottle of Stella before taking a sip. "Princess, when do I not know something?"

"I'm probably the only one that never met Boots." She spun her spoon in the chili she hadn't really eaten.

"Louis had his reasons for not introducing you two."

"He never let me around any of his friends."

Her father chuckled. "You never wanted anything to do with Navy men. Why would that be an issue for you?"

"Can you blame me?"

The tap of his bottle hitting the counter echoed. "I've never understood that. At first, I thought it was a teenage rebellion thing. The longer it went on, the more I put my energy into not taking it personally rather than understanding it." He cleared his throat. "I know I didn't do a perfect job with you. I tried, but girlie girl was outside my wheelhouse."

"Daddy." She shook her head. "Not that you were a bad dad, you're *not*. You did great even with the girlie stuff. You learned to French braid because I *needed* braids when I was seven and decided I wanted to be that American girl doll for Halloween. You read *The Babysitters Club* out loud to me, and took me to every princess movie that came out. You let me do makeovers on you and paint your nails."

Her father chuckled.

"You didn't flinch through my first period, or panic when I started dating. Even when I had to go to the gynecologist. You handled it as well as any of my friends' moms."

"Was it just the travel and the worry?" He leaned back on the stool.

She glanced away. "No, it's just no matter how great you were with *me*—women, relationships, weren't your thing. Or Howard, or Louis, or Donald."

"Now, wait," he started.

"Daddy, think about it. Louis never had a girlfriend. Howard is currently separated from wife number three because he keeps cheating. Donald is on his second wife. You all act like relationships are a burden on you. And you never could commit to any woman."

"Enough." His sharp tone shocked her. His blue eyes pierced into her. "I did commit to one woman—*your mother*. And it's a tragedy that you never got to meet her or see our relationship. But she had my whole heart. Still does. Which is why I've never committed again. I've never found anyone who captures my heart the same way your mother did." He reached across the counter and wrapped his fingers around her forearm. "But Moey, don't doubt that if your mother was still alive she'd be here, next to me, because it wasn't a burden to be married to her. *It was a joy*."

There was a passion in her father's voice she didn't hear often.

"I wish I'd gotten to see some of that," she said honestly.

"I should have talked about her more, but it never seemed fair for me to dangle something you couldn't have in front of you," he admitted, and leaned back in his chair again. "And I know you assumed it was Donald's fault his marriage ended, but Caitlyn ended things."

"What?" Her mouth fell open. Man, she had to stop assuming things.

"In fact, he begged her to work out their issues, and she refused. Neither one of them cheated, but she didn't want a military life, and he wasn't ready to leave at that point."

"Wow." Morgan shook her head.

"For the record, there are bad eggs, like Haley's dad. And I hate to say it because he's my son, but Howard needs to figure out his shit." Her father growled. "But there are good ones. And that man out there." Her dad pointed out the window.

The lights had been turned on, and people moved around the yard. Nick stood in the middle of all of it on the phone, pacing. His hand was moving as fast as his mouth.

"Who said anything about Nick?" she asked, but glanced back down at her chili, unable to look at her father anymore.

"I did. Because that man out there is steady as sun, fiercely loyal, supportive, and determined. He's the type of guy I've prayed you'll find."

"So I'm out of your hair," she joked.

"No."

She glanced up at him.

"Because I want you to be happy."

26

"I DON'T SEE why the fuck not," Nick snapped into the phone at his brother.

He was pacing in the backyard while the FBI team on scene swept the back for any sort of chemical compound. As Nick sat at the counter with Morgan, he'd realized Reed had been in the backyard before Nick found him. It needed to be checked because something wasn't sitting right with him. Reed was entirely too happy and sure that he'd won for there not to be something. It didn't take long to plant a bomb. Just the time Nick had been inside eating would have given Reed the opportunity.

"You've got to be kidding me," Danny yelled in his ear. "I've been busting my ass on this case. It's huge for me because it's Admiral Johanson's daughter. He's a liaison to the president and my bosses are breathing down my neck not to mess it up. And you've been all up on me, riding me, to do it right."

Nick's hand flung into the air as he spoke. "You're all the way in fucking Jersey, so who is questioning this asshole?"

"Not you, that's the point. In no world is it *you*."

Nick growled.

"Why the fuck not?"

Danny took a deep breath, but his voice sounded like he was talking through gritted teeth. "Because you're in love with the woman he's trying to kill."

Nick almost missed his footing and had to right himself.

In love?

No. Love was slow and took time. It was something you built and worked for. Not something that happened in a week. He and Morgan might have the start of something, maybe. If she wanted to try—even with the fact that he lived in Ambra and it sounded like she was coming back to Florida, but she'd been pretty clear that she wasn't interested.

"Listen, I'm getting on a plane. I'll be there in four hours and I promise you I will talk to this guy. And if you have certain things you want me to ask, I will ask them. But you will be happily at home with Morgan while I do it." Danny didn't give him time to answer. "Now I've got to go."

The line went dead.

"Shit," Nick mumbled. Glancing around the yard again, he saw most of the agents had moved toward the front. They weren't finding anything. Which was good, because it meant Morgan was safe, but the itch wouldn't go away.

"Lieutenant Evans?"

Nick turned to see one of the young agents headed his way.

"We checked the admiral's car, but the rest of them came with you guys, right? They're clear?"

"Yeah," Nick agreed. "None of ours were here before Reed was cuffed."

"Here are his keys if you want to give them back to him." The young woman placed the key fob in his hand.

Nick glanced down at the red and yellow shield like design before dropping it into his pocket. He did a lap around the front, and asked a few more questions before heading into the empty backyard to make another call.

"Gimpy." Bex picked up on the second ring.

"Hey, listen, put your legal hat on a second," Nick demanded.

"Hey, Bex, how are you? I know it's the middle of bedtime routine with the kids, but I needed a question answered, and I hoped you could help me." Her voice was teasing, but it also had that air of a mom tone that pointed out he was being a dick.

"Hey Bex," he said and rolled his eyes. "I know it's in the middle of bedtime, but we just caught Reed, the guy stalking Moey and I need your help, please."

"Why? What happened?" The teasing disappeared, replaced by worry.

"I want to talk to him, and I need to know how to do it. Because Danny said any defense attorney will have a field day with me talking to their client. Probably get anything I get out of the fucker thrown out."

There was a long pause before she cleared her throat.

"Nick." Her tone was careful. "Why do you need to talk to him?"

"Something is not right. He gave in too easily. I feel like we missed something." Nick pulled at the back of his neck. "If he's rattled a bit."

"No," she interrupted. "I get that someone should talk to him, but why *you*?"

The answer was easy. Because he could do it better. Not only because he had more training than most, he was trained to interrogate in seven languages, for fuck's sake, but because as Reed saw it, Nick had the one thing Reed wanted.

"You know what I do?"

"Yes, but Nick, you've never been close to anyone like you are with Morgan—"

"Are you kidding me? We've been friends for twelve years. You were literally the person I called to come to Germany to fly home with me when I shattered my leg."

"Yes, and you're one of my best friends too, but I've seen you panic once in the entire time I've known you, and that was the moment you didn't know if Morgan was okay."

Nick vividly remembered that moment. It felt different from anything else he'd been through.

"And what happens if this guy tells you something you don't want to hear? The reason we keep people that are extremely emotionally invested out of cases is because love —"

"Love?"

"Nick, you are entirely too self-aware to not know where you're headed. Now stay out of Danny's case; let him do his job. Hang out with Morgan. It sounds like she had a rough day. Go give her a hug."

"Why do people keep telling me to hug her?"

"Because you're a man of big action, but sometimes the best course is the simple gesture. Just stop panicking."

"I'm not panicking," Nick said, but the line was dead.

"I don't think you're panicking," Seabass said from behind him, and Nick turned. "But everyone's packing up—they found nothing."

"Overreacting then," Nick mumbled.

Seabass's head tipped. He kicked the grass with his boot. "Honestly? Because I don't think you're going to like it."

"Yeah." It came out harsher than he wanted, but he and Seabass had too many issues already this week.

Seabass wasn't happy with the fact that Nick had slept with Morgan. And Nick got where he was coming from. Everything became a grey area once that line was crossed. But Seabass wasn't his father, and Nick didn't want another lecture. It was his life and his company. Nick did however, need Seabass's objective opinion about the current situation.

"I was worried, man, after the issue at the resort. I didn't know how you'd handle this."

"Fine, I don't see why you're beating around the fucking bush, but I get it. I'm not seeing things right," Nick snapped. He spun back to the water, trying to force away the itch that said something was wrong. His mind flicked back two years, to Syria. To a fight with his guy, Jeremy about his fiancée, T-cup, riding with him. Nick didn't believe Jeremy could be objective where T-cup was concerned, and that seemed to be what Seabass was now calling Nick out on.

"No, Nick," Seabass said. "Since we got here, you've been on point. Focused. I had a fucking heart attack when Reed said he'd won. My mind pictured a hundred ways he had Morgan. But you didn't blink."

Nick's stomach bottomed out when Reed had said those words. If Reed had pulled Morgan out or said he had the house triggered to blow, Nick's legs would have given out.

Slowly, he turned back to Seabass. Shocked that Seabass wasn't ripping into him. But he just stood arms crossed, watching, braced for Nick's reaction.

"You stayed focused, did the job. I sent you in because I thought you'd be out for blood, but you were calm as fuck. I'm impressed as hell, because if he was talking about my girl, I would pound his ass until he wasn't breathing."

Nick wasn't sure how to take that, because he had those

thoughts, but of course he hadn't acted on them.

"You acted exactly how you've been trained to." Seabass walked closer. "I'm saying if you feel like there is something, then I believe you. If you need one day, hell, five days to figure it out, I'm here with you. Your instincts have saved my ass too many times to not trust you."

"And if I'm seeing ghosts?" he asked.

Seabass's black eyes met his straight on. "Wouldn't you rather be here and wrong than home and right?"

Nick pulled at the back of his neck, wishing he could piece together what he was missing. But the teams had swept the house twice. There were no chemicals inside, and they did the permitter and the backyard. They couldn't find anything. Maybe he was off. Maybe it was nothing. And then there was a tiny voice in his head asking if he wanted it to be something for the simple reason of not wanting to leave Morgan. Because if it was nothing, he had no reason to stay.

"Look, neither one of us really ate, and we've been up since three a.m. Maybe we need to eat, sleep, and reevaluate." Seabass rocked back on his heels as he spoke.

Nick nodded, but two hours later, even with a full stomach and a shower, he'd lain in bed unable to sleep.

He kept flipping through the details. Reed had been dirty, but there was a smell that lingered on him that Nick couldn't place. And looking back on it, the mud almost looked like grease. They checked the admiral's car. Reed was talking to someone across the yard that wasn't there. But they knew he was working alone. There wasn't anyone else.

He picked up the pillow behind him and adjusted it, trying to make it more comfortable. Howard's old room was fine. But he'd spent the past few nights with Morgan and the bed felt cold without her. He kept listening in the silence to catch her breathing and he missed the scent of lilacs that followed her.

His body missed the soft warmth of her touch. It hadn't been many nights, but he was already accustomed to her being beside him, and it felt wrong being alone. But the admiral had shown him up to Howard's old room, with the expectation that he'd stay here. What was he supposed to say?

"Hey admiral I know I'm bailing soon, but I need to sleep with your daughter while I'm here because it doesn't feel right without her."

Yeah, Richard Johanson would love that.

Nick rolled over and circled back to Reed again when the door cracked. He was on his feet before the door was all the way open.

Morgan slipped inside the room, closing the door behind her. "It's just me."

"What's wrong?" he whispered.

"I just—" the words died, and she shrugged.

He remembered what Bex had said. He'd spent the entire night trying to find a big action; he'd forgotten the small gestures.

"Come lay with me for a while." He settled back into the bed and she moved next to him in an instant. Her leg draped over his, and her head rested in the crook of his left shoulder. His body eased as the scent of lilac filled the air. Just having her here relaxed him.

"Are you leaving tomorrow?" she asked. Her fingers danced along his chest, and his stomached clenched.

"I'm not leaving until I'm sure you're safe, Moey." His hand came up and rested over hers. Her diamond pressed into his palm. He wasn't sure what to make of the fact that she hadn't taken off her ring. A part of him wondered if she'd just forgot she was wearing it. He hadn't, just like he knew his band still sat on his finger. Twice he almost mentioned it to her, but if he did, he thought she'd take it off. And he hated that idea.

"If he's in jail, and the drug ring guys pleaded, then why do you think I wouldn't be?" she asked.

Nick sighed. This was more than he should probably say but he wanted her to understand. "Since I speak multiple languages, a big part of what I did was interrogation." He paused, trying to assess how she'd take that. She didn't react in any way. "A huge piece of my training is how minds work; normal people, hostages, terrorists. I was taught to understand what makes them tick, to get into their mind, and to learn how to turn it against them."

"It's why you handle your PTSD so well," she said.

Nick had heard that many times from his therapist. Understanding how the mind worked definitely helped.

"Maybe, but people like Reed, someone who's massively intelligent yet twisted and obsessed, they don't give up. Not until they have you in checkmate."

"And you're wondering what he thinks he has over me?" Her voice quivered at the end of the sentence. Nick instantly regretted the conversation. He wasn't trying to scare her; he just didn't want her to see this as a secret.

"I don't know Moey, it could be nothing. I'm not currently at my best, and I know it." He swallowed wishing he was in a better headspace. Because he was almost positive there was still an ax dangling over her head.

"Nick, I'd take you at your worst over anyone else at their best any day of the week."

27

THE EGG FELL into the pan and she sprinkled another layer of the clear crystals into them. It was early, barely six thirty. But Nick woke up to a three-a.m. phone call from Danny, letting him know they'd found Reed's car on base. He'd had Morgan's gate clicker to the side entrance of the base that led directly into her father's neighborhood. He couldn't get on the main base from that entrance, but he could access the housing.

There was a lot of yelling about how that could have happened, but Morgan didn't think it was farfetched. Her car had sat in front of her former Florida apartment for weeks before her father finally moved it. Reed could have gotten her clicker at any point. And thinking back on it, he probably came by her father's multiple times to check to see if she was there.

She shivered and dropped some more salt onto the eggs, and she stirred them in the pan.

"Send someone to check the storage unit, but be careful. If there was a trace of mercury fulminate in the car—" Nick paused. "I know you're not an idiot, Danny. I'm just saying, the only other place she has stuff is that unit. If he didn't rig something here at the house, it's probably there."

Morgan lifted the pan of scrambled eggs off the stovetop and spooned them onto the three plates. She gave them a final sprinkle of salt and pepper before she added a fork and passed them out to the guys on the counter.

"Thanks," Nick said as he hung up the phone. "If the storage unit clears, they have nothing. Everything in the car could be tied back to the firebomb he used in New York or what he took from the lab in Pennsylvania. And they had to medicate Reed because he became manic. Danny doesn't think he's lucid enough to plan something."

"Or," Seabass added. "Whatever he did made him manic."

Nick scooped some eggs onto his fork as Wyatt turned to his breakfast. Both took a bite at the same time. Morgan knew she messed something up without either of them saying a word. Seabass looked from Nick to Wyatt, and then dropped his fork back onto the counter. Wyatt spat into a napkin.

"Whoa," he said, his eyes cut to Nick, who swallowed harshly. "That just answered my question. You don't swallow that shit for anything but a 'the.'"

"What?" Morgan asked.

"Easy on the salt next time," Wyatt said. "Unless you're trying to keep a ghost out, no one needs that much."

Her father chuckled from the doorway, "I warned you when she offered. I'll pick up breakfast sandwiches at the deli now." He sipped his coffee.

"Three sprinkles. That's what you told me last time. Once just as they go in, once when I mix them, and once on the plate." She'd followed her father's instructions.

"With a light hand," he reminded her.

"I give up, I just suck." Morgan sighed, dropping into the seat next to Nick. His hand came up, rubbing her back.

"They aren't that bad." His face, as he picked up the fork again, made her laugh.

"Please, Nick don't." She shook her head. There was no need to torture him. "I'm not doing anything. I'll just go get you all something." She pushed out of the chair to an echo of *nos* from around her. "Why not? There is no way Reed could plan that I'd go to Maggi's Deli to pick up breakfast at seven a.m. today. And he's not here to follow me."

"I'll go with you," Nick said, also pushing to his feet.

"Fine, but I'm buying. It's the first time I've been able to pay for anything since I met you guys." Morgan ran upstairs.

When Danny called, she had left Nick's room and tossed on a pair of old cutoffs she still had in a drawer in her old room, along with Nick's Navy hoodie. She was pretty sure her father knew she'd stayed with Nick last night, but he'd never been one to butt in to her relationship choices. He'd already given her his two cents about Nick, and now he'd left it up to her. That was one thing she loved about her dad.

Her old flip-flops were still in the closet, so she slipped them on before grabbing her debit card and driver's license from the top desk drawer where she left them months ago so she wouldn't be tempted to use them in New York. Her keys sat on the dresser, and she swiped them before heading back down.

Nick was waiting at the bottom of the steps.

"I'm driving," she announced as she passed him on her way to the front door.

"I'll drive," Nick corrected.

"Don't be all alpha male. You don't even know where you're going." She laughed, heading for her Acura in the driveway.

"Moey, you don't have the keys. That right there tells you

who should drive," he teased with a chuckle, but she raced ahead of him.

"Wanna bet?" she said, making the car beep as she unlocked it. She jumped in, slamming the door behind her. She expected Nick to be exasperated, but as he glanced from the key in his hand to her his face was frozen in horror.

"Morgan! *No!*" he shouted just as she put her foot on the brake and pressed the button.

The car clicked, but nothing happened.

Nick yanked the door open. "Don't move and don't take your foot off the brake," he demanded frantically. "This is your car?"

"Yeah, Dad's Cadi is in the garage," she said, nodding to the key fob in his hand.

"Fucking mistakes. Over and over," Nick mumbled.

"What?" Her heart raced and her hands started to sweat as she gripped the wheel, but Morgan didn't get the problem. "What did I do?"

"Nothing. When I said we cleared the cars, I didn't mean this one. And fuck, I'm sure no one checked it because I thought this was your father's. Just don't move," Nick repeated as he carefully looked under the seat. "*Fuck.*"

"What's wrong?" Wyatt asked from behind Nick.

"Look at me Moey." She met his slate-gray eyes and saw the sheer terror reflecting in them. "It's going to be fine," Nick said, but his eyes told another story. "Wyatt." Although he called him, Nick's eyes didn't leave hers. "I need you to go inside and call the bomb squad. She's sitting on a live device."

Morgan's heart stopped.

IT WAS ALL happening too fast. She knew she couldn't panic because this was a crisis. But she felt frozen. Terrified. Unable to process the directions being given to her. At some point, Nick had moved to the passenger seat and was holding her hand. He might be talking to her. She knew other people were. But she was just focusing on her quivering leg, trying to keep the pressure on the brake pedal.

Nick squeezed her hand, and she looked over at him.

"They'll be here any minute, okay?" Nick assured.

She nodded blankly.

"You know what would be funny?" Nick asked, but his voice sounded tight.

"What?" Her voice barely worked.

"Imagine if you were my Uber driver. I was on my way to the airport, couldn't miss my flight. But the car broke down. We were waiting on AAA." Nick's words penetrated her haze.

"Are you giving me a meet cute?" she asked. "Now?"

"Tell the story with me, Moey." He let go of her hand, reaching across to place his palm on her thigh, helping to hold down the break. Her muscles relaxed slightly, and her shoulders sagged. "That's it. I got it for a minute. Just tell me about the Uber driver."

"I guess I would need to make him a total alpha-hole, right?" She swallowed and shut her eyes. "It would probably be better if she picked him up from the airport and he was trying to get home for a Zoom meeting or something, but it started to snow. The car broke down. I'd have to research what about the cold would make a car not work."

"I'm sure you could figure it out, freckles."

She opened her eyes, glancing around. Men in naval uniforms had created barricades keeping everyone back. She saw her father, and Wyatt with Seabass just inside the line, talking to someone. The guy was wearing a weird tan outfit, almost like an astronaut with a large helmet in his hand. It took her a second to realize it was bomb gear.

Her eyes welled, and she blinked a few times.

"What's the alpha-hole's name?" Nick asked.

"Nick, I don't want to do this." Her voice cracked, and she shut her eyes.

"I know you don't, baby." Nick sounded calm. His voice was a balm to her soul. "But I need you to do this with me. Because we're going to get you out of here, but I need you to not panic. So, tell me the alpha-holes name."

"Hawk." A deep voice called and Morgan opened her eyes to see the bomb squad guy moving toward her open car door.

"Garrett," Nick answered. "I'm hell of a glad you're not deployed."

She glanced over to see Nick's tight smile.

"Morgan, your dad tells me you got yourself into some trouble," Garrett said, his voice as calm as Nick's. "I'm going to take a look, then I'll get my helmet on and call for some help. Okay?" He waited for her to nod before turning to Nick. "I'm also going to need you to get out."

"Nope," Nick said. "I'm good."

"Hawk." Garrett shook his head. "I know you want your wife out."

Wife? She glanced down at her leg. His left hand rested on her bare skin, the silver band on his ring finger clear as day. Her eyes flicked to her own hand.

They'd never taken off their rings.

"I get it. I know how I'd feel if it were Steph, but we need to be able to get in both sides, and . . ."

He didn't finish, but she knew. And if the bomb went off, they needed to minimize casualties. She turned her head back to Nick. His eyes ran over her face, and he shook his head. But he had to leave the car. If this bomb went off, he needed to be far away. She thought about his brothers and sister, his nieces and nephews, the guys that worked for him. There were a lot of people who needed him. She couldn't imagine a world without Nick Evans in it.

All the parts of him she'd come to know and love flashed through her brain. And the thought of anything happening to him was worse than the idea of this bomb blowing her up. She *loved* him, so he needed to get the hell out of the car.

Morgan looked deep into those expressive slate eyes. All she wanted to say was "I love you." But she couldn't put him on the spot like that, especially if he didn't feel the same way. So instead she gave him the one thing she could give him: strength.

"Get out of the car, Nick." His head started to shake again, but she went on. "I'm okay. I've got this. I'll name the alpha-hole, and later, you can tell me if it sucks or not. We can even continue the debate about honey pot."

He scoffed.

"I know you hate that term." She forced a laugh. "Get out of the car, Nick." Her voice cracked, and she swallowed as she saw his eyes give in.

"I'm going to lift my hand," he said, and she tightened her own muscles, holding down the brake pedal. He said nothing else as he climbed out the door and walked around the car. Garrett nodded once and then stepped away from the driver's side.

Nick squatted down in his place, pulling her hand off the wheel. He pressed something hard into her palm and closed her fingers around it. The flat metal was warm in her hand.

"For two years that's been my touchstone, the thing I clung to get me out of a car I didn't want to be in." Nick swallowed. "Now it's going to get you out of the car I don't want *you* to be in." He leaned forward and pressed his lips against hers for one brief second. "Your job is just to bring my touchstone back to me."

"I won't drop it," she promised.

"At the moment, I don't give two shits about the dog tag, Moey," he said.

TURNING AND WALKING away from her was the single hardest thing he'd ever done. But he needed to give her the best chance to get out of the car safely, and that meant Nick needed to let Garrett do his job.

The key fob. If he had realized just two minutes sooner that it didn't belong to the Acura, none of this would have happened. He headed straight for the guys on the barrack line.

"What did he say about it?" Nick demanded at Seabass.

"Nick, there is no excellent answer here. You know about home-made bombs. They need to get in and look," Seabass said. "Garrett is the best."

Nick nodded. And took a few steps away, surprised when the admiral came up beside.

"I can't believe you want to stand here with me," Nick said. "Why?"

"I killed your son, and now I left your daughter sitting on a bomb," Nick said, pulling at his neck. His heart pounded, and he swore he couldn't get a good breath. But he couldn't swallow the lump in his throat either. If something happened to Morgan—

"Nick, look at me," the admiral demanded. Nick turned. Worry etched lines around his eyes, but he was calm. Everything about his demeanor was the opposite of Nick's. "I read every report, heard all the intel about that day. You all followed orders, ran the route we sent you, did your job. You *didn't* kill my son."

"Exactly, had I been driving, had it been *my call*." Nick's hand fisted, remembering. "I would have bucked the system and said fuck the out-of-town route—taken my guys the safer way. And that's why I lead the team, because I knew when to be a sheep and when to be the shepherd." He turned back to Morgan and the car.

"Why weren't you driving? Why was Alpha Two still in charge if you were there?"

Nick whirled on him. "Because I flew halfway around the world for my sister's wedding for eighteen hours before I flew back. I was tired as fuck and not at my best."

"So, as a team, you decided to let him take the lead?"

"Yes."

"Again sounds like you followed protocol and did everything right. You didn't kill him. A terrorist who hated our country enough to blow up soldiers bringing food and water to women and children in their cities killed him. And he died a war hero."

"Yeah, I know," Nick admitted, but sometimes it was easier to blame himself than to deal with the fact that he couldn't have done anything to change it. But he wasn't a machine. Nick couldn't save everyone. He needed to let go of the idea that he could have changed anything. Because the truth was a different road, a different car, could have killed Lewie just as easily. And none of it was Nick's fault. The grief would always sit like a weight on his shoulders, but he had to stop carrying the guilt.

"You do not need to live with survivor's guilt, because I know you didn't kill him. And I can't imagine Morgan thinks that either."

Nick scoffed. "She said I was ridiculous. Got mad at me about it."

"She's a smart woman."

"Hell yeah." His eyes flicked back to the car and the four men in bomb gear. His hand shook as he lifted it to pull on his neck.

"Nick, can I tell you a story?" Admiral Johanson asked.

He pulled his eyes off Morgan and turned back to the admiral.

"I asked Louis to invite you to a family BBQ when you were both home on a leave the last time. You'd just come back from spending the Fourth of July with your family, and the unit wasn't heading back out for another five days."

Nick thought back, trying to remember the time. His sister had just started dating her husband, Marc. But he didn't recall

Lewie inviting him over for a family thing. In fact, Lewie almost never invited Nick over. With the admiral as his dad, and how closely the admiral and Nick worked together, Nick always assumed it was weird for Lewie.

"He said he would." The admiral seemed serious, but Nick honestly didn't remember the invitation. "After the BBQ was winding down, Louis was sitting out on the dock alone. I walked down, saying it was too bad you didn't show up."

He wished he could remember why he'd blown off the invitation, but at the same time, his eyes flicked back to Morgan and the car.

"Nick, you know as well as I do Louis didn't invite you over that day," he said, drawing Nick's attention back to him.

"I can't remember that he did."

"He admitted he didn't." The man paused, and Nick was confused as fuck about the point of this story. Nick started to turn away again to check on Morgan. "Nope, look at me sailor," he demanded and Nick obeyed the order without question. "This is the important part. He said he didn't invite you because Morgan would be there."

Nick's jaw dropped open in shock.

"Yup, said you weren't ready to meet her yet—you had two years left on the teams before you left active for the higher ranks."

Nick's eyes widened. "What?"

"Finding your wife wouldn't work for you yet. And when I laughed, he told me I didn't understand. The second you two saw each other, that would be it. You'd both fall. And my son was rarely wrong. So, is there something you want to tell me?"

Nick turned to the car and found Morgan's gaze. His eyes locked with hers. She nodded once and then swallowed, not breaking eye contact. She was scared. He knew that, but she was also in control, determined. All the things he'd come to love about her. He stared into the deep aqua depths of the eyes he never wanted to look away from.

"Nick?" the admiral repeated and Nick turned back to him.

"Admiral." One of the bomb squad guys called as he moved their direction. "We need to push back the perimeter about twenty feet."

Nick's body felt heavy at those words. His heart sank knowing what they meant. An unstable bomb they weren't going to be able to defuse. He knew the protocols; all the ways they could protect the person in the car: Kevlar, blast shields, fire bags. He only half listened as the man explained the plan to Morgan's father.

People moved around him, but he simply stood at the barricade, waiting.

He ended up moving down the row. Alone. Away from the chaos. Even though he was as close as they would let him be, it wasn't enough. He wanted to hold Morgan's hand. Be there for her as multiple people in full bomb suits repositioned shields. He knew they hoped to get Morgan behind a shield before the bomb blew. His fist clenched. Hope wasn't good enough. If anything happened to her, he wouldn't be able to function.

Nick reminded himself to take a breath, to not storm back over to the car and demand to be part of the plan. Because he wasn't a bomb expert. Nick couldn't fix this.

He couldn't see her face anymore because of the bulky helmet on her head. He needed to see her eyes. He wanted her to know he was right there with her. But as the shields moved into place, he couldn't even see her outline. Never in his life had he felt this helpless.

His heart clenched in his chest just as someone came up behind him, and a heavy hand suddenly rested on his shoulder. He turned.

Danny.

"I'm here with you, bro, and everyone else is here in spirit," he said. Nick gave him a quick nod before starting to turn back to Morgan but a second hand came to rest above Danny's.

Seabass, and three guys from his SEAL team stood directly behind Danny. At first, he thought they were going to back him up. Together. But instead, each gave him a clipped nod and then placed their right hand on the other's left shoulder.

"We're with you, bro," Seabass said.

A hand hit his right shoulder before he turned away from Seabass.

"So are we, boss," Wyatt said as he stood, left hand on Nick's right shoulder, with Donovan next to him. Donovan even flashed his phone to show Bex, hands clasped under her chin. "Love you," she mouthed and blinked a few times.

"Moey's got this," Howard said as he and Donald came up behind Wyatt. Resting his left hand on Wyatt's.

"And we've got you," Admiral Johanson came up behind his sons.

"I love her." The words rushed out of Nick's mouth. "I know it's too fast and not rational and crazy. I'm not nearly good enough for her."

"I know that," the admiral said and Nick finally turned away from the car.

"But I will spend every day of my life attempting to be the man she deserves."

His face broke out in a smile. "I know that too, son."

Nick's throat tightened as he looked around at his brother, his brothers in arms, his brothers at NAE Securities, and Lewie's family. A week ago, these guys would have represented the most important people in his life. But Morgan had burst into his world like his personal sun overshadowing everything else. And she wasn't okay.

The hum started from the guys to his left, but he wasn't sure which of his former SEAL team started it. It was Seabass's words that echoed around them.

Nick's eyes burned at the lyrics that his best friends used to belt out.

"I won't be afraid, just as long as you stand—stand by me." Seabass squeezed his shoulder.

They all stood around him, singing his best friend's song, as the bomb exploded thirty yards away and Nick just watched. Not being the hero for the single most important person in his life, unable to save the only person he truly needed.

29

IT WAS HOT. Her body hurt in ways she couldn't describe. Almost like something had hit her from the inside out. And then from the outside in. The helmet on her head only did so much to stop the force as she slammed into the concrete.

Having someone tell her they were going to detonate a bomb around her was crazy.

They had precautions. And once they found out the brake pedal wasn't triggering just the panel under her seat, it got easier. They removed the car door. They spun her so her legs were out of the car. They got the fire shelter over her legs and carefully, over the course of ten minutes, she worked it up under her ass to bring it high enough to meet the other half.

The thing looked like an aluminum foil sleeping bag, but they promised her it deflected the radiant heat. Once again, she put on the Kevlar vest, and this time, a helmet too. They gave her a Kevlar plate to keep over her back. And then they zipped her and the shield into the bag. The directions were clear. Fall out of the car, onto the concrete, face down. Keep the shield over as much as her as possible and wait.

Smacking into the concrete wasn't the worst—it was the wave that smashed through her. That was the worst. But now she just ached, and it was hot.

The air seemed to get thick. The fire shelter would work for one minute, they said. Hold in the breathable air for one minute. Protect her airways from super heat that would blister and char them and kill her instantly. But even the thick air seemed hot enough to burn every breath.

And the bag itself seemed to get heavier although she didn't know how that was possible. But every second, it pressed closer around her. All she wanted was to get through this, to see Nick again. She clung to the flat dog tag he'd pressed into her hand. Praying that she would get the chance to tell him all the things she needed to say about how she was feeling.

After what seemed like much longer than one minute, she felt something pulling on her. The bag dragged, with her inside, until finally clear, cool air rushed about her body.

"She's breathing," Garrett announced. "Morgan, can you hear me?"

"Yes," her voice croaked.

The gear around her was carefully being removed, and questions about what hurt were rapid fire around her. But she pushed everyone back, standing up. She yanked the sweatshirt over her head, trying to cool her body down. Behind large temporary walls her car still burned.

"Morgan," Nick's voice called, and she turned.

She was in his arms before she took a step. And the sob caught in her throat. Tears she'd held in for entirely too long welled in her eyes.

"You're okay, I've got you. It's over," Nick promised and held her.

"Sorry," she sobbed, unable to stop the tears but Nick just wrapped her tighter in his arms. There were so many things she wanted to say but at the moment all she felt was safe, and loved.

"Cry as long as you need, Moey. I'm here."

She opened her hand to show him her brother's dog tag. "Your touchstone."

"No." Nick's head shook against her hair. "You're my touchstone, the only thing I need to pull back from the edge. I know life with me won't be easy, and there are parts of me that are forever broken, but I love you, Morgan. And I know you don't want a hero, so if you need me to sell NAE Securities, I will. Because all that matters is I have you."

She snuggled herself tighter in Nick's arms having everything she needed wrapped around her. "I love you too, Nick. You don't need to quit anything. You're more than just a hero. You're my hero."

30

"HEY, MOEY, I'M home," Nick said as he shut the door to his house. Although, at this point, it didn't resemble the place he used to live. Morgan's touches filled every space to make the place a home in a way it never used to be.

"You're early," she called from the kitchen.

He headed to the back of the house, sniffing. "What's that smell?"

"Haley dropped off spaghetti sauce. Don't worry, I didn't so much as stir it, so it'll be edible." She rolled her beautiful aqua eyes at him from the reclaimed wood kitchen table where she sat in front of her laptop.

His poker table was one of the first things that made the trip down the stairs to what was becoming the man cave. She didn't mind poker night, she just liked the idea of a family kitchen table for dinners. Dinners he planned on cooking.

He loved his girl, and having her in his house, his space—best thing that had ever happened to him, but the woman couldn't cook worth a damn. It was a special skill to be as crappy at it as she was.

"How are you feeling?" he asked, moving to the table to drop a kiss on her lips. Today, that question didn't bring up the awful memories that had haunted him for a few weeks after watching that car bomb explode. Morgan had been lucky that she came through it with only a few bruises and some first-degree burns.

"I'm perfect."

"That you are," Nick agreed.

Even with Haley and Morgan's super planning, the soonest they could get it done was April, which was still three weeks away. But that didn't matter. The wedding was more for her than him anyway. In his mind, she was already his forever.

The wedding band he'd put on in the car back in January still sat on his finger. Although their ceremony wasn't until next month, he didn't care. He'd belonged to her since the moment he'd slipped that band on his finger. Even if he didn't realize it at the time. He'd replaced her fake diamond engagement ring with a real one two days after they'd returned to New Jersey, and he had a diamond wedding band he couldn't wait to slide on her finger.

Morgan turned back to her computer and sighed.

"Story trouble?" he asked, moving to the stove to check on the sauce Haley made and start some water to boil for the noodles.

"Are you going to be weird about it again?" Her eyes got that cranky flash he loved.

"Moey, come on. You used my idea for the Uber driver book and then named the cranky alpha-hole Nick." He sighed. "And then when you read me something 'Nick' does, I can't help but take it personally."

Morgan laughed. "Would you rather I name him Wyatt?"

Nick growled.

She lifted off the chair and came over to wrap her arms around him. "I've told you a million times, it's an honor to have a character named after you. I did it because he's the guy who broke my anti-hero streak."

It thrilled Morgan's agent that she was trying her hand with an alpha-hero this time. And Morgan was enjoying it so much that she was talking about turning it into a series. If she did, Nick could appear in books again and again.

He gave her crap about it, but secretly, he'd loved that she named him Nick. Honestly, every book she wrote from now on could have a hero named Nick, and he'd be happy as a pig in slop because he wanted to be her only hero.

"I really think this one is going to do better than Bar Hop," Morgan said as she settled back at her computer. They would see but Bar Hop, her last romcom that released a few weeks ago, was still sitting in the top ten in a few categories on Amazon. And he was proud as fuck of her. "Oh, and Trish called. She said they're only staying with us on Saturday night because Grant doesn't want to miss two days in the spring. Especially when they are coming back in a couple weeks for the wedding."

"Oh shit, I forgot about the twins' baptism this weekend." Nick pulled at the back of his neck. Marc and Beth's twins, Payton and Colten, were only five weeks old, but her father was dying for the publicity that some family photos at their baptism would give him.

"And Dad's staying with us too because Beth's dad invited him," Morgan reminded Nick.

"Are your brothers coming?" he asked and braced himself.

"Yeah," she said.

He winced. Although he got along fine with both Hewie and Dewie, and always had, it was slightly different being the brother-in-law. He found himself having to stand up for his girl with stuff like, "of course we need nine throw pillows on the sofa" or "dude, just use the disposable towels on the back of the toilet. The ones on the rack are only to look cute." Then hear the brunt of it for the next two days, because they both thought he was pathetic as fuck.

He glanced over at Morgan. She was smiling at something she'd written. She'd read it to him later, he was sure. But the smile was an easy reminder that he didn't care how pathetic he seemed to anyone because she was "the girl" for him. The girl he'd take all the shit for, the girl he'd take care of, the only girl he ever needed.

Epilogue

NAVY PANTS AND shiny shoes. Normally his shiny shoes went with his dress whites, but today was something different. Even the gold tasseled epaulets were the polar opposite of anything he was used to wearing.

He glanced in the mirror and shook his head, but couldn't stop his smile. It said something about the changes in his life that he was excited about this outfit. So much was different in the last few years, and the sharp cry from behind him seemed to accent that point.

He spun and walked toward the sound.

"What do you think, Ellie, is it so bad you need to cry?" His little girl was three days old and already had him wrapped around her finger as much as her mother did.

He lifted the tiny pink bundle and balanced her into the crook of his elbow. Tonight was the first night Ellie and Morgan would be home, and he was thrilled. It had been hard leaving them at the hospital. If he hadn't had a good reason to come home, he would have just slept a second night in that god-awful reclining chair just to be with them.

He'd come a long way from the guy who couldn't walk into a hospital. His triggers were few and far between these days. What used to feel like a scab that would never heal felt more like a scar he'd always carry. And Moey got a lot of the credit for that. Not that he didn't have to keep working every day to let go of his demons, but his wife gave him multiple reasons to want to keep moving forward. One of whom was currently resting her head full of dark hair against his white polyester shirt.

His daughter's tiny mouth opened as she searched for something to latch onto.

"We'll have to find Mommy if you're hungry, Ellie. You should feel special since you're the only person in the world she can actually feed."

"Haha, you're hysterical." Ellie's eyes worked their way open at the sound of her mommy's voice and he turned to find Moey leaning against the doorjamb of their bedroom.

"Do you see your Mommy?" He smiled down at his daughter. "Isn't Mommy beautiful?"

Morgan shook her head. "Maternity leggings and your hoodie doing it for you tonight?"

He walked over to her and brushed a stray red lock of hair that had fallen out of her ponytail off her forehead. "You know it doesn't matter what you wear, Moey. You always do it for me."

"I swear, Nick, if you say anything about—"

He lifted his finger to her lips.

"Hey, I learned. You get back rubs and flowers, and lots of compliments about what an amazing, beautiful woman you are for at least two months before I even hint at sex."

She rolled her eyes, but he leaned down to give her a light kiss.

"Beth and Marc here with the twins?" he asked, and she nodded. "And she's ready?"

"Yup. I'll take Ellie, but I'm going down first because I'm getting this on camera."

He gave his wife a minute to hurry down the stairs before he made his way down. He headed down slowly, smiling as his daughter's blue eyes widened.

"Daddy!" Sadie called. The sequins on her green tail shimmered, reflecting light as she jumped up and down, causing her red hair to bounce around her shoulders. She'd be three in two weeks, but she was already the spitting image of her mother. "You look perfect!"

"Oh, I think you're the perfect one." He knelt down, seeing Morgan out of the corner of his eye, snapping pictures on her phone. "What a beautiful Little Mermaid you are."

"Can we go now?" Sadie asked, grabbing her bag. "Uncle Marc and Aunt Beth are already outside." She pulled on his hand.

"Wait, wait," Morgan called. "I want one where you're both looking at the camera."

Sadie sighed and her shoulders slumped. "I want to go twick or tweat."

He scooped up his little princess and stood. "Smile at Mommy and then you and I can go for as long as you want, just like I promised."

"Because I'm your favorite girl." Sadie batted her little eyelashes at him.

He resisted the urge to chuckle over his daughter's jealousy of her new sister. "You're my favorite big girl."

"And Ellie's your favorite little one." Sadie's head flopped onto his shoulder dramatically. "But you can't be her prince. Only mine and Mommy's."

This was his favorite part about having girls. Everyone assumed he would want boys. But from the second Morgan told him she was pregnant with Sadie, he imagined a house full of redheaded princesses just like their mom. And if he could get Morgan on board, he wouldn't mind a few more girls filling his house.

"How come I can't be Ellie's prince?"

"She has brown hair like you, Daddy," Sadie said. "Only mommy and I are Ariel."

Nick paused, trying to find a flaw in that logic, but Morgan jumped in.

"Daddy's pretty committed when he wants to do something. I'm sure he'll figure out a way to be Ellie's prince." Morgan smiled. "He even figured out how to borrow Prince Eric's clothes for you."

Nick had called six costume stores before he found Prince Eric's suit to wear for Trick or Treating with Sadie today. But her smile made it worth it.

"You're my hero, Daddy," she said, giving him a kiss before she wiggled and Nick dropped her to her feet.

"Mine too," Morgan said before she came over and added softly. "And a very sexy Prince Eric."

He loved being their hero, their prince, anything his girls needed.

Dear Reader,

First, let me just say a massive THANK YOU! Thank you for reading More Than a Hero. Thank you for supporting me. It's only because readers exist that writers get to live out their dreams.

This book was harder in so many ways from others I've written. Trying to capture all the sides of Nick and do justice to what special operations forces face and have to do to move forward from all they experience was a challenge. And I'm very grateful to the many guys who talked me through so much of this. As promised not mentioning names.

And creating the perfect heroine who understood, could handle, and could help Nick move forward wasn't easy either. In the end, I think Morgan and Nick fit perfectly.

I know some of you are thinking *what about Bex??* Don't worry she's got her happily ever after coming!

If you want more of Nick and Morgan check out my website www.Jennibara.com for bonus epilogues as well as my reading group on Facebook Jenni's World.

If you love the Evanses, check out my website for pre-order information for More Than a Story coming spring 2022. Which brother will be next? And for even more of a bonus, check out the new spin-off series featuring the guys you love from NAE Securities, coming later in 2022.

Finally, remember: Live in your world, fall in love in mine.

Jenni
www.jennibara.com

Acknowledgments

Thank you, my wonderful readers, for reading my work and loving the Evan family as much as I do. Thank you to my street and arc teams for all your sharing, your reviews, your support. You are all amazing!

Haley, thank you so much for all your help. For making my awesome graphics. For always getting stuff done even when I don't give you enough direction. For helping me with this launch, for managing all my teams. For reading and helping me with changes. For helping with the blurbs and teasers. Wow you do a lot- I probably need to thank you more often! You are the best.

Katie, as always, I couldn't do this without you. Thank you for working with my timelines dealing with me being behind and then finishing quickly because I had to get this book out. Your edits as always made this book so much better than it could have been without you. You are my hero!

Amy, thank you for making me finish this darn book. For being insistent that Nick needed his own book and for helping me with all the fixes for it. Basically, for loving Nick a million times more than I did through most of this process. Thank you for all the times you made me work on this when I tried to do anything else. For listening to me whine about all the changes I didn't want to make.

Bonnie, thank you for pushing me to work on this, for setting up sprints and for the photos of "Nick." I'm so lucky to have you as a friend and fellow author. Amanda, thank you for all your edits and sharing. I love having you as part of my author support team, and I'm so looking forward to the next Nighthawk Novel! Even if you won't give me the one I want to read most. Kim, thank you for all your support and the promoting you do for me. I love having you to bounce things off and to chat about what else we can do. Raleigh, thank you for reading the start of this book so many times and helping me with it, and then going through the entire thing for me. Thank you for all your comments and edits and sharing!

All my posse friends: Thank you for your support and sharing and for being amazing authors I can learn from.

Erica, thank you for bringing me into your circle, showing me so much support, and being an inspiration of determination.

All my author friends, thank you for being supportive and inspiring writers. JL Reed, Garry Michaels, Kat Long, Jane Poller, Annie Charms, Daphne Elliot, Lizzie Stanley, Lydia Chelsea, Blye Donovan, Bethany Smith and so many many more.

A big thank you to my wonderful husband, who has the patience to deal with me living in another world half the time. You can laugh when I zone out thinking about a scene in the middle of our conversation and love me even with all the voices in my head. All of me loves you! To my kids who have to hear, "Hold on a second, mom is writing."—it takes a lot for you all to deal with my writing, but you all are awesome about it.

Thank you to my parents, who support me in all I do all the time. I couldn't get through life without you guys. Being able to count on you both all the time for help or support, or encouragement, is the best gift. Thank you for being examples I can strive to be with my kids and for being the best grandparents ever.

Beth, thank you for being so flexible and understanding with this book. For being amazing with your edits and proofreads and checking everything twice! Your communication is wonderful keeping me in the loop. You are always a joy to work with.

Stephanie, I love the interiors, you are awesome. And the fact that you deal with my million emails to make sure we are on track with patience is amazing. Thank you for all you do.

Kari, your cover is incredible, and your patience with me asking for changes was unending. I sing your praises to everyone.

Jeff, thank you for being the final nit-picky check to make sure everything is perfect. Becoming a romance reader wasn't on your to do list, but I'm grateful you did it anyway!

Moey, thank you for letting me borrow your name. For becoming a reader just in time to read my book, for sending me an endless number of funny memes that make me seem fun on social media, helping me run Jenni's World, posting about my books whenever and wherever. Also I'm so lucky to have you not only helping me with this but as a "sister."

And big thank you to the rest of my friends and family who have helped me with encouragement and feedback. I love you all and am so thankful for your support.

About the Author

Jenni Bara lives in New Jersey, working as a paralegal in family law, writing real-life unhappily ever-afters every day. In turn, she spends her free time with anything that keeps her laughing, including life with four kids, or five, if you count her husband. She is just starting her career as a romance author, writing books with an outstanding balance of life, love, and laughter.

9 781737 560050